Tales of the Were ~ Grizzly Cove

Wolf Tracks

BIANCA D'ARC

Copyright © 2020 Bianca D'Arc
Published by Hawk Publishing, LLC
New York

ISBN-13: 978-1-950196-38-8

He's a tracker, following danger is his job. She wants to save his life. When worlds collide, can they ride out the storm together?

Jim is a tracker, newly hired by SeaLife Enterprises to find a man who was involved in sinister blood magic. The miscreant has fled the scene of the crime and it will take all Jim's skill to locate him.

Helen is a healer, part of a highly magical family. When the clairvoyant in the clan sends her to Jim, armed with fireworks and a directive to save Jim's life, Helen does what she has to do to get the job done. She's too attracted to Jim to let the man die. Not on her watch.

Outfoxed, but not undone, Helen and Jim set off together to corner their prey near the town of Big Wolf, Texas, where a showdown is on the agenda. Thrown together by fate, Helen and Jim can no longer deny the sparks that flare between them, but is a relationship between them possible? How can they make their very different backgrounds blend? And, can they bring down the evil operation just outside of town, and find a missing boy before it's all just too late?

DEDICATION

Dedicated to my Dad, on the occasion of his 95th birthday. He doesn't read my books, and frankly, I'm glad of that, but I do like to acknowledge his love and emotional support, which makes it possible for me to continue to write in these worlds.

Special thanks to Lila Dubois, who helped keep me on track to finish this manuscript when all I really wanted to do was take a nap. LOL. Thanks also to my editor, Jess, and my dear friend, Peggy, who helps spot continuity errors before these books make it out into the world. Any errors that may dare to remain after all our combined efforts, are purely my responsibility.

PROLOGUE

In the enchanted glow of a decidedly fey garden, a family of werebears, reunited with their lost little girl, accepted the hospitality of their new friends. The papa bear, Martin, was a retired Marine whose specialty was tracking. He'd tracked his cub from the schoolyard in Southeastern Pennsylvania where she'd been abducted, to the Blue Ridge Mountains of West Virginia, where she'd been found. The trail had been tricky. Deliberately fouled by evil magic. He'd been stumped several times, but the belief of his human mate and the love they both felt for their missing cub propelled him forward.

He had kept the faith that little Melissa would be found alive, and she had been, just that afternoon, by a mixed group of shifters and other magical folk, who had contacted him and his wife. He'd driven straight to the little town and the paper mill on its edge, finding his cub, much to his great joy and relief.

Martin Ebersole and his wife, Lisa, after much excitement, were now sitting in the fey garden of a cottage rented by one of their cub's rescuers. The woman, like his mate, was non-magical, but she had wisdom about herbs and had played a role in ending the evil bitch that had kidnapped his child. Kiki Richards and her newfound werebear mate, Jack Bishop, sat on the other side of the patio table, holding hands. Kiki's sister, Helen, who was a healer, sat beside the younger of two ex-military werewolves, with a human Navy SEAL filling out the group that had saved his little girl. He owed them.

After the family had been reunited at the mill, Kiki had generously offered her cottage to Martin, Lisa and Melissa, so they could clean up and rest a while before heading back home. Her generous heart had touched Lisa, and she'd decided for the family, taking Kiki up on her kindness. Which was how the small family had ended up having dinner with the group in the backyard of that cottage with the magical fey garden.

Melissa had shifted into her bear form and was curled up, asleep, on her mother's lap while the ladies drank some after-dinner tea. The men were drinking beer, but not heavily. They were all just relaxing after a very trying day.

In the case of Martin and his wife, they'd been on the road for weeks, going from place to place, following the faintest of trails to find their daughter. They'd been close when the call had come in from the Lords, relaying that Melissa had been found. Martin had driven them as fast as he could get away with toward the mill where he'd been directed by those he could trust, and sure enough, Melissa had been there. A bit thinner than she had been. A bit weaker than she should be. But alive. Thanks be to the Mother of All.

Apparently, the team had found her in a laboratory darkroom, restrained with a silver chain that had burned her tender skin, silver being poisonous to many magical creatures. Helen had taken away the marks with her healing power, and Jack had offered to sell the pure silver to a group of Native American artisans who would melt it down and turn it into trinkets for the human market. In that way, they'd be turning something that had been made for evil purposes into something harmless. The money from the sale of such a huge hunk of silver would go toward Melissa's recovery and future education, which was an even more generous offer.

Martin had called the Lords directly when they'd driven away from the mill and headed for this cottage and learned that these people were able to make such expensive decisions and were as good as their word. Overwhelmed by the generosity of spirit of these people, Martin had taken his wife and cub into his arms when they reached the safety of the fey cottage, and all three had just held each other for a good long while. His wife had cried. Melissa had cried. And, yes, Martin wasn't too proud to admit there might've been some tears of joy and relief in his own eyes, as well.

They'd had a few hours to relax and regroup at the little cottage set in the middle of the most fantastic garden. Martin and Lisa had been on the road for a long time, and it was nice to just sit still, secure in the knowledge that their baby girl was finally safe, with them. Lisa had taken charge, leading Melissa to the bathtub for a long soak. Not long after the girls emerged from the bathroom, smelling of bubble bath and flowers, the others had arrived with bags and bags of take-out food for an impromptu celebration.

They'd taken every chair in the little house out onto the patio in the garden and sat together for a delicious Italian meal. They had talked about general things. The men had compared their military service dates and locations. Martin had been a Recon Marine in Viet Nam. Extended shifter lifespans meant he was still in the prime of life, though he'd been out of the military a long time. Shifters had to move around a bit to conceal the fact that they had much longer lifespans than the average person.

Arch Hanson was a little older than Martin. He'd been a Navy SEAL around the same time and was still considered a legend in Special Forces circles. His nephew, Jim Hanson, had also been a SEAL, though a lot more recently. Both men were werewolves from a reputable Pack in Iowa, and both were friendly with the lone human Special Operator at the table.

Ben Steel was a former Navy SEAL, as well. He was a regular guy who had gotten mixed up with shifters while on an op in South America. Once he'd learned about the secret world of shifters living under the radar, he'd been recruited by an ancient order of watchers known as the *Altor Custodis*, or *AC*, for short. He'd worked for them for a few years before realizing that there was something desperately wrong with the organization. Now, he was working to set things right, which was something Martin could respect. Ben had called Arch and Jim for help when he'd realized they were dealing with some seriously bad magic at the paper mill.

Of the others, the three men were all bear shifters, like Martin and his cub. Ace, King, and Jack Bishop had been jokingly referred to as the three little bears sometimes, but seldom where they could hear it. King, in particular, had been known to take offense at the moniker, and a few teeth had been knocked out from other people's faces as a result.

All three of the bears had found mates recently, which was plenty cause for celebration. Ace had found himself a weather witch named Sabrina, who had a sweet disposition. King had found his mate in a shy werewolf named Marilee, who had originated in a Canadian Pack. Both couples now lived in Grizzly Cove.

That left Jack and his new mate, Kiki of the enchanted cottage, who had apparently only just become mates during the recent crisis at the paper mill. Kiki didn't have much of a magical gift of her own, but she came from a magical family, and her sister, Helen, was a healer of great ability. Martin knew he owed them all for rescuing and then taking such great care of his daughter. They had all impressed him, and he was trying to come up with a way to pay them back.

The opportunity arose when Melissa fell asleep and the talk turned more serious. The men started discussing what had happened at the paper mill and the loose ends that still needed to be tied up. They had until Monday to clear the site and get it ready for the human workers to go back to work. If they had to take longer than that, their cover story blaming everything on a chemical leak might fall apart, so it was in everyone's best interest to get things cleaned up as quickly as possible.

"We need to figure out what to do with the freezers,"

Sabrina said, looking pointedly at Melissa, asleep on her mother's lap. They all knew what she meant, though. She didn't have to spell it out.

Jack had told Martin that, among other things, they'd discovered a few bodies that had been mutilated in various ways, including exsanguination, stored in freezers in the warehouse. Those bodies couldn't just be turned over to human authorities. For one thing, they still had to identify a few of those poor victims first.

The creature of evil that had kidnapped Melissa had also been abducting adults and killing them. Stealing their power and using their blood and body parts to fuel her sick, twisted, evil potions. If Jack hadn't already killed her, Martin would have enjoyed ripping her limb from limb and dancing on her entrails.

"Some were employees," Kiki said softly. "We identified them from their personnel files. They'd been fired—on paper, at least—and none listed any next-of-kin."

Jack picked up where his mate left off. "We suspect the witch had been singling out loners and people with no family. Nobody to miss them or raise an alarm when they disappeared."

"That's so sad," Lisa said. Martin reached out to take his mate's hand, squeezing softly in reassurance.

"We can trace the employee victims back through their personnel files and see if there's anyone who might want to be notified of their passing," Ace went on. "Some of our government contacts might be of help there with paperwork and such. It's the ones we haven't been able to identify yet, that are going to be the bigger challenge."

"I might be able to help there," Ben piped up. The lone human male at the gathering, he probably had connections the others knew nothing about. "That janitor that was supposed to be watching the plant for the *Altor Custodis* was taking copious notes. He might have something in there about it, but there's a lot of material to sort through."

"Digital or analog?" Lisa asked, earning some surprised

looks from those gathered at the table. They didn't know his mate, after all. Martin sat back and let her educate them, feeling pride in his ultra-intelligent wife.

"A little of both," Ben replied warily.

"If you can get me a scanner and internet access, I might be able to help you," Lisa said, her confidence in her chosen field clear in her words and expression. "We can take the digital records and set up a search algorithm that might help find the information you want faster. Likewise, we can scan in the handwritten pages and run optical character recognition. It's not perfect, but it's not as bad as it was in the past. I have some personal tweaks that I've made to handwriting analysis that might make it easier and a little more accurate, as well."

"Is this what you do?" Kiki asked, clearly intrigued.

Lisa nodded. "I own a company that assists large law firms with the discovery process. We analyze lots of data all the time. I have a few hundred employees who all work remotely, each working with specific, dedicated client accounts, to avoid any possible conflicts of interest or possible leaks of information."

"That's fascinating," Sabrina said, looking impressed. Actually, they all looked impressed. As well they should be. Martin was very proud of the business Lisa had built. She was a powerhouse. A computer nerd and loveable math geek. And she was all his.

"Do you have to get on the road right away tomorrow?" Jack asked, a hopeful note in his voice.

Martin looked over at Lisa and knew she wanted to repay these people for their help in finding Melissa as much as he did. Also, helping them clean up the mess that witch had left behind was the right thing to do for everyone.

"We hadn't planned that far ahead, to be honest," Martin told them all. "We've been on Melissa's trail for weeks, so staying in one place for a bit to regroup is appealing."

"And we really want to help you," Lisa put in. "You've all been so incredibly kind." Lisa's eyes teared, and she stopped talking. Martin squeezed her hand again.

"I can have whatever equipment you need delivered first thing in the morning," Jack promised. "There are scanners and computers at the plant, but I wouldn't ask you to split up or to take Melissa back there. You can work from the cottage, if you want. Or the hotel, if that's easier. I can get you a suite, no problem. In fact, you can have mine, since I'll be with Kiki." He reached into his pocket and took out his hotel key, handing it over to Martin. "Come to think of it, you'd probably be more comfortable there. It's a big suite with a couple of private bedrooms, a kitchenette and dining area. We could set up the computer equipment on the big table in the main room, and there are plenty of outlets."

"Something this cottage lacks, unfortunately," Kiki said with a cringing smile. "Though, it does have other compensations, there's no WiFi here."

"We're all staying at the hotel, too," Helen put in. "All our rooms are next to each other, in a block. It's very safe and clean. They also have nice amenities, including a pool, hot tub, and sauna."

"The hotel sounds perfect," Lisa said, having reined in her emotions. "Thank you. I'll just jot down what I'll need."

She reached into her purse with one hand, taking out a small memo set that had a pen clipped to one side of a small pad. The logo of her company was emblazoned on the front as she flipped it open and started to write. While she did that, the others kept talking.

"There's also the matter of Buford Somersby," Jim mentioned. "The warehouse worker who wanted so desperately to get into that freezer section. He had to be in on it with the witch. He wasn't under her spell. He was part of her organization. Had to be." Jim's expression was grim.

"He already skipped town," Arch put in, looking disgruntled, but resigned. "Trail is either clouded by dark magic or getting cold by now. Or both."

And that's where, Martin realized, he could be of some help. Since it looked like they were staying for the weekend, he would do his best to use his superior tracking skills to help them find their target. He could at least get them headed in the right direction before he took his small family home.

CHAPTER 1

Jim Hanson, ex-Navy SEAL and nephew of Arch Hanson, a legend in his own time, stepped on the gas of his pickup truck. He was part of a small convoy, following both the Ebersole family's truck and Helen Richards' compact car as they all got on the highway, heading east. Jim was really following Martin Ebersole's lead. Helen was just traveling with them as far east as the trail led them, for added safety. Her sister, Kiki, had insisted.

Oddly enough, Kiki and Helen's mother had called last night to discuss Helen's return travel arrangements. Their mother was clairvoyant, so when she suggested Helen tag along with the trackers, Helen had agreed without argument. After their mother had hung up, both Kiki and Helen had exchanged a knowing look and explained that it was just easier and usually better to do what their mother asked them to do. She always had a reason, and things always worked out better if they listened to her casual advice.

They'd started out early this morning from the hotel. Jim's uncle, Arch, was going to hang out with their human ex-Navy SEAL friend, Ben Steel, for a few days before heading back to Pack territory. The bear brothers—Ace, King, and Jack Bishop—and their mates were staying on at the paper mill in West Virginia for a while, just to make sure things settled down for the human workers of the plant, and that no uncomfortable questions were asked. Or, if such questions were asked, that they would be there to run interference and provide the right answers.

All three Bishop brothers were now working for SeaLife Enterprises, the conglomerate that owned the paper mill and many other businesses. It was based out of Grizzly Cove these days, Jim had heard, under new ownership. The story he'd been told had to do with a mermaid who had sought refuge in the cove and mated with one of the bear shifters who lived there. She'd inherited SeaLife Enterprises on the death of her stepfather, who had turned a once-legitimate business into something dark and sometimes illegal.

The new owners were working to fix that, one business at a time, which was why Jack Bishop had been sent out to West Virginia, in the first place. That he'd found his mate while uncovering the evil that had taken over the paper mill was a huge bonus. Mates were hard to find. Some shifters went their entire long lives without ever finding that one special person meant for them.

Arch was a lot older than Jim, and he'd never found his mate. Jim was at the age where he was looking to settle down, but it was in the hands of the Mother of All whether or not he'd find the special woman meant just for him. He prayed that it would happen, but he wasn't going to beat himself up if it didn't. He had a good life with a loving family and great Pack, though there was a complication that made mating—even dating—next to impossible most of the time. Jim sighed inwardly. Something would have to be done about it, at some point, but he'd been hoping the situation would resolve itself without him having to do anything overt.

If he found his mate, he'd have to act. Until then, he could let things ride and just keep on keeping on. Doing jobs with Uncle Arch and helping keep the Pack secure.

Uncle Arch was one of Jim's favorite people, and Arch had been teaching Jim everything he knew for years, which Jim really enjoyed. From time to time, they went on missions together. Arch and Jim had become sort of a team of troubleshooters. When necessary, they'd leave Pack territory to do side jobs for the Pack, friends of the Pack, or Others who needed their specialized help. They'd been finishing up just such a mission when Ben Steel had called for help, and they'd hightailed it right over to act as backup at the paper mill. Luckily, they'd already been near enough to the area to get there fast enough to help.

It had gone a bit like clockwork. They'd arrived on scene just in time to help with the mop-up, which was really the largest part of the job. There were a lot of confused human factory workers who had to be dealt with, and Arch and Jim had been able to arrive on-scene like the cavalry and played the role of first responders to all those dazed employees. It had worked like a charm.

They'd stayed on through the weekend, but the bear brothers had things covered once Monday rolled around and the plant reopened. The Ebersoles had stayed, as well, regrouping a bit after their long journey, with Lisa Ebersole working her computer magic on behalf of SeaLife Enterprises while Martin had done his tracking thing.

Martin had followed the missing employee's trail eastward to a neighboring town, just down the highway. They would start the hunt in earnest there, and make decisions about whether or not Helen would continue to travel with them. According to Helen and Kiki, though, it was very likely Helen would be with the hunting party for some time to come. If their mother told Helen to travel with them, Mrs. Richards had likely foreseen a large part of the journey already.

Jim thought about that as they drove along in loose formation. What must it be like to grow up with a mother who knew things before they actually happened? How could a kid have any fun—or get into any trouble—with a mother like that? Of course, she could also help a lot of people with her gift.

That Helen, too... She had a healing gift that was incredibly powerful. She was a good person, down deep inside. Her spirit shone as she used her gift to heal that little girl who had been so abused at the hands of evil. Helen had worked with little Melissa several times since she'd been freed, giving the badly drained girl a boost in energy and inner strength each time. Jim had witnessed two such sessions and been impressed with the power Helen wielded with such grace both times.

She was a beauty, too. Classical features and sunshine-blonde hair with pale blue eyes that looked almost gray. Fair Helen was gorgeous, both in body and in soul. Tall and willowy, she looked as if a good strong wind would blow her away, but there was also an odd sort of strength about her. Jim felt a keen attraction to the delicate healer, but he wasn't sure if she felt the same.

Who was he kidding? A woman like Helen had her pick of male company. No way would she choose a hard-edged ex-soldier werewolf with complications in his life she couldn't even begin to imagine. Helen was so pure of spirit. So untouched. He wouldn't mar her life by trying to worm his way into it. He wouldn't be that cruel.

Helen drove along, between the two pickup trucks, wondering why her mother had been so insistent that Helen travel with the trackers as far as possible. She had driven to West Virginia all by herself and had managed all right. She didn't need babysitters to get her back to southeastern Pennsylvania and her family.

Mom had to have had ulterior motives. Mom always had ulterior motives. What they were might come clear in time. Or not. Mom's gift was cagey that way. Helen had, more or less, come to terms with being manipulated by an oracle since birth. When you were born into the Richards family, that was just the way things were. You learned to deal with it and move on with your life.

If Helen were to place a bet, she might think her mother's machinations were designed to let Helen spend as much time as possible with the dishy werewolf in the truck behind her compact car. Jim Hanson was the kind of man women had midnight fantasies about.

Tall, ripped, handsome as sin. The golden streaks in his dark blond hair invited her to run her fingers through the short strands. She'd had to sit on her hands to stop the impulse to touch him when he'd been sitting next to her on Kiki's patio the other night. She'd wanted to stroke his arm, hold his hand, touch him any way she could, but she mustn't. He was a werewolf and had not invited such liberties.

She didn't know much about shifters, but she had heard that they didn't like to be touched by strangers without an explicit invitation. She figured that was reasonable. She didn't like it when strangers touched her without permission, so it was only fair. It's just that he looked so...so...pet-able.

She could only imagine what his wolf side must look like. He probably had soft, silky fur in those shades of brown and gold, like his hair. And those striking blue-green eyes that reminded her a bit of the ocean. He'd said he had been a Navy SEAL. She could see that. His eyes spoke of the turbulent depths of the Atlantic, and it was clear from his physical form that he was physically fit. Fitter than almost anyone Helen had ever seen, and she lived among farmers who labored all day, every day, on their farms.

She'd seen her share of physiques sculpted by hard work, but Jim Hanson's body was honed like a fine-edged blade. Sharp, dangerous and devastating to the opposite sex.

He could have his pick of female companionship, and probably did. She didn't blame him. Shifters were of the earth, and they had instinct and impulses that were probably a lot stronger than most people. Since learning about shifters living among the regular population in secret, Helen had been fascinated by the very idea of them. She'd learned all she could from the available sources, which were few and far between. Her magical tradition didn't have much to do with shifters, in general. Which was unfortunate.

She wanted to know more, but she knew asking flat out was not the way it was done. She'd have to ask Kiki to share some things, but that would take time. She wasn't about to bombard her little sister with questions during what was essentially her honeymoon period, even though they hadn't had the official wedding, yet.

Part of what Helen would be doing when she got home was planning a big country wedding for Kiki and Jack. Once things settled down at the paper mill and it was safe to leave for a while, they were going to head home to the family farm. They'd hold the wedding so Kiki would be married in the eyes of their friends and neighbors, though from what little Helen had been able to learn about shifter culture this past weekend, once mates found each other, they were considered *mated* as soon as they let their friends, family, and any leaders of their Packs or Clans know.

Helen wasn't completely clear on the Pack or Clan thing. The bears had a Clan, she'd heard them say, but the wolves spoke of their Pack. It made sense for the wolves. Non-shifter wolves ran in Packs, too. But non-shifter bears? She'd thought they were mostly solitary creatures. She'd have to do some more research, now that her little sister was mated to one.

She'd heard both Arch and Jim refer to an *Alpha*. It sounded like the Alpha was the leader of their Pack, which also made a certain amount of sense. But, having met Arch and Jim first, she would have pegged both men as Alphas, at least in the sense that she knew the word. They were both powerful, intelligent, and they had this aura of competence about them. They were leaders. Alphas. Though, it sounded like they both answered to someone they respected enough to take orders from. Helen would be afraid to meet the werewolf that could give warriors like Arch and Jim orders.

When the truck in front of her put on its turn signal, Helen followed suit. She looked into her rearview mirror and saw Jim do the same in his truck, behind her. They all got off the highway at the next exit, and Helen followed the Ebersoles' pickup into a large parking lot adjacent to a diner with shiny silver panels on parts of the exterior and large windows. It was nearly lunch time, and she hoped they might stop for a bite, but she'd do whatever the others decided. She was just along for the ride.

They parked in a row, next to another vehicle. Helen was aware that Jim positioned his pickup on the far side of the other car. Martin had parked between the other car and the diner. Helen's car was next to Martin's, adding another layer of obstruction between the diner windows and the car in the middle of the two trucks.

She got out of her car and stretched her legs. Martin helped Lisa and Melissa out of the pickup. By the time the family was standing in the parking lot, Jim had joined them all.

"That car is the one Buford left in. He dumped it here. I didn't touch it, preserving it so you could search for evidence, but I did pick up his scent trail and followed it back to the highway for a bit. He got a rental car at the lot just down the street and then went back to the highway. The trail goes cold at that point. At least for me," Martin admitted with a grimace. "I was thinking maybe you might find something in the car that would give you fresh sign."

"Good call. Why don't you all head into the diner while I take a gander at the car?" Jim suggested.

"Yeah, it's about lunchtime anyway, and we could use a pit stop," Martin agreed. He turned to his little family and shepherded them toward the door of the diner.

Helen hesitated a moment. "Shall I order food for you?" she asked Jim.

He seemed surprised by her offer. "I'd really appreciate that," he told her. "Roast turkey on rye, if they have it. No mustard. No mayo. Extra tomatoes. And fries. And a big glass of O.J. Maybe a slice of apple pie?"

"No problem," she told him with a smile, pleased to be able to do this little kindness for him. "It'll be waiting when you finish."

He paused to meet her gaze, a spark of blue-green making her want to catch her breath. "Thanks, Helen."

She nodded and turned away, unable to form words. She practically skipped into the diner, her emotions running so hot and...weird. Jim's simplest words made her feel all fluttery. Like some kind of teenager mooning over a heartthrob. She really had to get a grip.

Helen sat at the large table with the others, keeping a surreptitious eye on the parking lot to see if she could figure out what Jim was doing. Whatever it was, he was better at stealthy maneuvering than she would have credited. How did a big guy like Jim manage to keep such a low profile? It boggled the mind.

"Don't expect to see too much," Martin told her quietly, his eyes twinkling with amusement when she met his gaze. "That boy's a former Navy SEAL, and he's got a direct line to one of the legends of the Spec Ops community. I bet he knows more about stealth than just about anyone, other than his Uncle Arch." Martin looked past her, out the window. "Look, here he comes now. Boy doesn't give much away, but I'd bet he found something."

"What makes you say that?" Helen turned to watch Jim's long-legged amble into the diner.

"Because if he hadn't, he'd still be out there looking." Martin winked at her as he grinned. "That boy's no quitter."

Jim had no sooner sat down at the table with the others when the waitress came out with a large tray, delivering the plates heaped with food to everyone. Jim winked at Helen when the turkey sandwich he'd asked for was deposited in front of him, sending her a smile of thanks that nearly melted her bones. He really was the most attractive man she'd ever met.

There was just something about him that drew her like a moth to a flame. He was probably just as dangerous to her gentle soul as that fire was to a moth's tender wings, but she couldn't help herself. The longer she was around him, the more she felt this uncanny pull to be near him...always.

Conversation halted until the waitress left, but once they all had their food, they were able to talk, as long as they kept their voices low. Lisa was doting on her daughter, but Martin looked keen to find out what Jim had learned. As was Helen.

"This was stuck in a little crevice behind the door panel," Jim said, handing something over to Martin.

"Well, well, well," Martin mused. "Careless."

"There's every indication he cleared out in a hurry. Food wrappers all over the place. General grunge in the passenger area. This, however, was the only piece of even remotely identifying data left. He scrubbed the vehicle of anything that might lead us farther down the trail, only he missed this bit, in his haste." Jim looked smug as he took a big bite of his sandwich.

"What is it?" Helen asked, curiosity getting the better of her.

Martin handed her the little rectangle. It was a library card. She looked closely. A library card from Virginia Beach, with a man's name on it, that was *not* Buford Somersby.

"What does this mean?" she asked, puzzled. "Was this left behind by some other person, or does Buford have a friend named Gil Smithsby?"

"Gil Smithsby is likely one of Buford's aliases," Martin explained gently. Helen felt like a dolt when he said it. She should have realized.

"We can use that name to trace him. Maybe," Jim added. "I already texted the info to Ezra Tate in Grizzly Cove. He's running a computer search now."

"If he doesn't turn up anything, I might be able to make a few calls," Martin offered.

CHAPTER 2

As it turned out, Ezra was able to find out a great deal about Gil Smithsby. By the time they'd finished eating and were working on dessert, Jim had received a full dossier on Gil Smithsby, alias Buford Somersby, alias Gerald Settersby, alias, alias, alias. The man turned out to have a list of aliases longer than Jim cared to read.

Buford was the newest of his long line of false identities. The best part of being able to link Buford with the others was being able to trace any activity by the older identities. In this case, they were able to find out that Gerald Settersby had rented a car just up the road from the diner, paying by credit card. Ezra had used his investigating wiles, calling the rental place and pretending to be a credit card fraud investigator, he'd learned a great deal about what Buford/Gerald had said to the clerk—and, more importantly, what he hadn't said.

He'd told the clerk the rental would be for one night, that he was not leaving the state, and that he'd return the car tomorrow. Buford/Gerald had claimed to be visiting a friend in the area when the clerk had remarked upon his driver's license being issued by the State of New Jersey. He'd had a plastic bag full of papers in addition to three large suitcases. When prompted, the clerk had revealed that he'd noticed a few things. Like a map of Virginia among the other man's collection of papers and a quickly glimpsed luggage tag on one of the cases that had a Virginia Beach address on it.

"Could be a setup," Martin mused. "Though I can't think of any reason they'd want to lure people to Virginia Beach. I hadn't heard anything about that area being a hotbed of sinister activity, but then again, I'm not really in the game anymore these days."

"I haven't heard anything negative about Virginia Beach either. Nor had Ezra and his sources," Jim said as he ate his pie. "Thing is, I know the general area pretty well. I spent some time in Norfolk, which isn't too far away as the crow flies, when I was in the Navy. I may still have a few friends in the area."

"Then, it would be a good idea to call on them," Martin said with finality.

"That's the plan," Jim agreed. "But I'm going to head in that direction while I do that. I have a feeling that's where I need to go."

"Then, I suppose we're going to part ways sooner than I expected. We head northeast from here," Martin said, regret clear in his tone.

"And I'll be going southeast," Jim replied, nodding. "It was a pleasure meeting you and working with you," he said formally, to the older man.

"Likewise," Martin responded warmly. "You have my number. If I can help in any way, just call, okay?"

"Roger that, and thanks." Jim nodded again, and the waitress came over with their check. Jim picked it up. "I'm officially on an expense account from SeaLife Enterprises, so this one's on them," he told them all with a grin. "Ezra told me to pick up the tab for you all, and I'm happy to do so."

Martin nodded, making polite conversation as Jim offered up a shiny new company credit card to the waitress. Lisa left the table with Melissa, heading for the ladies room, but Helen stayed with the guys. She was feeling a bit panicky and sad, knowing this might be the last few minutes she ever spent with Jim. How had he grown so important to her in such a short time?

They all stood and began heading toward the exit once Jim had filled out the credit card receipt with a generous tip for the waitress. He handed it to the woman on their way down the aisle toward the door. There was a small vestibule where they waited for Lisa and Melissa to rejoin them, Martin's eyes on the inside of the diner, through the glass of the doors.

Helen saw Lisa and Melissa heading toward the door about the same time the men did, and Jim opened the outer door for Helen. She went through it, out into the late afternoon sunshine. With any luck, she would be home before full dark had fallen.

Jim paused at the bottom of the stairs with Helen while Martin waited for his women folk in the vestibule. This was, perhaps, the last moments she would ever have alone with Jim, but she couldn't figure out what to say. Luckily, he seemed to have something to tell her as he turned to face her.

"It's probably best if you continue as far as you can with Martin and Lisa. I'm sorry I can't travel with you all the way, but duty calls."

"I understand. I'm sorry we didn't get more time together," she said, feeling bold.

Jim's smile lit her insides. "Me too," he replied in a low voice, his blue eyes holding her gaze as if he could see within.

Maybe he could. Maybe that was some secret werewolf thing. Or a Navy SEAL thing. Helen couldn't be sure. But whatever it was, Jim had that magic touch, and it sent her senses spinning.

"Will you text me when you get home, just so I know you made it there safely?" he asked. She had his cell number. They'd all exchanged contact numbers before setting out on this little convoy.

"Oh, I was just thinking that I'd probably be home before it got really dark. But yes, I'll send you a text. I—" She had been going to tell him to call her anytime, but Martin and his family rejoined them, halting her words. Darnit.

"We're not too far from home now, either," Martin added, no doubt having heard what Helen had just said. She still had to get used to shifter hearing. "We'll be taking Route 78 northward, then we get off at exit 10."

"So do I," Helen told the bear family with some amazement. "Our farm is just outside Frystown."

"You're kidding," Lisa piped up. "We go farther south, past Shaefferstown, near the wildlife preserve."

"I go there in the fall to watch the migrating birds," Helen said, excited by the idea that this nice family lived so near to hers. "You should stop in at the farm and have dinner before heading home," she offered. "We always have plenty to eat, and I'm sure your house has been closed up for a while, right? You probably don't have anything fresh in the refrigerator."

"We were going to stop at the supermarket on the way home," Lisa admitted.

"Don't do that. I'm sure my folks will send you home with plenty of farm-fresh provisions. At least enough to get you through until you can get your house up and running again."

"Are you sure they won't mind your inviting strangers over?" Lisa asked, seeming hesitant.

"Mind? Are you kidding? Mom is probably already packing a cooler of goodies for you to take home. She has a gift of foresight, you know." Helen chuckled. It was no less than true, as these people would learn when they met the matriarch of her family.

"You've already eaten their food," Jim put in. "All that meat and dairy at Kiki's was from their farm and their neighbor's dairy.

Martin actually groaned. "That was some good food," he added.

"All organic," Helen offered, grinning. "Just don't be surprised if they want to ask you impolite questions about being a bear shifter. We only have wolves in the family so far, and they're a very new addition. They're also quite distantly related, so we don't see them much. I know my folks, and my siblings, are really curious."

"We don't generally talk about ourselves, you know," Martin said, but she could tell he was going to accept because the food had already won him over.

"That's okay," she assured him. "I just wanted to warn you that they might ask, but if you choose not to answer, they'll respect that. We all know what it's like to have a secret that needs keeping."

"Well, all right, then. We'd be pleased to accept your offer of hospitality," Martin replied formally. "We'll just follow you, once we're back on the road, okay?"

Helen grinned. "Sounds like a plan."

Martin shook hands with Jim in farewell. Lisa and Melissa gave Jim hugs, and then they headed for their vehicle to get everybody settled before they got back on the road. That left Helen with Jim for one final, all-too-short moment.

"I'm glad they're going with you," he said. "That was nice of you to invite them. That couple has been through the ringer looking for their little girl. I suspect you're right about their cupboards being bare."

"My family will take good care of them," she promised. She had to say something before they parted, but there was no time. "Will I ever see you again?" she wondered aloud.

Jim paused, his stunning blue-green eyes catching her gaze as warmth sparked between them. "I hope so, though I'm not sure if it would be wise." He stepped closer to her and took her hand in his. "You're an intriguing woman, Helen." His voice dropped low, and she felt it in her bones as he moved even closer, his head lowering toward hers.

She saw his kiss coming a mile away, but she didn't want to stop him. No way, no how. Helen had been wanting to discover what Jim's kiss felt like since soon after meeting him.

He moved closer still, and she finally found out. His kiss felt divine. It tasted sublime. And it made her feel finer than she ever had before.

Her head was still spinning a moment later when he lifted his lips from hers. She met his gaze once more, and she thought she saw a glimmer of regret in his eyes. Helen was feeling a boatload of regret, herself. Not for the kiss, but for the fact that he was leaving, and despite what he'd said, she might very well never see him, ever again.

"Be well, Helen," he said, his tone intimate.

"Stay safe, Jim. And, when this is all over, call me sometime. Okay?" Her heart rose in hope, but his noncommittal answer didn't give her much to build on. He stepped away and headed for his pickup.

Devastated by the kiss and the sheer drop off the cliff when he failed to agree to call her when things were calmer, she went to her car. She had to get a grip. She would be seeing her family shortly, and it would never do to let them think that her emotions had been so churned up by a man she'd only just met. If they even suspected, she'd never hear the end of it, and she could do very well without the teasing that would follow from her siblings, or the concerned looks from her parents.

Sliding behind the wheel, she started her car and looked over, just one last time at Jim. He was already in his truck, with the engine purring. He was looking her way, too. Was it her imagination, or did he have a wistful look in his eye?

She raised her hand to wave, but Martin had already pulled out and honked once—in farewell, she supposed, to Jim. Jim looked away, sticking his hand out his window to wave at Martin, Lisa and Melissa. Helen realized she was supposed to go in front of the family's car, so the time for dawdling was over. She put her car in reverse and backed out of the parking space.

She pulled in front of the family's much larger vehicle, and her view of Jim was eclipsed. Shaking her head at what might have been, she drove out of the parking lot and headed for the highway they'd left earlier. They would continue on their northeastward trek while Jim headed for another highway ramp a few miles away, which would take him away from her...possibly forever.

A couple of hours later, the sun had disappeared below the horizon, but there was still enough light to see the farm fields as Helen turned into her family's driveway. Down the long gravel road, she drove with the Ebersole family following behind, past tall corn and waving wheat then, finally, to the fifty-tree orchard that was closer to the house.

The yard was lit up, awaiting her arrival, and as she pulled her little car into its accustomed spot, her family spilled out of the house to welcome her home. Her mother came first, of course, having known already exactly when her baby girl would return. She gave Helen a hug and a look that said more than words could ever express, of pride and commiseration...and hope.

Mom always knew everything, so she probably had foreseen something about Helen's reaction to Jim. Helen would have to question her mother later, but first, there were the guests to introduce and make welcome. Helen watched as Martin approached cautiously, parking his car outside of hers, even backing into the spot, so he could make a quick getaway, should that prove necessary.

She didn't take offense. Magical folk and shifters didn't mix. As a general rule, none of the Other races mixed much in modern times. Though shifters and mages, and yes, even bloodletters had been allies in the far, distant past, their camaraderie had not lasted the centuries. Each group had kept to themselves for as long as anyone living—except maybe a few of those immortal bloodletters—could remember.

Martin's caution was understandable, especially considering what he and his family had just been through at the hands of an evil mage. That he'd accepted her offer of hospitality at all had said a lot about his willingness to trust her based on his recent association with both Helen and her sister, Kiki. The fact that Kiki was now mated to a bear shifter had probably gone a long way toward Martin's willingness to give Helen the benefit of the doubt. That and the way Helen had taken to little Melissa, healing her wounds and befriending the child.

"Mom, I want you to meet Martin Ebersole, his mate,

Lisa, and their daughter, Melissa," Helen said, escorting her mother over to where the family was slowly emerging from their vehicle.

"I'm so glad to meet you all," the matriarch of the family said, her smile beaming as she extended the hand of friendship to the newcomers. "We've got dinner almost ready. Come on in, and you can freshen up a bit before we sit down to eat."

The meal was a great success, and they sent the little family on their way with a cooler full of perishables and several boxes of preserves, fruits and vegetables from the family's stores. They'd even taken little Melissa out into the kitchen garden after dinner, which was just outside the back door, and let her pick some herbs she liked. The fact that it was dark out didn't deter the little werebear cub. She could see better in the dark than just about anyone present, except for her father.

Helen put her arm around her mother's shoulders as they watched the family drive away. "I think we made some friends here tonight," she said, feeling happy and wistful all at the same time.

"It's a good thing," Helen's mother said in that dreamy sort of a voice that sometimes indicated a moment of prophecy. Helen listened closely. "We're going to need all the alliances we can get in the trials to come. What has grown apart will need to reunite, and all creatures who serve the Light will have to work together to defeat the threatening darkness."

Helen felt chills run down her spine. When her usually happy mother spoke in such dark terms, it was time to batten down the hatches and prepare for…what sounded very much like…war.

*

Jim felt every mile he put between himself and Helen like a tear in his soul. He knew he had to be imagining things. He couldn't really have grown so attached to the woman on such

25

a short acquaintance. Could he?

He'd grown up hearing about shifters finding their mates through arduous trials that tested their commitment to each other. Or the lucky ones found their mates in long-time friends. A few of his extended family had mated within the Pack to other werewolves they had known all their lives until, one day when they were old enough, the mating instinct kicked in, and they realized they had always been meant for each other.

There were many singles in the Pack, too. Uncle Arch wasn't the only bachelor, nor would he be the last. The sad truth was that most never found their true mates. While some went outside werewolf circles to find their one true mates, it was rare. There were only a few humans who had been brought into the Pack in the past fifty years.

Some even found mates among other species of shifter. There were two werecougar mates—two sisters who had mated with two cousins. The cousin having met the sister at the mating celebration for the first couple. There was also a red fox shifter, a hawk shifter, and the most recent had been a lynx who joined the Pack several years ago.

Of the humans, none were magical. Jim wasn't even certain it was permissible, according to Pack law. Their Pack had a rocky history with mages, and even though Helen was a healer, she came from a long line of very powerful magic users. The Pack might frown on any association with someone like her.

He wanted to tell himself that he didn't care what the Pack thought. If Helen really was his mate, he'd go total lone wolf to be with her, if he had to. He'd cut ties with the Pack and live out his life unaffiliated—alienated from his own family. He cringed. Never to see or talk to Uncle Arch again? His family? That would be really hard.

Wolves were social creatures, for the most part. Jim knew for a fact that his wolf thrived when surrounded by its family—its Pack. To forsake his Pack... He wasn't sure he could survive that.

Of course, if Jim had a mate, and a family of his own, that might make such a sacrifice easier. And, in time, he might find another Pack willing to accept a magical human mate. Helen certainly had gifts of her own to share. Her soft heart was a joy to be around, and she gave of her power to help others. That had to count in her favor.

But it didn't matter right now. Jim was on a mission, and Helen had probably already forgotten all about him. It wasn't like humans had the same mating drive that shifters had. She'd probably thought he was interesting at the time. An oddity in a world she hadn't really known existed. She'd admitted as much to them all while they were eating dinner one night.

Helen, and the rest of her magical family, had only learned about shifters being real when her distant cousin had married into a Canadian wolf Pack a few months before. Until that event, all they'd had were old stories from the family archives, and rumors that they couldn't verify. Even with the new matings in the family, they still knew very little about shifters in general, though they'd been trying to learn more about the Pack that had married into their line. Due to shifter secretiveness, they hadn't been able to find out much.

Of course, that would all change now that Kiki had mated to a bear shifter. She was a daughter of the house, not some distant cousin. She'd tell her folks, and her siblings, all about life in a bear Clan. Of that, Jim had little doubt. He wondered if they'd realize how very different bears were from werewolves. They might both be shifters, but they were different species, and their animal halves needed different things. Bears were mostly loners—or had been, before the Grizzly Cove experiment. Wolves were Pack creatures. Family was ultra-important to a wolf. The Pack was a living, breathing unit within which the individuals helped and cared for each other. It was much more involved than the casual relationship shared by the bears who had banded together out in Washington State. At least, that was Jim's take on the matter.

But why was he worrying about this anyway? He must've been mistaken. No way Helen could be his actual mate. Sure, he'd felt drawn to her. Who wouldn't be? She was gorgeous and kind-hearted and intelligent. He'd always liked that kind of woman.

Surely, this attraction was just a normal consequence of being around a very beautiful, gifted woman. No way was she really his mate, and any silly thoughts he had to the contrary would, no doubt, fade with time…and distance.

Still, he felt every mile he put between them down deep in his aching heart.

Jim ignored it. He had a job to do. Mission first. Mixed up feelings later. Much, much later.

CHAPTER 3

Helen's mother knocked on her bedroom door in the middle of the night. Helen roused out of a restless sleep to find her mother entering her room, her face pale, her hands trembling.

"What is it?" Helen asked, her head clearing as worry set in.

"You have to go," her mother whispered urgently. "You have to go to him. Go now."

Helen guided her mother to sit on the side of the bed. "Mom," she said gently, recognizing that her mother was in a state, probably still half in the vision and half in the real world. She had seen her mother like this a few times before and had learned to deal with it as calmly as possible. Arguing or shouting at her mother would produce no results. "Mom, where do I have to go? What do I have to do?"

"The werewolf boy. He's driving into a trap. He's going to die unless you go help him."

Helen caught her breath. Jim was going to die? If her mother said something so dire, it wasn't an exaggeration. Her mother was always very particular about the words she chose to express her visions. She wouldn't make such a pronouncement unless it was absolutely true—as she saw it.

"On a dark beach. An ambush. In roughly twenty-four

hours." Helen noticed her mother was looking at her now, coming more out of the vision as time passed. "You have time to get there and be ready, if you go as soon as you can. He will be hurt. There's nothing that can stop that, but you can save him. You can heal him and let the enemy think he's out of play. Then, the two of you, working together, can turn the tables on the enemy."

"Me? I'm no soldier," Helen protested. She could do the first part, of course. She could save Jim's life. But helping him fight the enemy? No way. She was a healer, not a fighter.

"You have all that you need to help him do what's right," her mother insisted. "Just don't let him leave you behind. You must go with him, when he leaves the beach."

Helen was confused but knew enough not to argue. She would go to…wherever her mother wanted her to go. Possibly Virginia Beach? Jim and Martin had talked about that location before they'd all parted. Helen knew she would be able to pin down the location better in a few minutes, when her mother was ready to answer questions about details in her vision. Landmarks would help them figure out exactly where Helen needed to be.

*

Helen followed her mother's instructions to the letter. She'd learned long ago, not to argue when it came to her mother's visions. Loading up her car with spare clothing from her brothers, medical supplies, towels, wipes and whatever else she could think of that she might need, including a cooler full of prepared food and bottles of water, she headed out at first light.

She made a few stops to get gas, use the facilities and stretch her legs, but other than that, there was only one thing her mother had demanded she do. That little task was the oddest of the odd things Helen had done that day, but she didn't question. She merely stopped at the fireworks store near the state border and picked up an armful of some of the larger fireworks—particularly the ones that were on sticks and could be sort of *aimed*.

When her mother had suggested rather strongly that she pick up a large number of those, Helen had begun to understand what her mother had in mind. She didn't come out and explain every step of what might happen, because that could alter events in a bad way. However, she had made suggestions that Helen had learned to read, over the years, and Helen would be very much surprised if she didn't end up aiming the fireworks she'd purchased at someone or something later that night. She'd been sure to get a long-necked lighter, as well. And a backup. Just in case.

She wasn't a big fan of fireworks, generally, but she would use them if she had to.

When she pulled in to Virginia Beach, it was nearing dusk. Using the first bits of twilight, she trolled up and down the famous strip, searching the parking lots for Jim's pickup. She was about to give up when she spotted it, at the very end of the strip, in the parking lot of the last high-rise hotel. Pulling into that lot as night began to fall in earnest, she decided to book a room in the hotel. She was tired, and according to her mother, the attack wouldn't come until much later.

Helen wanted to clean up a bit and refresh herself before the work of the night. Luckily, it was off season, so she was able to get a beach-front room for a very low price. She asked for, and received, a room on the first floor, with a sliding glass door that led, after a few easily-overcome obstacles, to the beach. She knew within moments of entering the room—which was located on the far corner of the building—that the room next to hers, and several after that, were not occupied. Perfect.

She brought in her supplies and took a quick shower. She didn't worry about trying to find Jim. His truck was parked right next to her little car, and she'd even put a small note on his windshield, instructing him to call her when he saw it. She didn't really expect him to call. What she did expect was that, at some point in the middle of the night, there would be a confrontation of some sort on the beach. Then, she would have to act.

She set up her supplies near the sliding glass door for later, then went out to get the lay of the land and scout the beach a little while there was still a bare hint of sunlight. If she ran into Jim before everything kicked off, so much the better, but she doubted it would happen. When her mother had a vision this strong, things usually occurred according to what she'd seen.

*

Jim didn't like what he'd found in Virginia Beach. The town was not filled with holiday makers, which was a relief, since the year was turning toward winter, but it was still a big place, with lots of nooks and crannies. He remembered better times spent here while he'd been in the service, among friends, but those days were long gone. The place was filled with the ghosts of memories past, friends lost in conflicts around the globe, and good times that would never come again.

Maudlin. How had he let himself get into such a depressing mood? Jim realized a lot of it had to do with leaving Helen behind in Pennsylvania. His inner wolf was in mourning, howling in his soul, wanting to turn around and go back to find her.

Ridiculous. She wasn't his mate. How could she be? For one thing, she was much too good for the likes of him. She was a princess, and he was certainly no prince. He was more the palace guard, fit only to serve and protect, not to become romantically involved with the beautiful lady in the high tower.

And now, he was waxing poetic. Jim shook his head at his own fanciful notions.

He'd been on the phone with Ezra Tate, back in Grizzly Cove, and they had established that the paper trail definitely led here, to Virginia Beach. Buford—using two more of his many aliases—had paid for gas, using a couple of different credit cards, under a couple of different names, all the way here.

Jim just had to find him. It sounded so simple, but in

32

reality, it was proving difficult. Jim decided to prowl up and down the boardwalk, the strip, and the beach. Hell, he'd even check out the ocean, if he had to. No way was he letting Buford—or whatever he was calling himself now—get away from him.

Jim had been up and down the strip three times already when the sun set. He paused to eat dinner at a beachfront restaurant, so he could keep watch on the darkening waters and the long strip of beach, sparsely populated at this time of year. When the sun set fully, the darker parts of the beach would be perfect for clandestine operations. Jim decided he would prowl the sands after dinner, for as long as it took. He had a strong feeling that he would find his prey there, in the dark.

Hours later, he was almost ready to give up. He'd been up and down the beach a number of times and had found nothing. There were a few good vantage points near the hotel where he'd reserved a room, basically to have a safe place to park his truck. He went down to the waterline and back, hoping to catch a scent—any scent—that might somehow indicate he was on the right track.

Alert at the first cackle, Jim was nonetheless caught by surprise when, of all things, a hyena Pack descended on him from downwind. He hadn't scented them because their pungent odor had been carried away from his sensitive nose even before it could go much farther than a few feet from the spotted animals.

That they were shifters, he had no doubt. They were as big as he was in his fur, which was to say, larger than their wilder cousins who had only the one form. With no time to strip, he shifted into his wolf form, his clothing tearing off in bits around him. It wasn't ideal, but he'd fought like this before. It wouldn't hamper him.

The hyenas were organized as they came for him. They'd hunted together, like this, before. They even looked a little alike. Perhaps they were a family of hyena shifters, living in the area, though he'd had no intel saying there were any dominant shifter claims on this part of the country. If there had been an Alpha claiming this place as part of his territory, Jim would have at least thought about seeking the Alpha's permission or even cooperation, depending on what sort of guy he was. But there had been no Alpha. Ezra had double checked with the Lords.

Hyenas weren't native to North America, though a few had to have immigrated over the years, Jim was sure. Still, they weren't common, and if a Pack had taken up residence here and claimed it as territory, somebody would have mentioned it to the Lords, even if the hyenas themselves were reluctant to do so. Which meant, these were rogues. Either they were living nearby, under the radar for their own nefarious reasons, or they'd come here to do a job.

Killing a werewolf sounded like the sort of job a group like this might take on. Jim had met their kind before, when he was a SEAL, deployed to Africa. They hadn't been exactly warm and cuddly then, on their home ground. They were even less so now, as they stalked him, surrounding him.

Jim didn't even consider changing back to his human form, but he did think about the right moment to unleash his battle form. The in-between state that only the most powerful shifters could hold for any length of time offered all the strength of the animal and the opposable thumbs and other useful features of his human half. He wondered if any of those facing him could manage to hold their battle forms for any length of time.

Four against one, they could take turns, even if they couldn't manage to hold it as long as Jim could. He had to be four times as strong as any of them…and then some. Good thing he'd stopped for dinner. He'd need the fuel to fight, though he wasn't at all certain of the outcome. These hyenas were moving as a practiced unit. Jim might have just bitten off a little more than he could chew, but he knew one thing for certain… He'd walked right into Buford's trap.

The trail had led him—by the hand, practically—to this. Buford had been a lot smarter than Jim had given him credit for being. Jim just hoped his mistake wouldn't prove to be fatal.

One of the hyenas made a feint, and then, the one behind Jim charged, morphing to battle form even as he ran. Jim half-shifted, as well, ready for the clash of fists and claws. He would try to pace himself, and even if he couldn't win, he was going to make these bastards bleed for what they were about to do to him.

*

Helen had a large beach bag full of fireworks, the two lighters, bandages and other supplies as she set out from the hotel, at midnight. She decided that the beach was too well-lit on the strip where light spilled out from the many businesses that were on or close to the beach. If anything was going to happen, it would likely be away from the tourist area, where the beach faded into the inky night.

She noted the wind direction. It was blowing toward her, so her scent wouldn't carry to anyone in front of her right now. If she didn't find Jim on the outbound trek, it would be much harder to sneak up on any shifters that might be in the area on the way back.

She heard snarls and a chilling laugh that sent shivers down her spine before she noticed a smudge of activity in the darkness in front of her and closer to the water. Something was churning up the sand. A fight.

Dropping to her knees in the scrubby brush behind a low rise of a sand dune, she reached into her beach bag. She'd worn dark clothing, and her bag was dark, but the moment she lit the fireworks, the night would light up. She just prayed whatever it was that was attacking Jim would get scared and run away—and not attack her. It was going to be pretty obvious where she was once the fireworks went off.

Maybe they'd just think it was teenagers out to have some fun. Maybe they'd get spooked about being discovered and just leave. That was her fervent hope. She decided to shoot off the first rockets toward the sky, just over where she thought the fight was happening. The flash of light might give her an idea of what Jim—and she—was up against.

Putting action to her thoughts, she stuck the little sticks of five rockets into the sand at the top of the low dune and lit the fuses before backing away and going a short distance down the beach. She could aim the sticks, to a certain extent, and when they went off, she wasn't looking at the fireworks display, but rather at the beach.

What she saw made her gasp. Thankfully, the bangs and booms of the fireworks hid the sound. Shifters had really good hearing, and she was in enough danger just being nearby as it was. Setting up her next round, even before the last sparkle faded from the sky, she lit those and moved again.

She could see more each time a shell exploded overhead. There were at least five figures on the beach. One was in the center. He was enormous. Furry. Not a man, but not quite a wolf. He looked like the werewolves in the old movies—half-and-half. He was bleeding profusely, but still standing.

Around him circled a pack of...hyenas? In Virginia? It didn't seem possible, but she thought that's what they were. The inhuman cackling made sense as they communicated with each other. Three of them were full-on animal form while one engaged Jim in that half-and-half state. She hadn't realized they could hold that shape, and it certainly was effective for fighting.

Even as she realized all this, she saw the nervous glances of the hyenas at the fireworks. They were pacing, probably wanting to kill Jim before they left but getting antsy about the possibility of discovery. That was good for her. She just had to get a little bolder before they managed to hurt Jim so badly that even her powers couldn't heal him.

She aimed her next rockets carefully, even as the last embers of the previous round faded in the sky. This time, she wasn't aiming for the sky. No, this time, she was going to singe some hyena fur, Goddess willing. Sending up a prayer for protection, she lit the fuses and moved again, knowing she didn't have much time.

She was headed down the beach, toward the hotel each time she moved. Just a few yards, but enough to change her viewpoint. There was a parking lot behind her now, and she decided to raise the stakes again. Picking up some of the rocks around her as soon as she lit the fuses, she threw them as hard as she could at the cars most distant to her position, setting off at least five car alarms as she moved position yet again.

Then, the rockets flew, and the cackling laughter of the aggressive hyenas turned to screams and whimpers as the rockets flashed past them, singeing their fur. Her aim had been true, and in the light of the rockets, she saw the hyenas scatter. The one who was fighting with Jim paused, looked over at the parking lot and all the flashing lights and honking horns and let itself shift to full-on hyena form before running after its packmates, up the dark beach, into the night.

People were milling around the far end of the parking lot now. Helen didn't have much time. She had to get Jim to safety while the darkness on the beach covered them and the people wondering about their cars were looking elsewhere. She slung her bag over one shoulder and ran out to where she'd last seen Jim in the darkness.

She almost stumbled over him, but he was still breathing when she found him, kneeling on the sand. He looked bad. Even she could smell the copper of blood all over him. He raised his head, and his eyes widened when he saw her.

"Did I die?" he asked in a ragged whisper.

"Not if I have anything to say about it," she muttered. "Can you stand?" She reached out to him, putting one arm under his, trying to help him without hurting him more.

His shirt was in shreds, so she took it off completely, rolling it up and stuffing it in her bag. His torso wasn't the source of the heavy bleeding. No, she thought maybe the blood flow was coming from a vicious leg wound. A little zap of her healing energy eradicated all the little marks on his torso and turned the blood into vapor, removing it from his body.

She calculated that the fight had been near enough the water that the approaching high tide would erase all evidence of the altercation within the next hour or two. Hopefully, nobody would happen across the scene before then. As dark as it was on this stretch of beach, it was unlikely.

Jim leaned heavily on her, but he stood. Shaky, but standing, she tried to make a quick assessment of his condition, but it was just too dark to see anything useful. She infused him with a steady flow of her healing power, hoping it would stabilize him enough to get him into her hotel room. She needed light to see what she was doing, and privacy in which to do it. She'd set up the room. Now, if she could just get him to it, she might have a shot at saving him.

"Come on, now," she encouraged. "See that big hotel over there? I've got a room on the ground floor, all ready for you. We just have to get you there."

CHAPTER 4

Jim tried. He really did. Helen could feel him making the effort. She gave him a bit more of her healing power, and it seemed to help. He was able to stagger, with her support, toward the hotel. She kept a wary eye on the beach behind them, but she didn't see the hyenas. Of course, she didn't have shifter night vision, so she had no idea if they were watching her or not. If they were, she'd have to cross that bridge when she came to it. Right now, her main concern was getting Jim to the hotel and making sure he lived.

She knew he was leaving a blood trail, but she could use a little jolt of her healing power to deal with that once she had him inside. She would do her best not to leave a trace of what had happened, but the commotion she'd created with the fireworks and car alarms had definitely drawn the attention of the local human population. Even as they neared the corner of the hotel where her room was conveniently located, she saw flashing lights down the beach. Someone had called the cops. Good. Maybe that would keep the hyenas at bay for a bit longer, if they were still in the area.

There was video surveillance on the outside of the hotel, but with Jim's arm around her, she hoped they would look like a partying couple returning well after hours. With any luck, the cameras were low enough resolution not to show the full extent of Jim's injuries. They were both dressed in dark colors, so the blood wouldn't show on their clothing, and maybe the rips in his pants could be explained as a fashion choice rather than the result of a battle to the near-death. Shirtless men were common on this beach, though probably not at this time of year. Still, with the torn pants, she hoped he would be seen as an eccentric, if anybody bothered looking at this footage at all.

With any luck, nobody would.

Helen had taken the chance of leaving the sliding glass door of her room unlocked so they wouldn't have to actually enter the hotel through the public door or walk down the hallway that undoubtedly had cameras all over it. As they stepped over the low barriers and staggered toward her door, she hoped anyone who might see them would think they were just a drunk couple, sneaking in late.

They made it to her door without a problem. Now, to get him inside. But first, she sent a little sizzle of her power along the blood trail he'd unintentionally laid, using magic to turn the blood to vapor, erasing the trail and allowing the molecules to float away on the wind.

Task done, she slid the door open and helped him inside. She aimed him straight for the bed and was unsurprised when he collapsed, face down, on it. She'd already stripped off the bedspread and put a white plastic tablecloth she'd brought with her over the top of the mattress. She would leave as little evidence as possible of their presence here and would do her very best to leave no traces of what would happen here behind when they left.

Helen cleaned as she went, erasing the blood by the door before pulling the heavy drapes over the locked sliding glass door. Only then, did she turn on the bedside light.

She gasped when she finally saw the ruin of Jim's left thigh. How had he been walking on that? It was still bleeding, and if she didn't do something soon, he could easily bleed out from that horrific wound. Mouth set in a grim line, she set to work.

*

Hours later, Jim roused from his unconscious state, instantly wary. He didn't recognize his surroundings as he cautiously peeked out of half-closed eyelids. He gazed around the dimly lit room, realizing he was, most likely, in a hotel room. The furnishings and their arrangement told him that much. He kept going, noting everything he could see from this position.

Jim's eyes opened completely when his gaze landed on Helen, sunny blonde hair mussed, asleep in a chair in the far corner, next to the bed he was laying on. He moved and heard a crinkle. Only then did he realize he was lying on plastic. White plastic that was stained red in places with his blood.

Memories he thought had only been fanciful dreams, or hallucinations, came to him. Helen had found him on the beach and made him get up. She'd supported him and given of her incredible power to allow him to walk for what felt like miles, but had probably only just been a short distance up the dark beach from the place where he'd been ambushed to the last hotel on the strip.

She had saved him. And healed him, judging by the lack of wounds on his torso and the big wad of clean white gauze wrapped around his left thigh. That had been a killing bite when it had been made. Jim had known it but had refused to accept it. He hadn't wanted to go down to a Pack of hyenas. No way. No how.

Yet, when he'd been on his last dregs of energy, he'd seen fireworks. He wasn't sure if that was a memory or some sort of delusion, but he could've sworn he'd seen actual fireworks chasing the hyenas away. Then, Helen had come. Had she set off the fireworks? It seemed crazy, but that might just be what had happened. He'd have to ask her when she woke.

Right now, she looked exhausted. Beautiful, of course, but also drained. As if she'd given all her energy to him. Hell, she probably had.

Jim tried to lever himself up into a sitting position on the side of the bed, but his body didn't really want to cooperate. He laid back down and tried again, a few minutes later. This time, he was able to scooch up to sit against the headboard, his legs stretched out in front of him. Good enough.

He could feel strength returning to him slowly as he woke more fully. His shifter constitution meant he healed faster than most. His Alpha nature added to that inner strength. It was also what allowed him to hold the battle form through all the challenges he'd faced last night. Still, four against one had been rough odds with trained fighters working in concert the way the hyenas had been doing.

Jim would have to get on the phone to Arch and see if he could get any intel on a hyena mercenary group working in the States. Those bastards had been too disciplined to be just a random group of shifters. Plus, Jim knew, from his time as a Navy SEAL, that quite a few of the hyena shifters in Sub-Saharan Africa were well-trained fighters who had gone from war to war in their native land. A few of them had, no doubt, made the move across the ocean to try their luck as soldiers of fortune in the Americas.

Jim wondered if the four men had been paid for their efforts last night or if they had dedicated themselves to the *Venifucus* cause. He would be disappointed, though not surprised, to find that some shifters chose the path of evil, seeking worldly gain. Some—like the hyenas he had run across during his time as a SEAL—just liked the chaos of warfare. It appealed to their predatory nature. The freedom to indulge in killing was something every predatory shifter worked to control, though some embraced it. As a result, Jim thought those kinds of shifters were just one level up from feral.

No impulse control. No reason. No discipline. They allowed their inner beasts to rule over their human instincts when the real goal should be a perfect partnership between the two sides of a shifter's nature. But that was too hard for some people, apparently. Or they had been raised in chaos and knew no other way to live.

It was a shame, really. Shifters could be so much...*more*...if they learned how to use the strengths of the predator and the cunning of the human. But their hearts had to be in the right place, and they had to want to use their abilities for good. Serving the Light was the best path for any being, and like any race, there were some among the many shifter species that served only themselves. Or worse, they chose to serve the darkness and tried with all their strength and cunning to overcome the Light.

Jim sat there, pondering these deep thoughts, not wanting to make too much noise, lest he wake Helen. She deserved her rest after what she'd done for him tonight. He felt a bit guilty that she was so very obviously drained after healing him. For, he was certain, there was no other way he could have healed to this extent already if she hadn't given of her own energy to heal him magically.

Hell, he probably wouldn't have even been able to make it to the hotel without her infusing him with magical strength. He owed her. Big time. She had—he had zero doubt—saved his life.

Jim spied his phone on the bedside table. He reached over to snag it, and after only a vague consideration for time zone conversions, he fired off a few pertinent text messages. He wanted others to know what was going on with him and Helen, just in case the hyenas came back before he was fit to deal with them.

Answering texts came back almost immediately. First, Arch wanted to know where, exactly, he was and if Arch should scare up a cavalry unit. Jim thanked his uncle for the offer of support but replied that what he most needed right now, was help with intel. Jim told his uncle all he could remember about the hyenas, knowing Arch would put out feelers in the morning to his extensive network of contacts.

Jim also thought Arch would probably put out warnings along those same lines for anyone who might cross paths with the team of hyenas. If they were working for the

Venifucus, they weren't to be trusted or afforded any sort of concessions when crossing anyone else's territories.

When the phone in his hand rang, Jim answered it, though he hadn't wanted to make too much noise. Still, he wanted to talk to Ezra Tate, his point of contact at SeaLife Enterprises, who had hired him for this gig. Jim spoke in low tones, but before the call had progressed too far, he saw Helen stir in her chair. By the time he ended the call, she was awake and looking at him, even as she yawned.

"You're looking better," she said as he lowered the phone and met her gaze.

"You saved my life." He hadn't quite intended to say that so baldly, but it was true, nonetheless.

Helen blushed a little, the spots of color on her cheeks stark against her pale face. She looked a bit like a ghost of herself, which meant she'd given *a lot* of her own energy toward keeping him alive. He'd have to protect her while she recouped her energies. He owed her that much.

"I'm just glad those things were scared off by the fireworks," she said, modestly.

"So, it was you with the fireworks," he marveled. "I almost thought I'd imagined that part."

"Nope," she assured him with a small grin. "I lit up the skies, and I think I singed a few of their hides, too."

"Good for you," he praised her, glad to see her smile, even if it was faint.

She looked so pale, so in need of energy. He wanted to wrap her in his arms and protect her from all harm, but he knew he was in no position to do that just now. They both had some healing to do before they would be at full strength once again.

"What made you think of fireworks? For that matter, what made you come here?" he asked, curious. Grateful, of course, but really, really curious.

"My mother sent me. She had a vivid dream vision yesterday night, and she sent me off in the morning with the instructions to stop at the fireworks shop just over the border and stock up before I got here." She let her head roll back to rest on the back of the wide chair. "I had no idea what she had in mind at the time, but when it all started to happen, I suddenly knew what the fireworks were for. I'm just glad it worked to scare off those... Were those hyenas?"

"Hyena shifters," he confirmed. "I've come across them before, but never in the States." He frowned at his phone. "I was texting Uncle Arch about them. They're common in parts of Africa and a few other spots in the world, but it's unusual for a trained team like that to work on this side of the Atlantic. Arch is checking to see if there's any scuttlebutt about a mercenary group hiring out to someone in the States."

"Do you think we're safe here?" she asked, her eyes looking a bit haunted.

"We don't have a lot of choice right now, considering the state of us both, but I think we're okay for a while. That was Ezra on the phone, and he's turned up some interesting data about the man I'm tracking. Ezra's going to arrange a private plane so I can fly out of here to a place in Texas where he thinks I might be able to pick up the trail," he told her.

"I'm going with you." There was no doubt, no hesitation in her voice.

Jim wasn't sure what to make of her insistence. He'd assumed she'd go back home after her very timely intervention, but apparently, she had other ideas.

"I'm not sure—" he began, but she cut him off.

"I am. Coming with you. Mom insisted, and if you knew my mother, you'd understand that she only insists when there is absolute necessity." She looked a bit embarrassed, but he wasn't going to argue.

Even though it might be dangerous, he couldn't bring himself to send her away. The truth was, he wanted to be with her, no matter what. He wanted her by his side, where he could keep an eye on her and make sure she didn't drain herself, as she had, ever again. He could almost be mad at her for allowing herself to get into such a delicate state, but she'd done so saving his life, so he found he couldn't complain.

"It's not really safe, but..." Yeah, he was a total scoundrel for feeling satisfaction that she wanted to go with him into danger. What was he thinking? He should be doing everything in his power to protect her, not bring her along on an interstate manhunt.

"Good. Call Ezra back and tell him you'll need two seats on that plane," she instructed, then stood and walked, somewhat unsteadily, into the bathroom.

Jim could only stare after her, marveling at the way she'd managed to issue orders. He hadn't thought she'd had it in her, but she'd surprised him, yet again. Happily. He liked a woman with gumption.

Helen felt awful. She'd just barely made it into the bathroom on her own two feet, but she'd made it. She sagged against the counter, holding on for dear life. Saving Jim had taken all her skill and all her energy. But it had been worth it. The world would have been a sadder place without him in it, and she wasn't altogether certain she wanted to live in such a place.

She used the bathroom and then splashed cold water on her face from the sink. It felt good. She would've liked to take a shower, but she didn't think she had the strength to stand up that long. As it was, she'd been able to clean the blood off her hands before falling in a heap into that big chair at the side of Jim's bed, but little else. A change of clothes would be nice, but she'd left them outside.

Jim was out there, too. She'd have to face him again, and do her best to hide just how drained she was. She could feel the concern radiating off him in waves, but there was nothing really wrong with her that time wouldn't heal. She just needed to let her reserves rebuild naturally. A good night's sleep ought to do it. Most of it, anyway.

She was just afraid the hyenas would come back. It had to be pretty obvious which way she and Jim had gone when she'd hauled him from the beach. She'd erased the blood trail, but she wasn't sure her work was shifter-proof. They could probably smell things on a much deeper level than she could erase magically.

"Helen?" Jim's voice came to her from the other side of the door. "You all right in there?"

"Fine. I'll be right out." Surely, he wasn't standing up already? Though, his voice had sounded as if he were standing just on the other side of the door.

She'd been told that shifters healed faster than regular folk, but other than the little bear cub they'd rescued from the paper mill, she'd never had occasion to really use her healing gift on a shifter. She'd definitely felt Jim's innate magic sparking off her own when she'd started working on his wounds. It had resisted her, at first, but there came a point where her energy meshed with his and began to work in tandem.

The effect was kind of amazing and allowed her to do far more healing on him than she would have been able to do on a non-shifter. Something about his metabolism or his wolf or his magical core allowed her to direct almost double the energy at his wounds than she otherwise would have had. It hadn't all come from her. No, it was clear to her, at least, that a good portion of that magic had come from him. His wolf, his psyche, his soul...she wasn't sure. But it had definitely come from him. Somehow.

She gathered what was left of her strength and stood up straight as she grasped the door handle and turned. She'd have to face him, and she'd have to convince him that she was all right, except for a little drain. It wouldn't do to let him know just how much of herself she'd given in order to keep him among the living.

It had been well worth it, of course. She wouldn't have been able to face it if she hadn't been able to save him.

She opened the door, and there he was. Standing. Right in front of her.

CHAPTER 5

He shouldn't have been able to stand yet, but apparently, his will was greater than any wound he might have received. His muscles rippled as he lifted one hand to touch her cheek.

"You look tired," he said, his voice holding a note of gentle care that she hadn't really heard from him before.

"I am tired," she admitted, "but I'm okay."

"You need some sleep," he said, turning to escort her toward the bed, his muscular forearm under her hand. How had he managed to maneuver her into that position?

He was limping, and she immediately grew concerned. "You shouldn't be walking on that leg," she scolded gently.

"It's feeling much better already," he told her, pausing as they reached the side of the wide double bed. He turned to face her and looked down into her eyes. Her breath caught at the tender look on his face. "Have I thanked you for saving my life yet?"

Mutely, she shook her head. She wasn't sure what was happening here, but it felt...big. Important. Life-altering.

His head lowered, and he placed a gentle, chaste kiss on her lips. Then, he drew back, meeting her gaze. Her lips tingled where he'd touched them with his. Never had she had such a visceral reaction to a man's kiss.

"Thank you, Helen. You saved me, and you gave of

yourself to do so. I will never forget your courage or strength." That sounded sort of…final. Like he was planning on leaving again. No way was she going to let that happen. He might be on a mission, but so was she.

Without thinking about the consequences of her action, or why she thought it was a good idea, she reached up and dragged his head down for another kiss. A very different kiss that was far from chaste.

She sucked on his lips, demanding he engage fully with the tempest inside her that yearned to get out. He hesitated maybe half a heartbeat before succumbing and joining his lips to hers in a kiss that was anything but tepid. No, this was full-on heat. Desire. A sparking fury of passion.

His tongue swept into her mouth, spiking her excitement higher. Lost in his kiss, she felt her energy replenishing at an astonishing rate. Was this all it took to rev her engines? A kiss from a shirtless, hot, devastatingly attractive male?

Somehow, she didn't think just any male would do. There was something incredibly special about Jim. Something she couldn't quite define but knew was extraordinary. She clung to him, running her hands over his skin in the way she'd longed to do before but hadn't allowed herself.

She'd touched him, but only to heal. She'd kept her attentions as professional as she could, regardless of her attraction to him. He'd been unconscious and near death. That had been no time to run her fingers over his chest the way she was doing now. Her restraint had been rewarded with the most amazing kiss she'd ever experienced.

All too soon, he drew back. She was glad to note that he was breathing as hard as she was. He had not been unaffected by their kiss.

"I wish it were otherwise, but we don't have time for this right now," he told her, his voice low and gruff.

"What do you mean?" Instantly, she was on alert. Even as her lips tingled in the aftermath.

"I was going to let you grab a few minutes of sleep while I arranged things, but Ezra called back while you were in the bathroom. He's got a plane for me." He looked reluctant to say the rest, but he went on anyway. "And Uncle Arch texted me back about the hyenas. His intel is mostly rumors and hearsay, but it's nothing good. His advice was to get out of town as soon as possible."

Helen saw the wisdom in that. She'd been worried about the hyenas finding them again, too. She nodded.

"I called down to the desk and checked out of my room," he went on. "I didn't leave anything in it, so I don't need to go back there."

"I can be ready to go in five minutes," she told him, and surprisingly, she knew it wasn't a boast.

Whatever else their kiss had accomplished, it had somehow given her a jolt of much-needed energy. Where before she'd barely been able to stand to get to the bathroom, after their kiss, she felt ready to walk. She wouldn't be turning cartwheels for a while yet, but at least she felt good enough to leave and get to the airport, or wherever this mysterious plane of Ezra's was waiting.

"Are you sure?" He looked at her as if she were a bug under a microscope. She didn't like that. She shrugged out of his hold.

"I'm sure. Let me just clean up and get my stuff together." So saying, she set to work.

Jim watched her for a moment before shrugging and limping into the bathroom. When he came out, he was a bit cleaner. He'd rinsed off the blood she hadn't already taken care of last night. He'd also washed his hair. It stood in dark, spiky strands going in every direction as he rubbed a towel over his head.

"I brought some clothes for you," she said, tossing a T-shirt and pair of sweatpants in his direction.

"Thanks," he replied, an odd note in his tone, as if men's clothing was the very last thing he'd expected her to pull out of her bag of tricks. She discovered that she liked surprising him.

He'd been wearing boxers—the only item of his own

clothing that had survived his encounter with the hyenas. He sat on the side of the bed to aid himself in sliding the pants on without jarring his bandaged leg too much. Helen would have helped, but she was familiar with the male ego from dealing with her brothers. Also, she really did need to sanitize this room, erasing as much of their presence from it as she could. It wouldn't do to leave a trail for the hyenas—or anyone else—to follow.

She pulled a travel-sized box of black garbage sacks she'd brought with her out of her bag. Opening one of the large garbage sacks, she put all the remnants of Jim's torn clothing, plus all the bloody garbage she'd accumulated treating him. The plastic tablecloth from the bed went in, as well, plus anything else that might have traces of his blood on it. She squished that down to a surprisingly small bundle, once the air was out of the sack, and tied it off. That went into her large beach bag as she looked around the room to make sure she hadn't missed anything.

She took the television remote control and switched the set to the remote checkout option. Leaving the key cards on the table next to the TV, she opted to have the receipt sent to her via email. That done, she cast her eyes around the room again.

Helen judged she had enough magical energy left to give the room a quick zap, using her affinity for blood and anything that came from the body, to vaporize any residual evidence of their presence. There wouldn't be a single strand of DNA left to identify them once she was through. She went to the door of the hotel room where Jim was waiting for her, an odd expression on his face as he watched her.

"You're doing some kind of magic, aren't you?" he asked, a note of suspicion in his tone.

"Just a little zap," she told him. "My healing ability gives me an affinity for anything that comes from a living organism. I can use my power to zap it—even on a microscopic level—so that nothing identifiable remains. No DNA. No trace that could identify either of us."

"Seriously?" He looked genuinely surprised...and impressed, if she was any judge. She nodded in answer. "Wow. Okay." He looked around. "I guess if you can do that as we leave, then we're good to go. Does it drain you?" he added, concerned, which made her feel oddly touched.

"Very little," she assured him. "As long as I have at least some reserve energy, I can spare a bit for this. It doesn't take much."

"That's...handy," he said. She had the impression he would've said more, if they'd had time, but he was already peering out the peephole in the hotel room door.

"Wait," she told him, reaching into her giant bag again. She pulled out baseball caps and handed him one. "Hotel hallways all have cameras these days. It's not much, but at least if we keep our heads down, they shouldn't get a clear shot of our faces."

"If you pull a trombone out of that bag next, I wouldn't be surprised," he observed with dry humor. She laughed and shook her head.

"Sorry. No musical instruments, though I was tempted to pack the kitchen sink, but my mother needed it at home." He chuckled in reply and resumed looking out the peephole.

"It looks clear," he said a moment later. "Stand back behind me. The range of view is limited on these things."

She moved back and remained alert as he opened the door. He stepped out and looked around casually, as if turning to escort her out of the room. She had to hand it to him. His motions didn't look the least bit furtive and wouldn't raise any eyebrows if anyone happened to be watching the hallway at that moment—or looking at the recording sometime later.

Keeping their heads down, they walked out the exit door at the end of the hallway. Their vehicles weren't far. It looked like nothing had been disturbed, and the small, nearly-invisible string Helen had tied as a telltale around her door handles was still intact. She was reasonably certain that nobody had messed with her car in the night.

"We'll take both vehicles," Jim announced. "We shouldn't leave either of them here in the public lot, but we can leave both safely at the airport hangar. It's owned by an ally."

"Okay. I'll have to follow you because I don't know where we're going," she said, already heading for her door.

"Just stay right behind me," Jim cautioned. "I'm going to take some back roads. I was stationed at Norfolk for a couple of years and used to spend some of my leave here on the beach, so I know this area pretty well."

"Glad one of us does," she muttered as she opened her car door. She heard his chuckle as he did the same with his pickup.

"You have my cell number if you need to talk to me," he reminded her just before they got into their cars.

"I do," she replied, meeting his gaze over the roof of her car. He seemed so serious all of a sudden.

"All right then, follow me." He got into his truck and started the engine as she did the same. She got the sense that he wanted to say more, but he opted for making tracks instead, which was probably a good idea.

She followed him out of the parking lot onto the strip, where traffic was picking up as the morning matured into midday. Even in the off-season, the businesses here were being patronized by the locals and the few folks who came to visit even when it wasn't prime beach weather. Helen stuck right behind his pickup through the traffic and onto the road that would lead them away from the beach. From there, he turned off onto side roads that she never would have dreamed of traveling if she'd been on her own.

The roads twisted and turned, going from larger roads down to two-lane cow paths at times, as he used shortcuts and switchbacks. She figured he was trying to make it difficult for anyone trying to follow them. Still, he eventually brought them to a small airport.

Helen had been imagining a commercial flight from a larger airport. This was no more than a rural airstrip with a few hangars where small planes were housed. There was an airstrip very similar to this near her family's farm in rural Pennsylvania. She'd never flown in a small plane, but she'd seen them flying around the area often enough. One of her brothers had even taken a few flying lessons from one of the fellows at the airfield but hadn't pursued it beyond the first few lessons.

Helen followed Jim's pickup truck into the airport and then toward a hangar on the far end of the airstrip. As he approached, the door to the massive building slowly opened, revealing a well-lit interior that was mostly empty, except for a somewhat larger airplane than the others parked around the field. This one, while still a small plane, boasted two prop engines, one on each wing. It also had little windows down the body of it, as if it was able to seat a number of passengers.

Jim gave someone inside the hangar a hand signal out the window of his pickup and then drove slowly into the gaping doorway. Helen followed close behind. He pulled his pickup to the far corner of the building, and Helen did the same, parking right behind him. He got out, and she waited to see what would happen before doing the same.

A woman came out of the shadows behind the plane, wiping her hands on a rag. She nodded to Jim and gazed over at Helen before turning back to Jim. They exchanged a few words while Helen got out of her car and made sure she had all her things. She didn't know when she'd get back to her little car or how long it would sit here, among strangers, so it was important to take everything with her.

Jim motioned her over when she shut the door of her vehicle. She walked the twenty feet or so to where he was still chatting with the woman. Tall and fit, the woman had to be a shifter of some kind. Helen felt short and distinctly small compared to both Jim and the Amazon, but she did her best not to let her intimidation show.

"Helen, I'd like you to meet Leslie. She's loaning us her airplane and will be looking after our vehicles for the next few days."

Leslie smiled and held out a hand. Helen reached forward

to shake the Amazon's hand and felt a little jolt of shifter magic. Yep. The lovely Leslie definitely had a furry side.

"Pleased to meet you, and thank you for your help," Helen murmured, feeling outclassed by the tall, blonde beauty.

This was the kind of woman Jim belonged with. Not some short mage who had no offensive capabilities to speak of. He needed a warrior by his side, not a healer who had to be protected. Feeling a little down from her own thoughts, Helen was surprised when Leslie turned her full attention toward her.

"You're the healer," she said, smiling. Helen looked more closely. It was a nervous smile. A cautious smile. Helen grew concerned.

"I am." Helen saw no need to hide her ability. Someone had to have briefed this woman about Jim and Helen and given the information to her. "Is there something I can help you with?" Sometimes, patients had to be coaxed.

"If you would be so kind," Leslie said hesitantly, "it's my father. He's human, you see. He's been coughing an awful lot, and I'm really afraid it's something bad, but he won't go see a doctor." Helen heard the heartbreak and fear in Leslie's voice, and there was no question in Helen's mind that she would try to help.

"Take me to him," she said without hesitation.

"He's in the office," Leslie said, pointing to a little room built into the side of the hangar on the opposite corner.

Helen didn't wait but started walking, and the others followed her. This was something she could do. She knew her abilities, and healing was her major gift. It was her *raison d'etre*. The reason she'd been born. If she could help this woman, and her father, in return for the help Leslie was giving them, it would go a long way toward clearing the debt.

But the feeling of owing them for their help was only a small part of it. Mostly, it was that Helen couldn't stand to see someone in pain or ill or in denial about their health problems, if she could do something positive about it. She had an immense power inside her that could heal all sorts of things. It would be a sin not to use it.

When Helen reached the door to the office, she stood aside to let Leslie go in first. The other woman gave Helen a nervous smile and opened the door, smiling brightly at the old man sitting at an ancient computer, scowling at rows of numbers.

"Hey, Dad, I've brought some folks to meet you," she said. "This is Jim Hanson, Arch's nephew, and his friend, Helen."

"Arch's nephew?" The old man's face lit with a grin as he stood from behind the desk. "You don't say!" He came around and shook Jim's hand eagerly as Helen watched the way he moved. There was definitely something wrong there, but it didn't look as dire as Leslie probably feared. Helen began to feel more confident about being able to help the man and relieve his daughter's anxiety. "I served with your uncle for a while," the man went on, grinning widely.

"You were in the teams, sir?" Jim asked politely.

"UDT they called us, in those days. Underwater Demolition Teams. Or frogmen. I always liked that one." He grinned. "You have the look. Are you in, now?"

"I was, sir. Retired recently. I've been working with Arch on special assignments since then," Jim admitted. "In fact, we're on one right now." He stepped aside to let Helen move closer. "This is Helen. She's not a shifter, but she's got other special talents."

Helen was surprised when Jim spoke freely about shifters, but then again, even if this older man was human, he had to have been mated to a shifter woman if his daughter was a shifter. He probably knew a lot more about the unseen world than Helen did.

"Sal Vaccaro," the man said, introducing himself as he offered his hand to Helen.

She took his hand in hers and then, she struck. Not in a bad way. But she used her power to freeze him in place while she did her work. If all went as planned, he would never know what she'd done. Jim was at her side as she worked.

She was aware of Leslie rumbling a warning, but Helen was too focused on her work. This was tricky but relatively easy for a talent like hers. Humans were somewhat trivial to fix, although sometimes they took a lot of her energy depending on what was wrong with them.

The contagion that was taking hold of Sal's lungs was aggressive, but it was no match for Helen's Light. She poured the Light of the Goddess into his lungs, destroying the thing that could easily have killed him if left unchecked. Even with modern medical intervention, he likely would not have survived, but she wouldn't tell his daughter that. Leslie was clearly worried enough without thinking about what could have happened.

A moment more and Helen released Sal's hand, letting him resume as if only a moment had passed. She had a split second of dizziness from the expenditure of her own energy, but it passed easily. It was well worth it to know that barring any other problems, Sal would live well past one hundred years of age. He had a good constitution. His good genes meant that he would live long past the age of most humans of his generation, and the magic of his daughter around him all the time would only lengthen that lifespan.

Now *that* was something she would be happy to tell Leslie. Helen figured it would ease Leslie's concern a little. It was no good to live worried all the time. If Helen could help alleviate some of Leslie's anxiety, she would do so, happily.

CHAPTER 6

"It's a pleasure to meet you, Mr. Vaccaro," Helen said as the older man stepped back.

"Please, call me Sal," he said, a twinkle in his eye.

"Sal," she repeated dutifully. "Is this your place?" she asked, looking around the office and motioning toward the open door to the larger space of the hangar.

"Leslie runs charters and, yes, I still own the air field, though it'll go to Leslie sooner or later," he admitted with a grin to soften his words.

"Later," Helen told him. "Most definitely later. You're going to celebrate a century and more, Sal. As long as you take care of yourself."

Sal looked surprised. Helen met Leslie's eyes and saw happy tears gathering there. Helen nodded and turned back to Sal.

"I'd listen to the lady, sir," Jim offered. "She's a healer of great power. Just last night, I was attacked by four hyena shifters and ripped to shreds. Helen brought me back from the brink, and I'm almost good as new today—and that's not all just due to shifter metabolism. She's got a gift, this one." Helen basked in the pride she heard in Jim's voice.

The older man didn't seem to know what to say to that, but apparently, the news of hyenas in the neighborhood caught most of his attention. He scowled. "Hyenas, you say?"

"Yes, sir," Jim said, taking the attention off Helen, for which she was grateful. She needed a moment to recoup her energy. "Four of them, working as a team. I haven't seen anything like it since my last mission to Africa."

"That's not good," Sal said, his eyes narrowing. "This why you need the plane?"

"Partially, sir." Jim looked uncomfortable. "I walked into a trap here. The hyenas were waiting for me on the beach, while new intel puts my target in Texas. I need the plane to get back on track. I can promise she'll be well taken care of while in Texas. I plan to put down at Big Wolf. I have Pack ties there."

Sal seemed to consider that then straightened and nodded once. "Well, that's all right, then. I've known the Alpha there for a long time. We fly a semi-regular route between here and there during the season."

"Why don't you two chat a moment while I help Helen get her things?" Leslie said brightly before Jim could reply.

Helen knew it was a ruse. She didn't have any luggage other than the giant bag she carried, but Sal didn't know that. Helen thought she knew why Leslie wanted to get her alone and wasn't overly concerned. She met Jim's gaze and nodded slightly at his questioning look.

"Don't go too far," Jim said, shooting a warning look at Leslie. "I want to go wheels up within the next half hour."

"Not a problem," Leslie assured him as she ushered Helen out the door. Helen wasn't surprised when Leslie started with her questions as soon as they were out of earshot of the office area. "What did you *do*?"

Helen smiled gently as they walked. "You were right to be concerned," she told the other woman. "He had a fairly nasty bug taking hold down deep in his lungs, as well as the beginnings of what might've turned malignant, but I zapped it all. He'll be right as rain after a good night's sleep. He'll cough up some of that nasty, but don't worry. It's all harmless now. His body will get rid of it in less than twenty-four hours."

Leslie's brisk walk slowed to a stop. Helen stopped as well, turning to look at the taller woman. She had an expression of stunned shock on her face and tears rolling down her cheeks. Helen reached out, putting one hand on Leslie's forearm, offering comfort.

"It's okay," Helen reassured the woman. "I meant what I said. He's got really good genes. Barring anything strange happening, he should easily make it to a hundred, if not more, and in good shape, too. He's got a remarkable constitution, and being around your magic can only help fortify that."

"Being around me?" Some of Leslie's shock turned to inquiry.

"Well, he's your father, right? When people are close—related by blood or sharing strong bonds of affection—I've noticed that they often give and receive energy from each other without conscious effort. It's pretty clear to me that your father has benefitted from your energy in recent years."

"Mom was so worried," Leslie said, the words making sense to Leslie, even though they came a bit out of left field. "She's going to be so happy when she hears this." Leslie turned and took both of Helen's hands in hers, joy dawning on her face. "I cannot thank you enough, Helen. I owe you. Big time."

Helen shook her head. "No, you don't. There is no price for my healing gift. Just be happy and do good things. That's all I ask on behalf of She who gave me this gift."

Leslie's eyes widened. "Are you a priestess?"

Helen shook her head. "No. I'm just a healer, but I serve the Mother of All." Helen didn't go into her own beliefs that when she healed using the Light only she could see—as she'd just done with Sal—that she was passing on the blessing of the Goddess.

"I've dealt with healers before," Leslie said, letting go of Helen's hands and stepping back respectfully, "but I've never seen anything like what you just did for my father. I felt the heat of your power. I scented the destruction of...something.

Something bad."

Helen nodded. "That was the stuff I zapped. I don't have your senses, but sometimes, I can smell it when I zap a really strong contagion. It smells like a lightning strike. Ozone."

Leslie was nodding, as well. "That's exactly it."

"That's why I call what I do *zapping*. It's like the sound of electricity or lightning." She grinned, and Leslie followed suit.

"You are something unique in my experience, Helen, and I'm really grateful for what you've done." Leslie would have gone on, but Helen held up a gentle hand.

"I'm grateful for your help, as well, though as I've said, there's no price to be paid for my healing. It is given freely. So, let's just call it even, okay? Now," Helen looked around the hangar, "is there anything I can do to convince your dad that we didn't just come out here to talk about him behind his back?"

Leslie laughed out loud at that question. It took a moment before she could reply. "Follow me."

Leslie led Helen into another room that had been partitioned off the hangar. This one looked like a break room, complete with a couple of tables, chairs, a couch along one wall and a kitchen area that boasted two refrigerators and a chest freezer.

"We offer catering on charters," Leslie explained as she led the way to the kitchen part of the big room. "Now that I know you're going to Big Wolf, I'd like you to take some things with you in the cargo area for the Alpha there. He's partial to Atlantic seafood." Leslie grinned. "And you'll need some supplies. I doubt either of you have eaten yet. Am I right?" In answer, Helen's stomach growled, and Leslie laughed again. "If you're that hungry, I can only imagine how your wolf is feeling. Hollow would be my guess."

"He's not my wolf," Helen protested. *Not yet, at least.*

"Please," Leslie scoffed cheerfully.

"Wait, if you're not a wolf..." Helen thought aloud. Leslie's tone and phrasing made Helen think wolves were something alien to the other woman. Leslie didn't quite say the word *wolf* distastefully, but there was a definite accent on it that had to mean something.

Leslie looked over sharply as she was hauling things out of the fridge. "You're kind of new to shifters, aren't you?"

"Does it show?" Helen felt a bit self-conscious. "I've known about magic all my life, but the whole shifter thing is a very recent discovery."

"Well, in general, asking what species someone is can be considered rude," Leslie informed her.

"Oh! I'm so sorry! I didn't realize." Helen tried to backpedal, but Leslie waved away her words.

"I can see that. I'm just letting you know for future reference. Somebody's got to explain the peculiarities of shifter culture to you if Mr. Wolf hasn't already."

"I only just met Jim a few days ago," Helen tried to explain. "Since then, it's been kind of a whirlwind situation, and we haven't had a lot of time to just talk."

Leslie was nodding, even as she loaded up some large freezer bags with boxes of lobster and crab, among other things. The cupboards in the kitchen area were well stocked with carryalls for both hot and cold things. Leslie nodded toward one of the insulated bags she'd removed from a cupboard.

"Go ahead and raid that fridge over there. That's where we keep the fresh stuff. Pack up anything you want and then triple the quantity for Jim." Leslie chuckled while she continued to fill up the freezer bags.

Helen set to work, feeling a bit odd about raiding someone else's refrigerator, but she was also really hungry, which helped allay her misgivings. She opened the door of the refrigerator and nearly groaned. It was chock full of things that made her mouth water.

"Take that whole platter of bagels, if you want," Leslie offered from where she was working. "We have a charter to New York and back all this week, and they're bringing me bagels like they're going out of style. That one is left over from yesterday, and we'll be getting a fresh delivery in about an hour."

"Say no more," Helen said eagerly, licking her lips as she took the plastic platter that had to have come from a deli or specialty bakery. The bagels looked really scrumptious.

The women loaded up a half-dozen large insulated bags, chatting all the while. Leslie gave Helen some pointers on how to interact with shifters, for which she was grateful. She was going into an area with a dominant wolf Pack. She certainly didn't want to insult anyone through her own ignorance of their ways.

Leslie took Helen over to the airplane and showed her how the door worked. Helen mentioned that she'd never been in a small plane before, and Leslie took the time to show Helen the layout of the cargo area while they were stowing the food she'd packed for delivery to Big Wolf. Then, Leslie showed Helen the passenger area, which was quite luxurious for a plane this small, with hidden compartments that held a bar and snacks, among other things. She also helped Helen stow the food from the other refrigerator in the small fridge in the passenger compartment and set things up so they wouldn't shift too much in flight.

Then, Leslie surprised Helen, by showing her the flight deck. There were only two seats up front—one for the pilot and one for the co-pilot. Helen had assumed she'd be sitting in the back for the trip, but Leslie casually dropped the bombshell that she wasn't coming along on their flight, so Jim could fly, and Helen could sit in the co-pilot's chair, as long as she knew what not to touch.

Leslie gave Helen a quick rundown of the controls, though it meant little to Helen. She was intrigued by all the instruments but didn't have the background to know much about how it all worked. Helen was sure she'd have questions for Jim when he actually got into the pilot's chair and started doing his thing. She hadn't really realized that he was a qualified pilot, but he must be if Leslie and Sal were willing to loan him one of their planes.

Helen guessed he must have learned the skill while he'd

been in the military, but that was just a guess. She'd ask him, if she got a chance, while they were in the air. Somehow, the thought that he'd be the one flying them to Texas was comforting rather than alarming. Having only been around him a few days, she still had this overwhelming feeling that Jim could do just about anything he set his mind to—and do it better than most people. He had a confidence that reassured her about his ability to get them where they wanted to go, and…when it came right down to it…she trusted him.

Sure, he'd made a mistake in following that false trail to Virginia Beach, but she'd heard him discussing it with Martin before they'd parted that first time. They'd both acknowledged that it could very well be a trap, but there hadn't been an alternative at the time. Jim had known the danger going in, but his mistake had been in underestimating the enemy. Of course, it was a bit farfetched to even think a low-level warehouse worker from West Virginia would have the resources to hire what had to have been a mercenary company to wait for a mark that might never show up.

From what Kiki had told Helen, the entire situation at that paper mill had been a case of hidden magic. What they called black magic. It operated in stealth and was incredibly hard to counter. Kiki's new husband, Jack, had underestimated his opponent in that situation, as well. Since this guy they were following was part of that sinister group, it made sense that he might have a few tricks up his sleeve that nobody had considered. She suspected Jim would think twice now, about things he otherwise wouldn't have entertained.

Live and learn. He almost hadn't. Lived, that is. Helen had to shake her head at her own thoughts. The Mother of All had to have other plans for Jim, which was why, ultimately, Helen was here. Leslie had almost finished the tour when Jim joined them.

"Almost ready to go?" he asked, spying them through the little door that led from the passenger compartment to the flight deck.

Leslie got up from where she'd been sitting in the pilot's

seat. "Just showing Helen around a bit," she said brightly. Jim made way as Leslie moved past him, and Helen followed suit. Only, Jim didn't really move out of the doorway, and Helen found herself brushing up against his tall, muscular body.

Was it getting hot in here?

She sidled past him, and the three of them exited the plane to stand on the hangar floor. Leslie looked at Jim expectantly.

"Did you do your walk-around yet?" she prompted him.

Jim shook his head. "Doing it now, captain." He gave Leslie a jaunty salute before jogging around to the other side of the plane to begin some kind of detailed inspection of the wings and other moving parts.

Leslie smiled after him. "Don't take this amiss. I've never met him before, but I can tell he's one of the good ones," Leslie said, turning the power of her golden gaze back on Helen. "Plus, my dad has told me stories about Arch Hanson all my life. If Jim is anything like his uncle, he's hell on wheels. You hang onto him, if you can, Helen, and you won't ever be unhappy."

Ending those startling words with a wink, Leslie went to join Jim at the nose of the plane. Helen watched the two shifters, both tall and muscular, and so in tune with everything around them. Helen had never really been that way. She'd always felt a bit like a square peg in a round hole around her family. All of them, except Kiki, of course, could do incredible magic while Helen was *just* a healer. None of them held it against her, but they'd often left her and Kiki in the dust when they'd been off practicing how to conjure illusions and other fun stuff that Helen just couldn't do. Her power didn't work that way.

Leslie waved to Helen as she left, and Jim finished his walk-around. He motioned for her to precede him into the plane, and she hopped up the stairs into the cabin. All the stuff she'd brought on board was already stowed, and Jim didn't have anything much with him, just a small bag he'd taken from the back of his truck that he placed behind the pilot's chair as he went into the cockpit.

He started flipping switches and put on a headset. "Why don't you keep me company up here for a bit?" he suggested.

Helen joined him, sitting in the co-pilot's seat. "I've never been up front in a plane before. It's pretty cool."

"It's about to get even cooler," he told her with a grin. "Here, put on this headset so you can listen in on the radio." Properly outfitted, he plugged her in, and she could hear some people talking about runways and wind speeds. "There's a charter inbound," Jim told her. "That's the tower talking to them on approach. We'll taxi out to the runway once they touch down, and be in the air before they even stop rolling."

The great doors to the hangar were standing open. Leslie stood at one corner, manning the controls of the power-assisted doors. She made some hand signals, and Jim responded. A moment later, Leslie was moving toward them, pushing a lawn mower shaped thing.

"She'll move us out of the hangar so we don't have to get the props spinning in here," Jim explained.

"What is that thing?" Helen asked as Leslie disappeared beneath the nose of the airplane.

"It's a motorized tug. Basically, powered wheels with a handle that's strong enough to pull the plane out of the hangar," Jim explained.

Helen felt a bump, and then the plane, started moving forward, out of the hangar. Leslie was walking backward, holding the handle of the tug, directing it. She moved the plane out of the large bay doors and onto the strip of tarmac in front, turning it to position it just so.

"She's moving us into a position so that when I spin up the props, we won't kick a few pounds of dust and debris into the clean hangar," Jim said with a smile, waving at Leslie as she walked away with the tug apparatus behind her. "Now, for the fun part." Jim hit some switches, and the propellers sputtered to life, one at a time.

Helen had never been in such a small plane, and the noise of the propellers surprised her. It was loud!

Jim started the plane rolling toward the big white lines painted at the end of the runway. As Jim positioned their plane at the end of the runway, Helen saw another plane come in for a landing in front of them. It touched down beautifully, and she heard the bored-sounding communications with the ground over the headset. Then, Jim spoke over the radio, requesting clearance. He got it, and they started moving down the runway, picking up speed as they rolled along.

She saw the other plane taxiing around, moving towards its hangar, even as the wheels on the aircraft she was in left the ground. Exhilaration filled her at the feeling of flight, as it always did, but this time, it was even more primal. The thrum of the propellers filled her body, and she felt so close to the outside, it was almost like being a bird.

CHAPTER 7

"This is amazing," she muttered. Jim, having heard her, even over the engine noise, turned and smiled his killer grin at her.

She saw the spark in his eyes. The excitement he felt at being in control of the machine that made the impossible, possible. This flimsy little aircraft allowed people to fly. It was still a wonder to her, after all these years.

The first half-hour of the flight passed in no time at all as Helen enjoyed the incredible views. She even took a few photos with her phone, intending to send one or two to her sister, later. Eventually, though, she started feeling hungry. They hadn't really eaten today yet, in all the tumult of leaving Virginia. Helen unbuckled her seatbelt and got up.

"I'm going to get lunch," she told him.

"Great. I'm starving," he replied, predictably. If there was one thing she was learning about shifters, it was that they could eat three times what she did and still be hungry.

Helen went back to the little galley area where she and Leslie had stowed the food. Helen took a few moments to unwrap a couple of sandwiches and put them on a tray, then added bottles of juice and headed back up to the cockpit. There was a little pull-out table on which she secured the tray. Jim looked over at her as she sat back down, and she could just about guess what he was thinking by the somewhat lost expression on his face.

"Don't worry. There's a lot more food back there. I just figured we'd start with this, and I'll go get seconds when you finish that," she told him. "There's really not enough room up here for more than this right now."

"Thank goodness," Jim said, chuckling. "I thought you were putting me on a diet or something."

"I wouldn't dare," Helen joked back. "I don't want to be locked in a small plane with a hungry wolf."

"Honey, you already are," Jim drawled. Suddenly, the atmosphere between them sizzled with intensity. His gaze held hers, and she felt like he wanted to devour her...not in a bad way.

Could he be feeling the same hopeless attraction? She'd thought he'd sort of given her her marching orders when they'd parted the first time. As if he'd decided that whatever it was brewing between them wasn't worth the hassle or complication.

Of course, then, she'd driven all day to get to him in Virginia Beach. She'd gone the extra mile—literally—and maybe he'd decided that things were different. She wasn't sure. The only thing she could be certain of were her own feelings, and they were yammering at her to grab on to Jim with both hands and never let go.

Whoa. Down, girl.

Yeah, her reaction to Jim had never been what she could describe as tepid. He'd revved her motor without even trying from almost the first moment they'd met. He'd alternately fascinated her and frustrated her, playing come hither and then pushing her gently away. As if he was fighting the attraction or couldn't make up his mind about whether or not to let this thing between them run its course.

Maybe he was trying to protect her. Maybe werewolves had some kind of kinky courtship rituals that would damage her in some way—either physically, mentally, or emotionally. She had no idea. She hadn't even been able to get the nitty-gritty details about Kiki's bear mate yet. There'd been no time for deep down sisterly chatting. Helen had hoped that after the honeymoon period wore off—if it ever did—she would get a chance to talk to Kiki and get all the dirty details.

Kiki's mate was a bear, though. Maybe wolves were different in their mating habits than bears. Once again, Helen had no clue. She could only go on instinct here, with Jim, and hope that she did the right thing.

Jim held her gaze for a moment longer, then something on the dashboard drew his attention, and he looked away. Helen was able to breathe again, as she started eating the bagel she'd prepared for herself. Jim had to make some sort of course change, so he was busy for the moment.

When he'd finished with the turn that put them on a more direct heading, he started eating. The two sandwiches she'd set out for him disappeared in short order. Helen wasn't surprised. She'd expected to have to get up a couple of times to keep him supplied with fresh sandwiches. Leslie had packed a bunch for them, probably knowing full well how much a shifter like Jim could eat.

Helen fetched two more sandwiches and another bottle of juice and placed them all on the tray next to Jim. He looked up and thanked her as she sat back down and went back to eating her bagel.

"So, did you learn to fly in the Navy?" she asked when he'd eaten the third sandwich and was starting to slow down a bit as he savored the fourth.

"Actually, Uncle Arch taught me when I was a kid, but the Navy gave me even more training on many different kinds of aircraft. I can fly anything from a single prop Beaver to a 787, but this little Beechcraft is a dream to fly. This is one really sweet ride," he replied, enthusing over the borrowed airplane.

"Really?" Helen looked around the interior of the craft. "I don't know much about small planes."

"This has to be Sal's baby," Jim replied. "The pressurized cabin. The engines. The trim. It's a very high-end version of a very useful aircraft. I'm actually surprised they loaned it to

70

me. Someone must have done some arm twisting."

"Maybe at first," Helen replied. "But, once Sal found out you were Arch's nephew, you were golden."

"Huh." Jim tilted his head as if considering. It was a very wolfish pose that made Helen wonder what his animal side would look like. "You might be right about that." He shook his head and grinned at her. "Plus, he knows that Arch would have my hide if I messed up this beauty."

"Does Arch still fly?" Helen asked, just to make conversation.

"He does," Jim confirmed. "We were talking about maybe building an airstrip on Pack lands, but it's a big commitment and not enough of the Pack members fly yet. Arch is teaching a bunch of the kids in his spare time, so maybe, in a few years, he'll be able to do something. He wants to leave a legacy for the Pack, and a small airport would be a good one." He finished the last of his fourth sandwich before continuing. "You'll see when we land. Big Wolf Airport is the grown-up version of what Arch wants to build. It started out like any other small airport, but it's evolved over the years to become a hub for the Pack that owns it, as well as a waypoint for other shifters in transit."

"Big Wolf Airport is owned by a wolf Pack?" She'd been told some of this already but wanted to get the full story, if Jim was willing to talk about it.

"The Big Wolf Pack. In Big Wolf, Texas. Just about everything in the town is named Big Wolf this or that. It's kind of a running joke that the Alpha, Joe, had no imagination when it came time to name the various businesses in the town." Jim grinned. "I think he did it on purpose. I mean, after he named the airport and the town, everything else became a joke. He oversees all the Pack businesses, but a lot of them are individually owned, and the people who started them named them. I think they were all in on it, naming everything the same as a show of unity and also as an inside joke. You have to admit, it is easier if every business in the town has basically the same name."

"Like Big Wolf Barber Shop? Or Big Wolf Delicatessen?" Helen asked.

Jim nodded. "And Big Wolf Bakery. Big Wolf Barbeque. Big Wolf Pharmacy. You have to admit, it is kind of funny in a nerdy sort of way."

"Will we be welcome in the town?" Helen wondered aloud.

"Oh, yeah. Our Packs are allies from way back. My Alpha already cleared our arrival with Joe Villalobos, the Alpha and mayor of Big Wolf," Jim explained. "He might be at the airport to meet us. I'm not sure. I do have an information request in to his sheriff, and I'm hoping they'll have more intel for us when we land."

"Do you want another sandwich?" Helen asked, stowing the napkin and paper plate she'd used for lunch in a garbage sack she'd brought with her from the galley. She reached for the refuse off Jim's tray, as well.

"Maybe just another bottle of juice, if you have it," he replied. "I'm looking forward to a good meal in Big Wolf when we land. Their barbeque is known throughout the area and by pilots all over the country. I'm hoping we'll have time to sit down and enjoy a meal there before we have to be on the hunt again."

That sounded nice to Helen. The past twenty-four hours had been jam-packed with tension and stress. She would enjoy a chance to wind down and sit in a restaurant for a little while, even if it meant she'd be surrounded by werewolves. She was getting to like being around shifters. They were so healthy, her gift rarely activated, which was a blessing. Normally, going out in public meant being pulled in multiple directions when her gift demanded she help everyone within a certain radius.

Which was the main reason why Helen didn't leave the farm much. Not that she minded healing people who would never know what she'd done for them. Her gift was freely given and happily used, but it did drain her. Sometimes, it drained her too much. Simple shopping trips to the grocery store had almost killed her, more than once, when she encountered someone so ill that she gave way too much of her personal energy to help them.

At those times, she would barely make it back to her car, where she'd call one of her siblings for help. Usually, her brothers would come to get her, taking care of the groceries and driving her car back to the farm where her mother and sisters would fuss over her until she regained a bit of strength.

Helen stayed in the galley for a bit, tidying up before she returned to the cockpit with Jim's bottle of juice. Leslie had packed a tray of cookies, so Helen brought a couple up front with her on a napkin. She figured Jim might want some, but if not, she wouldn't mind eating them all. Sweets were her downfall.

She offered Jim a cookie, but he declined, and she grinned. "More for me," she murmured, taking a big bite out of a chewy oatmeal raisin cookie. There was also a sugar cookie and two chocolate chip in the napkin.

"Interesting," Jim said, looking over at her with a grin.

"What is?" she asked, feeling a little defensive. Her brothers had often teased her about her love of sweets, to the point of real annoyance. Well, she was away from home now, and she wasn't going to take any guff from a guy who'd just wolfed down four humongous sandwiches.

"That you have a sweet tooth," he answered without rancor. "I find that intriguing."

She narrowed her gaze. "What? No comment about how I'd better watch myself eating so much sugar? How I'm going to blow up like a cow if I keep eating all the cookies?"

Helen wanted to stop the words coming out of her mouth, but something about Jim invited honesty. She realized only at that moment, how fed up she was with her brothers' snide comments. As if they had any right to pass judgment on what she ate or didn't eat.

Jim's expression sobered. "Aw, hell. Who's been saying such mean things to you?" he asked, right away, as if he would rush to defend her. She just shook her head. "For the record, I think it's cute that you like cookies. Sweets for the sweet. And you are, Helen… Sweet, that is."

His voice had dropped low, and his words sent shivers down her spine. She looked up at him from under lowered lashes, barely able to believe how the atmosphere between them had changed so sharply, so fast. From a teasing conversation about cookies, they'd jumped right into an intimate exchange where he was telling her how sweet he thought she was.

Didn't that just beat all? He thought she was sweet. She wondered how to take that. Sweet like sugar? Sweet like a little sister? Sweet like the most delicious thing he'd ever tasted…and wanted more?

There were a few different ways to interpret what he'd said, but she preferred to go with the steamiest connotations. Her heart fluttered a bit in her chest because she found him scrumptious, too. Not that she could say that out loud. For one thing, she could be totally wrong in her assumptions. For another, he'd probably think she sounded silly.

Helen had dated. Of course she had. But she'd never dated a man like Jim. His masculine presence and undeniable dominance was totally outside her experience. The men she'd dated in the past had been neighbors. Farmers, for the most part. Men who worked hard and had strong principles. Jim had that, as well, but there was something absolutely wild about Jim.

The wolf looked out of his eyes at her from time to time. She could see it watching her. She wanted to get to know it better. She wanted the wolf to come out to play, and she wanted to pet its fur and scratch behind its ears. She wanted to learn how it felt to touch the beast that lived inside him, and she wanted to see just how wild he could be.

The mood shattered when he cleared his throat and turned his attention back to his flying. Another course change was imminent, and he busied himself with that for a few minutes while she tried to calm her pulse and steady her breathing. Being trapped inside such a small space with Jim was proving very…stimulating.

Helen ate her cookies and said nothing while he dealt with the technical aspects of flying. When he was finished with the latest maneuver, he turned back to her. She was startled to find he hadn't forgotten their earlier topic of conversation.

"I'm guessing your brothers have been giving you grief about your sweet tooth. If you want, I can have a word with them when we get back. They shouldn't pick on you," he said in a low, serious tone that surprised her.

He *did* want to come to her defense. The idea floored her. Nobody had ever wanted to go up against her three brothers on her behalf. The men she'd dated had usually deferred to her brothers or, in a few memorable cases, been run off by one of them. None of her boyfriends had ever offered to be her champion.

A little warm spot erupted on her heart. A tender feeling that had Jim's name all over it. She tried not to let him see how deeply touched she was by his offer.

"It's very nice of you to offer," she replied when she could find her voice, "but it's not necessary. I try not to listen when they speak nonsense, which happens a lot more often than you'd expect, seeing how they're all grown men now, with wives and kids of their own."

"And they still find time to harass you?" Jim asked, smiling now.

"On occasion," she replied, the conversation back to an easy banter. "They might have grown up, but they're still boys at heart."

Jim laughed out loud. "Most of us are, sweetheart, but don't let the others know I admitted it." He gave her a conspiratorial grin, and she laughed, as he'd no doubt intended.

"Your secret is safe with me," she promised, crossing her heart with exaggerated motions.

They flew along in silence for a while. She yawned, feeling full with the nice meal they'd just eaten. Jim turned to her.

"I know you had a long night. If you're tired, why don't

you nap a bit? I can handle this on my own."

"Are you sure? I mean, I can't help you fly or anything, but I can fetch things if you need them," she offered.

"I'm sure. You're tired, and we're probably going to hit the ground running when we get where we're going. Catch a few z's so you'll have the energy to meet the Alpha or whichever members of the Pack we end up dealing with."

"If you're sure…"

"I'm sure," he told her. "Go in the back. Those seats recline. Buckle in and get comfy. See if you can nap. I'll take care of the rest. Trust me."

She stood and sidled her way out from the co-pilot's chair but stopped with her hand on the back of the pilot's seat. "I do trust you, Jim," she said, wanting him to know the truth of her words.

He looked up at her, but she didn't wait to see what he'd say. She'd seen the surprise in his eyes, and that was enough. She made her way into the small passenger compartment and slid into one of the chairs, buckling her seatbelt, as he'd suggested. She reclined the seat as far as it would go and let herself lean back into the cushiony softness of the chair.

The next thing she knew, the plane was on the ground, and Jim was touching her shoulder, shaking gently. "Wake up, sleepyhead," he said softly.

Shocked she'd slept through landing, Helen rubbed her eyes as she woke. "We're in Texas already?"

"We are," Jim confirmed. "We're at the hangar, and the plane is already parked. All we have to do is go outside and meet the locals."

"Wow." She found the control to raise her chair and did so. "I can't believe I slept that long. It was a couple of hours, right?"

"About two and a half hours," Jim confirmed. "I'm glad. You expended a lot of energy on my behalf last night. I'm happy you had a chance to rest at least a little."

"Well, I don't want to be rude and keep them waiting," she said, getting to her feet. Her bag was stowed nearby, and she went to retrieve it. "There's a bunch of stuff in the cargo compartment for the folks here," she reminded him.

"I'm on it," he assured her, "but first, let's get you outside and introduced. The Alpha himself came to meet us."

Helen's eyes widened. "Wow," she replied, still trying to wake up fully.

CHAPTER 8

Jim got Helen outside and onto the tarmac. She was adorably fuzzy from sleep, but he knew she would make a good impression, no matter what. Her inner goodness shone all about her, easy to see for anyone who looked close enough.

Joe Villalobos was an Alpha used to looking closely at everything that entered his domain. He and Jim had met before, many times. Jim liked to think they'd built up a certain amount of trust and respect between them, which was why Joe hadn't asked too many questions about the magical guest Jim was bringing to Joe's town. Jim was glad of that trust and would not abuse it.

"Alpha, this is Helen Richards," he introduced them formally. "Her sister, Kiki, just mated Jack Bishop, and one of her distant cousins mated one of the wolves from that Canadian wolf Pack that had the troubles a few years back. There's fey in her family, and her mother is a Llewelyn."

Might as well get it all out there in the open, Jim thought. He heard Helen gasp a bit as he revealed so much about her pedigree to a complete stranger, but she didn't stop him or make any outward objections. She trusted him. He was still a bit floored by that admission she'd made to him before leaving the cockpit. Having her trust meant...well...probably more than it should.

"Helen," Jim continued with the introduction, "this is Joe Villalobos, mayor of the town and Alpha of the Pack."

Helen offered her hand to the older man. "Pleased to meet you, Alpha."

"The pleasure is mine, Miss Richards. Jim told me you were a healer," Joe said, his tone inviting.

Helen nodded. "I am, and please, call me Helen." Her smile was sunshine on a cloudy day. "If anyone in town needs healing while I'm here, my gift is freely given," she told him. "I'm happy to help, if I can. Though, from what I've learned from the shifters I've met so far, you all are ridiculously healthy."

Joe chuckled at that and began walking. Helen fell into step beside him, and Jim brought up the rear.

"It's very kind of you to offer, but you're right. Most of us are in good shape. I wonder, though..." Joe trailed off as if in thought before continuing. "Can you do anything to ease arthritis pain? There's an elder in the Pack who has quite a bit of trouble when it rains."

"I'd be happy to take a look," Helen said brightly. "If it's something I can fix, I'd be happy to do so."

"That's great," Joe replied enthusiastically, then glanced back at Jim. "There's a spot on the edge of town that I think you should scout out, Jim. I've got the details back in my office, so we'll go there, and I can brief you."

"I'm much obliged, Alpha," Jim answered promptly. He would have suggested delivering Helen to someplace she could rest first, but this was a wolf town, and she was a lamb. He wasn't letting her out of his sight until he was certain the rest of the Pack knew she wasn't prey, and she definitely wasn't an enemy.

Joe drove them to his office in his SUV. Helen sat up front, and Jim took the back bench seat. Joe gave Helen an informal tour of the town on the way from the airport to the mayor's office, which she seemed to enjoy. Big Wolf really was a pretty little town.

When they finally were ensconced in Joe's office, with the door shut and the map of the town spread out on Joe's wide desk, Jim really went to work. Helen sat nearby, watching but not commenting much.

"This is the current boundary of Pack-owned land," Joe explained, pointing to a rough circle centered on the town of Big Wolf. "This area I've color-coded green is one large ranch that now belongs to a Pack member's mate and will eventually come to the Pack through their children." Joe's tone was laced with satisfaction as he pointed to a very large tract of land on one side of the town. "These yellow areas are owned by non-magical folks who have mostly been either friendly or neutral in their dealings with us."

"I'm guessing the red area is what you want me to check out," Jim jumped ahead, but Joe didn't seem to mind. The Alpha nodded.

"The red area has an old feed mill smack dab in the center of it that is pretty much derelict. The whole parcel—which used to be a working ranch, then became a feed lot for a while about fifty years ago, and then fell into disuse when the cattle market had a downturn—was purchased recently by some folks from California."

Joe took a stack of eight-by-ten aerial photographs out of a folder and scattered them over the map. Jim could clearly see a very large old building. It was weathered, and parts of it didn't look all that stable. Joe had photos of the area, including the access roads, parking areas and other buildings on the large tract of land. Jim studied them as Joe continued to talk.

"I've looked into it, and something about the entire transaction smells off to me. If I had known the land was up for sale, I would've bought it for the Pack, but the whole thing was done without anyone knowing until the deal was done. Just a tad too clandestine to be legit, to my mind. Of course, I've had people checking out the place as best we could, but they found nothing. I even went over there, in person, hoping to introduce myself to our new neighbors, but no one was about. Or, if they were, they didn't come out to see me. I left, feeling itchy about the whole place, but I can't put my finger on exactly what it was about it that bothers me. The old mill has been there for a long time. It's an old building with a lot of nooks and crannies. It's also huge. At one time, the feed lot was one of the largest in the state."

Jim studied the map and the accompanying aerial photos. The building was definitely of a bygone era and looked somewhat shaky in places, but there were also signs that someone had been fixing things in certain areas. There were a lot of tire tracks in and out of the place, and the paths into and out of the feed mill's doors were showing signs of lots of recent activity.

"How old are these images?" Jim asked.

"About seventy-two hours. I have someone going up tonight to do some thermal imaging, to see if there's anything new we can learn," the Alpha replied.

Jim looked up from studying the photos and met Joe's gaze. "I'd like to see those."

"Sure thing. I figured you might want to do some recon tonight, and we can reconvene in the morning to compare notes and go over the results of the imaging."

"That's a good plan," Jim agreed. "And, yes, I do intend to do a little prowling tonight."

"I'll inform Shane. He's our new sheriff. Good fellow, from out West, originally. He's out dealing with some youngsters who've been giving us a bit of grief lately, or he'd have come with me to meet you at the airport."

"I'll try to drop by the sheriff's office later," Jim replied easily, not offended by the other man's need to deal with Pack business. "I may need him in an official capacity, if things get interesting."

Joe chuckled. "I think you two will hit it off. He's ex-military, too." Joe started to roll up the big map since Jim was finished looking at it. "You can keep those photos. I have the digital files. If I need to, I can print up more."

Jim collected the photos and put them back in their folder.

"Thanks, I'd like to study them a bit more before I go on my prowl."

"Now, let me get you two settled in the B&B. It's in the center of town, and we only let Pack members and special guests of the Pack stay there," Joe explained as he came around his desk, heading for the door.

"We're honored," Jim replied. He would wait to see what kind of a reception the Pack gave Helen before he'd leave her on her own in this town.

Joe was solid, and his Pack was allied with Jim's, but Helen was human. Worse, she was a magic user from a long line of them, with a powerful family behind her. She might be a gentle soul and healer, but sometimes, werewolves objected strongly to the presence of human magic in their midst. If anybody had a problem with Helen's presence, Jim would definitely have something to say about it.

"The elder I mentioned earlier…" Joe said to Helen as he opened the door for her and waited politely, in the human way, for her to exit the office first, "…she lives at the B&B. Miss Felicity. She's a typical old granny who takes care of everybody who comes into her sphere of influence. Her great-granddaughter, Felicia, runs the B&B."

Helen walked with Joe as they left the mayor's office, telling him she'd be happy to see if she could do anything to help Miss Felicity's aching bones. Jim watched how Joe interacted with Helen. He seemed very at ease with her, which was a good sign. Jim knew Joe's Pack as well as he could know any Pack that wasn't his own, but he didn't know the nitty-gritty stuff about how they accepted—or didn't accept—humans or mages or any kind of Others that might cross their paths.

The B&B wasn't far. It was just down the street from Town Hall. A charming, sprawling Victorian monster of a house that looked like it had a lot of history. Just at first glance, Jim could see at least four places where it had been added to, over the years. The face of it that fronted Main Street was tall and sported a turret and high-peaked roofline with just a little gingerbread trim and moderately ornate corbels. It was painted a rich cream color with burgundy trim, and hanging plants graced the wide front porch that wrapped around the bottom floor.

The house looked deceptively normal—if very grand—from the front, but a glance at the side showed how far back it went. It was a truly massive building with plenty of room for guests and Packmates who needed a temporary place to live for whatever reason.

As they mounted the steps, a young woman came out to greet them. She was short, for a shifter, standing around five-foot-seven or so. She had wavy dark hair with a playful streak of purple running through it and warm brown eyes.

"Hi, I'm Felicia," she said, her personality as bouncy as her footsteps. "You must be Helen and Jim." She reached out to shake their hands, and Jim noted that Felicia gravitated toward Helen first.

Felicia seemed very open and cordial, and Jim thought her welcome was a real one. He breathed an inner sigh of relief. This could have gone either way, and if the person in charge of the B&B had taken a dislike to them, it would have made their stay in Big Wolf, and the work Jim needed to do here, much more difficult. He had a mission, but he also had to keep Helen safe. She was too innocent and gentle a soul to be left on her own among a Pack of hostile werewolves.

So far, the Alpha and the woman who ran the B&B seemed to be all right with her presence. If that trend continued—and with those two powerful presences already on Helen's side—Jim would be able to stop worrying about Helen's safety and get on with his work. Things were definitely looking up, and Jim started feeling very optimistic about his chances of going out and doing reconnaissance tonight while Helen stayed at the B&B, on her own.

Joe was making conversation, telling Felicia to make sure she took good care of his guests, which Jim appreciated. Joe didn't come inside, but left them on the porch, saying he had to see to town business, but he'd try to check in on them later. Jim shook hands with the Alpha as he left and then followed the women inside.

What he found within was surprising. In the front parlor—and it really was an old-style Victorian front parlor, complete with frou-frou furniture and fussy lace curtains—an old woman sat in splendor. That was the only word for it. She was one of the oldest wolf shifters Jim had ever seen. Her hair had gone silvery white with age and was worn tucked up in a bun on the back of her head. She wore a dark dress with little flowers in the design of the fabric and black leather shoes with buckles, like something out of yesteryear.

There was a cane at her side, as well as a well-padded basket with a little Westie dog sitting in it. The little pink tongue stuck out of its mouth, and its white fur shone with health, its ears pricking forward and its little black eyes watching the newcomers closely. It didn't bark, but it did pant happily, watching everything with great interest.

Jim approached cautiously, not wanting to give the little thing a heart attack. Dogs often reacted with fear to him because he was such a dominant wolf, but once they got over their fear and learned that he wasn't going to try to eat them, they tended to follow him around, wanting to be part of his Pack. This little Westie, though, seemed to be made of sterner stuff than most. Sometimes, little dogs had big personalities, and it certainly seemed the case with this little white fluff ball.

"Gran, please meet our new guests. This is Jim Hanson, younger brother of the Alpha of the White Oaks wolf Pack in Iowa, and his friend, Helen Richards," Felicia announced.

Jim was surprised that Felicia was aware of his lineage. Sure, he was the Alpha's brother, but that wasn't something most people knew or cared about. Most people cared more about his relation to his Uncle Arch than to his brother, the Alpha, but Jim supposed he'd been around mostly military vets for the past few years, and they all held Arch in very high esteem.

"Helen, Jim, this is my great-grandmother. Most folks around here call her Miss Felicity," Felicia told them with a twinkling smile.

"I knew your uncle when he was a little boy," Miss Felicity said to Jim without preamble. "How is young Archibald? Has he a mate? Pups?"

Jim was floored to meet someone who thought of his uncle as a youngster. He tried not to stumble over his own tongue as he answered her questions.

"Uncle Arch is just fine, ma'am. He and I work together, doing special missions for those in need. He never mated, I'm sorry to say," Jim reported, keeping his voice pitched to a gentle tone.

"That's a shame. He was a handsome lad, and so brave, too. He was in the Navy, as I recall. Which, I suppose, means you followed in his footsteps, if you work with him. He was on some kind of special team that called themselves after an aquatic animal. Otters? No. Walrus?"

Jim had to laugh. "SEALs, ma'am. Navy SEALs. It stands for Sea Air and Land."

He'd have to remember to tell Arch when he got back home about the *Navy Walrus*. This old lady was just too funny. He could see from the wicked gleam in her eyes that she knew darn well what the teams had been called. She was putting him on, and he liked her all the more for it.

"Oh, yes, of course. Navy SEALs. The frogmen. I always thought it was an odd occupation for a wolf. Did you work with any big cat shifters? I would think they like the water more than most." Jim was utterly charmed by the old lady.

"A few," he answered. "I knew a couple of tiger shifters, but there were also actual seal shifters. Selkies, they call themselves. Some of those guys started the teams with my uncle, back during the Viet Nam War."

"Ah, yes. Archibald always had an attraction to magic, and selkies are more magical than most shifters. I can see where he'd befriend that type of person." Those shrewd, twinkling eyes turned to Helen. "Which brings us to you, my dear."

"Me?" Helen practically gulped as the full force of that formidable personality turned on her.

"You're not a wolf," Miss Felicity stated. It wasn't a question.

"No, ma'am. I'm human. A healer. From a magical family with a touch of fey in the bloodlines, from what I've been told."

Helen seemed nervous under that gimlet stare, and Jim didn't blame her. He moved closer to her in an unconscious protective stance, and only realized what he'd done when Miss Felicity's gaze followed his movement. She gave him a knowing smile.

The little dog chose that moment to hop out of its basket and walk up to Helen, sniffing her foot before looking up at her. She looked down at the dog and her expression softened.

"Who is this?" she said, bending to offer the pooch her fingers to sniff.

"His name is Angus," Miss Felicity told them. "He seems rather taken with you, my dear. That's a good sign. Angus is an excellent judge of character."

"Hello, Angus," Helen crooned as the dog allowed her to stroke his head and scratch behind his ears. "Aren't you a handsome fellow?" Helen cocked her head to the side and seemed to study the dog for a moment. "There's something wrong with his paws," she said finally. "May I help him?" Helen looked to Miss Felicity for permission.

"Certainly, you may try," Miss Felicity replied, her eyebrows rising in apparent surprise.

Helen put both hands on the little dog, stroking his fur. A little zap of her magic that Jim felt only as a slight tingle since he was standing so close to her, and she looked up again, smiling. The dog jumped upward, and she caught him in her arms as she stood, cradling him close as he licked her face. She was grinning as she moved toward Miss Felicity.

"All better," Helen pronounced, putting the dog on the couch next to Miss Felicity when she patted the cushion. The little fellow walked over to its mistress and looked up at her adoringly as she stroked his fur.

Miss Felicity looked at Angus's paws in minute detail,

looking up at Helen with surprise. When she was finished with her examination, her expression had filled with approval and gratitude. Her whole demeanor softened.

"Thank you, my dear," Miss Felicity said to Helen. "That was kindly done. Angus hasn't been himself since he got hurt. Our Pack healer couldn't do much more for him. We just had to let him heal naturally. But you've returned Angus's vitality to him, and for that, I thank you."

"You're very welcome," Helen said, taking the chair at the side of the couch as Miss Felicity motioned for her to sit down. "How did Angus get hurt?"

"I'm not sure. He's an independent customer, is Angus, and he likes to prowl around during the day when I take my nap. He came back a few days ago with burns on his little paws, but nobody knew where he'd gotten them," Miss Felicity explained.

"Burns?" Jim asked, taking the chair on the other side of the couch, across from Helen. "Heat or chemical?"

Miss Felicity shook her head. "I'm not sure. By the time he limped home, any chemicals he might've gotten into—if that's what happened—were long gone in the dust and dirt of his travels."

CHAPTER 9

They spent a few more minutes talking with Miss Felicity, but before too much time had passed, Felicia reminded her great-grandmother that she had to leave for an appointment, and Felicia wanted to get their new guests settled in their room first. Helen hadn't gotten a chance to broach the subject of Miss Felicity's arthritis pain, but there hadn't been a good opportunity to do so. She would try again later. For now, finding a few minutes to freshen up sounded really good. She was also curious to see what the guest rooms in this grand old house would be like.

Felicia showed them to their rooms. It was a single suite with two bedrooms and a shared bathroom between them. The décor wasn't nearly as dated as the fancy front parlor that seemed to be Miss Felicity's domain, but it was lovely. Clean, crisp lines, and gentle earth tones in beige and cream with burgundy accents, echoing the trim of the house itself.

Felicia left them after pointing out the amenities and showing them a binder with the house rules in it, along with menus from various town businesses. All the information any guest would need about the town and its offerings were within the pages of that binder, and Helen looked forward to reading it cover to cover.

First, though, she wanted a shower. The flight hadn't been

that long—just over four hours—but it had been an eventful few days, and she was feeling a bit ragged.

"I'm going to freshen up," Helen told Jim, taking her bag and heading into one of the bedrooms.

She was in a bit of a daze from all the excitement, but she'd never felt quite so alive before. Her life on the farm, with her family, was predictable. It had evolved that way over time as her gift became stronger and required her to separate herself from most of the human world and only venture into it in small doses so she didn't end up burning out, or worse. She had known she was living like a hermit, but she hadn't known what to do about it. It seemed the only safe way.

Then, her mother had insisted she be the one to drive to West Virginia to help her sister, Kiki. That had been a surprise. Everyone in the family knew, though, to heed their mother's suggestions.

It was likely her mother had sensed that going to help Kiki would bring about all sorts of opportunities for Helen. First, she'd been on hand when Kiki and her new mate had found that poor, captive bear shifter child. Helen had been able to heal the little girl and return her in good health to her frantic parents.

Helen had suspected that had been the reason her mother had insisted that she go to West Virginia in the first place, but maybe there was more to it than that. Helen had also met Jim there, and even though they'd parted ways, her mother had sent her back to him, to save his life and help him on this quest. Helen had the startling realization that maybe Jim's life wasn't the only one to be saved.

This whole adventure had shown Helen some of what she'd been missing in her humdrum life on the farm. The farm was safe. Being out here, among people, wasn't. Being among shifters, though, was something Helen had never expected. They didn't drain her like other folk. They were all so rudely healthy and full of vitality. It was actually...refreshing.

She was beginning to realize that she could have a life

outside the safe confines of the family farm…if she dared. If she could find a group of shifters—like those in this town—or the ones she'd heard about in that bear town in Washington State. Grizzly Cove. That's what it was called. A town built by bear shifters looking for mates.

Kiki was going to Grizzly Cove, and Helen wondered if she could wrangle an invitation to go there, as well. She already knew Kiki's new in-laws, and they were great. Helen knew she could at least visit them, from time to time, and maybe not have to be so isolated on the farm anymore. It was a little ray of hope for a better life. Something she hadn't expected in a million years to come of her mission to West Virginia. Helen had the feeling that her mother had known, though. Mom always knew.

Helen smiled at that thought as she pulled the shower curtain closed and got under the spray of warm water. Boy, that felt good. Helen spent a good few minutes just letting the warm water work out the kinks in her muscles from all the traveling she'd done.

All the while, she was very aware that Jim was just a short distance away, in the other room. He might even be in his bedroom, with just a thin door between the steamy bathroom where she was standing naked and needy, and his hard body. Damn. Thoughts of the sexy werewolf she'd been traveling with were making her hot. Helen dialed the shower temperature down a bit, hoping to cool off.

A soft knock sounded on the door that led to Jim's bedroom. "Helen? You okay in there?"

"Fine," she called back. "I'll be out in five minutes."

Had she moaned? Damn. She bet she had, thinking about Jim of the Hard Body. Shifters had superior senses. She had to remember that and be more aware of her responses. How embarrassing.

Jim heard Helen moan, and his body immediately reacted, growing hard and ready.

Down, boy.

Her muscles were probably just stiff and painful from all they'd been through, and here he was having sexual fantasies over a barely-heard sound that could have been the result of pain as well as pleasure. His caveman brain was stuck on the pleasure side of the equation, and he began wondering what kind of sounds she'd make when he was inside her.

He got even harder and had to curse under his breath. This was getting him nowhere, except frustrated. Jim retreated to the main room of the suite and took a look at the guidebook to the town. He needed a few things if he was going to be here a while, so he set about identifying the local businesses that might have what he needed.

That occupied his mind well enough that he was able to answer the door without embarrassment when someone knocked. He found a tall man in a police uniform on the other side, carrying a shopping bag.

"I'm the sheriff. Sorry I couldn't meet you at the airport. Joe had me collect this and bring it over." The big man handed the shopping bag to Jim. "I think it's clothes," he added.

"Thanks. I'm Jim Hanson." Jim offered his hand for a friendly shake.

"Shane McClure," the sheriff responded, taking Jim's hand for a firm shake. "I just wanted to come by and let you know that I'm available for backup, should you need it. I've talked to Joe about your mission here, and he's concerned that this may impact the town, so he's given me wide latitude to assist as needed."

"That's great," Jim replied. "I'm not sure what I'll turn up, but I'll keep you posted if I find anything you should know about. So far, all we have is one of my target's aliases showing up on some of the paperwork associated with that old mill just beyond the town limits."

Shane nodded. "Understood. We don't have a big department, but I have a couple of deputies who could help out if you want to set up surveillance or anything like that."

"Thank you. I'm not sure yet, what we'll need, but I will

be checking that place out. Some of my contacts are still tracking down the rest of the paperwork, so they might come up with some new leads as well," Jim told him.

"Those contacts of yours wouldn't happen to be on the Washington Coast, would they?" Shane asked, a glimmer of laughter in his eyes.

"As a matter of fact, some of them are," Jim replied, nodding.

"I've heard a lot about the bear town out there. Big John and his guys were approaching legendary status before they retired," Shane observed.

"That they were," Jim agreed. He knew all about Special Forces legends, considering his uncle, but he wasn't going to volunteer that information if Shane didn't already know.

"Good group of men," Shane summed up his feelings. "Let me know what you need. Here's my contact info." He handed Jim a business card with the sheriff's office logo emblazoned on it, along with Shane's name, title and phone numbers. The handwritten number on the back was for his cellphone.

"Thanks," Jim replied. "I'll keep you in the loop. So far, it's observe and assess. If I go active, I'll try to give you some advanced warning."

"Good enough." Shane nodded and left.

Jim closed the door and took a peek into the bag. It was a change of clothing—things that would actually fit. Jim would have to remember to thank the Alpha for arranging this so he could at least go shopping in town today without looking like a vagabond.

Jim went back into his bedroom and changed into the new clothes. They fit well enough, and he didn't look like a bum. That would have to do. He had his wallet and phone, which was all he needed to resupply with the other things he'd need. He just had to go out and get shopping while everything was still open. Hopefully, he could pick up a few things before dinner.

He didn't hear any more noise from inside the bathroom,

so Helen was probably done with her shower. He went back out to the common room of the suite and knocked gently on her door. She opened it a moment later and took his breath away with the fresh scent of her skin.

She'd put on a slinky cobalt blue dress she must've had in that ginormous bag of hers, and she looked like a million bucks. At this point, if she pulled an entire wardrobe out of that bag, he wouldn't be surprised, but this dress had the look of something that would fold down to almost nothing. It fit her curves faithfully, in a way that made his mouth water.

"You look..." He had to clear his throat before continuing. "You look amazing."

She smiled brightly at the compliment. "Thank you. I've never worn this before, but it's specially designed for travel." She modeled it a bit, looking down and smoothing the fabric over one thigh. "It's so soft."

That's it. He was going to die, right there on the spot. She was killing him with her innocent sexiness.

"The color really makes your eyes sparkle," he said, looking for something that was both complimentary and somewhat neutral to hide the rather obvious reaction of his body to her presence in that form-fitting swath of fabric.

"Thanks," she said, stepping out of her room and closing the door behind her. She had left the big bag in the room and carried a much smaller floppy tote, instead. "I see you got a new outfit, too."

"The sheriff delivered it," Jim explained. "Joe sent it over. But I want to pick up a few more things on our way to dinner, if that's okay with you."

"Fine with me," she replied. "I'd like to get a chance to see a bit more of the town while I'm here."

Jim wanted to see how the town reacted to her presence, as well. So far, everyone had been welcoming, but they hadn't met that many people yet. Still, things were looking good for Jim being able to leave Helen on her own while he pursued his mission. He just wanted to see how the regular townsfolk responded to her. If all went well while they were shopping, he'd be able to leave her alone without worry.

They went out of the B&B without running into anyone, then headed down the street toward a clothing shop. That would be their first stop. Inside, Jim picked up two new pairs of cargo pants, one black and one camouflage patterned. He also got a few dark T-shirts and some underwear, as well as a web-gear vest that was a surprise to find in such a store.

While he shopped on the men's side of the store, Helen did the same on the women's side. He noticed she had a few things on the counter when he went up to pay. He nodded to the salesclerk and had them add her purchases to his.

"That's very sweet, but I can't let you pay for my stuff," Helen objected softly.

"You're here because of me, and I'm on an expense account," he reminded her. "It's my treat. Or rather, SeaLife's treat. And besides, you saved my life. This is the least I can do for you."

The clerk watched their banter with wide eyes.

"You saved his life?" the teenaged girl asked, seemingly unable to stop herself. "But you're…"

"Human," Helen supplied, smiling kindly. "It's okay. I know it seems odd. I just did what I could. Right place, right time, you know?"

"It was much more than that," Jim said, speaking to both Helen and the clerk girl. He figured building Helen's rep in this town could only help her. "She chased away a pack of mercenary hyena shifters using fireworks and then dragged my badly bleeding butt to safety before healing my wounds and quite literally saving my life." He rounded on Helen as he said the last bit, handing the company credit card that Ezra Tate had sent him when he'd signed on for this mission to the gawking girl.

"When you say it that way it sounds…" Helen was blushing so prettily Jim had to smile at her while the girl ran the credit card through her machine.

"Heroic?" he prompted. "Courageous?" He was enjoying this, he realized. "Badass?" He nodded as if to himself.

"Yeah, that was totally badass, Helen. You were amazing, and I will never forget the way you came to my rescue."

Their eyes met and held...and the moment stretched. Jim felt the pull of attraction, the joy of just being with Helen, and the need for more. So much more.

The girl behind the counter broke the spell, sliding the credit card slip across the counter for Jim to sign. He turned away and picked up the pen, scribbling his signature on the receipt. The girl then handed over a large shopping bag with both their purchases inside. Jim thanked the girl, took possession of the bag and headed for the door, Helen following close behind.

"You shouldn't have told her all that," Helen hissed as soon as they were back outside. "If she's like any other teenage girl, I bet she's already on her cellphone telling all her friends about the weird couple that was just in the shop."

"I hope so," Jim said, smiling smugly as Helen walked at his side. "I want this Pack to know not to mess with you. I owe you a life debt, which means if anybody messes with you, they mess with me."

He put just enough of his wolf's growl into his voice to make a man they were walking past jump a little. Jim dialed it back a bit.

"I didn't realize..." Helen's words trailed off, then she turned her head to meet his gaze. "Do you guys really take things so seriously?"

"Saving someone's life is always a serious matter," Jim replied solemnly. "And, I'll admit, I've been concerned about how the Pack would treat you. I want to be sure they know that, if someone treats you badly, they'll be answerable to me. Think of it as me extending my protection on your behalf."

Helen cocked her head to the side, and a smile lifted one side of her luscious mouth. "That's sort of sweet, but I don't think I'll have any trouble. Everyone here has been so great."

"Yeah, they've been good, and you have the Alpha, Felicia and Miss Felicity on your side. That's no small potatoes, but you never know. It's a big Pack, and there are always some idiots in every large group," he told her. At that moment, they passed a store he wanted to go into, and he paused. "Hey, do you mind if we duck in here for a moment?"

"No problem," Helen replied easily.

She was such a good sport about everything. He found it easy to be around her, which was a unique experience. Most of the time, he found himself craving alone time when he was around people other than Arch. Jim feared he was in danger of becoming a truly lone wolf. If anything ever happened to Arch, it might just happen. Even his brother, Brock, Alpha of their Pack, wouldn't be able to keep him in the Pack without that binding tie to Arch.

Somehow, over the years, it was Arch who had kept Jim coming back home. Not Brock. Not anybody else in the Pack. Just Arch. If not for his uncle, Jim probably would have faded away into a lone existence long before.

Helen had that same soothing quality about her. Being around her was different than being around Arch, but the same in that he felt a tug on his heart, a tie that was starting to bind him to her, similar but not exactly the same as the strong tie that bound him to his uncle.

He held the door for her as they entered the shop, and she went immediately toward a display that had a number of colorful pairs of sunglasses. It was a sporting goods store, and with any luck, they'd have what he was after—or something close to it.

Jim bellied up to the counter in the back where they kept the hunting knives and guns.

CHAPTER 10

Helen tried not to notice what Jim purchased, but it was pretty hard to miss the giant Bowie knife and all its little friends that went into the shopping bag as she joined him at the checkout counter. She hadn't found anything she wanted in this store, but they had lots of outdoorsy sorts of items on display.

"So…I hate to ask, but what are you going to do with all those sharp things?" she asked as they got back on the street. The sun was much lower now, on the horizon, and it was getting close to dinnertime.

"Hopefully nothing," he replied, his expression sincere. "But, when you need a knife, you need a knife, and it's best to be prepared. I lost a bit of my personal equipment in Virginia, so I replaced that and then some. Just in case. If they'd stocked any decent firearms, I'd have bought some of those, as well." Helen shuddered. She couldn't help herself. "I'm sorry if that bothers you, but you know I was a soldier. I'm well-trained in all sorts of weapons. That's been part of my life for a long time, and that doesn't really change now that I'm out on my own."

"Guns don't really bother me," she said, a bit more forcefully than she'd intended. "My brothers all have rifles on the farm. Sometimes, you need them what with the animals and all. I just don't have much personal experience with them because, you know, healer? I have a hard time with anything that can cause injury."

Jim seemed to consider her words then nodded, just once. "That looks like our destination," he said after a moment, pointing to a bustling entryway where two groups of people were passing each other—some going in and some coming out. She saw the sign above the door.

"Big Wolf Barbeque," she read aloud. "That sounds good."

"It smells even better," he agreed. "Wait 'til you get closer and get a good whiff of what they're cooking inside. This place is well-known among pilots. They deliver out to the airport, and some people just fly in for the ribs then fly back out again."

Dinner was every bit as delicious as Jim promised. They were seated quickly because the restaurant had a deceptively large dining room with other rooms branching off from the main one. What she'd assumed was just one store in a row of them was probably more like the whole block, spread out in interconnected rooms and a very large state-of-the-art kitchen.

Helen hadn't quite realized just how hungry she was until they got there. She ordered a shifter-sized portion of ribs and ate every last piece. She didn't remark on the fact that Jim still ate way more than she did, but he was grinning at her steady consumption all through their meal.

"Stop that smiling," she told him at one point. "Haven't you ever seen a woman eat before?"

"I've never seen *you* eat like *that* before," he replied quickly, still smiling. "I'm just happy to see it. Shifters like feeding the people they care about."

He cared about her? That was…interesting…and exciting.

"That's nice to know." Let him figure out if she meant it was nice generally that shifters liked to feed people they liked or, more personally, by implication, that he cared for her. She smiled at him, hoping he would say more to clue her in on which it was.

"I hope you'll join me in dessert," he said, pushing the plate of assorted pastries that had been delivered to their table toward her. "I hear the bakery in town recently got an upgrade. Some fancy baker from New York joined the Pack and has been teaching classes for some of the teenagers who want to learn the trade."

"Teenagers made all this?"

Helen was impressed by the variety and fanciness of the little treats. Now that she looked around, just about every table had a similar plate of goodies on it, and everyone was partaking with gusto. She picked a small cake with a lacy sugar decoration on top and put it on her plate.

"So I've heard," Jim replied, taking two of the treats for himself. There were still two more on the plate, but knowing how much Jim ate, she knew they wouldn't go to waste. He was probably just being polite in not grabbing the whole plate right away. "My brother is in pretty close contact with Joe."

"Your brother, the Alpha of your Pack?" Helen repeated what Joe had said, inviting Jim to explain more.

"Brock is... Well...he's great. He's my older brother. A few decades older than me, so we both grew up, to some extent, independently, but we're close friends now, of course. He's been the Alpha for a while, but he's still relatively young for an Alpha of a big Pack, like ours. Joe has been sort of mentoring him over the years, which is quite a coup for our Pack. Joe runs one of the largest, most successful Packs in the country. He's a great role model for Brock and his ambitions for our home Pack."

"That's really nice. I didn't realize there could be so much cooperation between groups like that," she said, taking a bite of the little cake. The flavors danced on her tongue, and she had to stifle a groan of delight at the incredible taste. "Sweet Mother in heaven," she said instead, once she had swallowed. "This is amazing. Whoever is teaching a bunch of kids to make *this* is some kind of culinary genius."

Jim took a bite and nodded. "Agreed. Amazing," he

replied after a moment. "Just like you." He took a sip of his water, watching her over the rim of his glass with half-hooded eyes that she found incredibly sexy.

Was he flirting with her? Sweet Mother of All. She really thought he was flirting with her! Helen tried not to panic and to just go with the flow. She knew she'd be a goner if he so much as crooked his little finger at her, but she hadn't thought he'd really noticed her as a woman. Well...not much. He'd kissed her last night, of course, but he hadn't really made any more bold overtures all day, and they'd been together for most of it.

Then again, they'd been really busy flitting from Virginia to Texas and then getting things settled here. When had they really had time, before this sumptuous dinner, to explore a little more flirtation?

They had ordered a peppery red wine with their meal, and the rich flavor of it had paired perfectly with her meal. Both the food and the wine had left her feeling mellow. She'd had a nice long shower, and all three things combined to finally relax her enough to enjoy the adventure.

Her healing power lay dormant, for the most part. Everybody seated around them were shifters, as were the waitstaff. They were all obscenely healthy and didn't pull at her gift, which let her enjoy the night as she usually couldn't enjoy a dinner out in public. She couldn't remember when she'd had a better meal or environment in which to enjoy it. Or better company.

Jim proved to be both intelligent and witty—a combination that attracted her greatly. She hadn't been sure what they would find to talk about, but he'd surprised her with a discussion of his travels and the various cultures he'd been exposed to while globe-trekking in the Navy. He'd proven knowledgeable on a wide variety of topics and had explained about how the Navy had offered classes in all kinds of things to him, from mechanics to languages, flight training to chemistry. He had an impressive array of knowledge, but he wasn't conceited about it.

She'd had a bad experience with a university professor she'd dated for a while when she was in her twenties. He'd been an out-and-out snob and had made fun of those without the advanced degrees he had undertaken. Eventually, his attitude had poisoned their relationship because Helen was a farm girl at heart. The things she knew about were of the land and of magic. They weren't learned in ivory towers or from hoity-toity profs with high opinions of their own intelligence.

He'd seen her more as arm candy than a living, breathing, thinking person. He'd liked the way she looked next to him at faculty events—a pretty blonde foil to his dark good looks—but he never really valued her as her own person. Once she realized that, she'd broken up with him. It had hurt, but she knew she'd been better off without him. After that, she found it easier to just stay on the farm and only mingle with people who knew farm life and could appreciate both her and her family's background. Not that anybody like that really knew about their magic.

That was a whole other problem. Being one of the heirs of a long-standing family legacy of magic wasn't exactly something she could explain to the average farmer in rural Pennsylvania. No, she had to keep that—and her healing ability—under wraps for the most part, though she did sometimes act as a midwife for the local Amish and Mennonite community when there was great need. For the most part, the groups handled births among themselves. Most babies were born at home, the way their great-grandparents had been born at home.

Only if there were bad complications did they call for Helen, and she was usually able to pull off a miracle by giving of her own energy. Not that they realized it. Or, if they did, they didn't really speak of such things. They just blessed her for helping and sent her home in a buggy with payment in produce or dairy goods.

They were good, hardworking people, and she was glad to help save lives when that sort of thing happened, but sometimes, she despaired of the fact that they wouldn't allow the advances of modern medicine to prevent some of the problems before they happened. Leaving everything up to the Divine was not always the best answer. Helen was more of the belief that the Divine—whether you called it God, Goddess, or whatever—had blessed people with the ability to help themselves. Denying the existence of science, and especially medicine, was just silly.

It was their religion. Helen tried not to be too judgmental. Live and let live was her philosophy. Only when religious belief endangered health and wellbeing did she really begin to question it.

But being here, in Big Wolf, was a blessed relief. She knew most shifters believed the way she did—in the Goddess, the Mother of All—and they were so rudely healthy, there was precious little tug on her gift. She felt almost...normal. For the first time since her gift had risen in her early teen years.

Then, there was Jim. Sexy, smoldering, sumptuous Jim. A more intriguing man she had never met. A more interesting fellow she couldn't even imagine. With every bit she learned about him, she wanted to know more, until she'd explored his every secret thought and desire.

That was the crux of it, right there. Desire. Never had she felt so drawn to a man. Even her nerdy professor hadn't lit her fire with his most suave seduction the way a simple smile from Jim did. All he had to do was look at her, and she was instantly rapt. Ready for whatever he might say, whatever he might want.

She feared she'd be the easiest woman in history if Jim simply asked her to sleep with him. She'd say yes in a heartbeat and suspected she'd never have any regrets. She was beginning to think that her only regret would be if she never made love to him.

They finished dessert, splitting the last two of the variety of small cakes that had been on the plate. Then, Jim paid the bill, and they headed back up Main Street toward the B&B. Jim was holding the bags from their shopping spree earlier as they strolled along. The town had a festive vibe at night. It was welcoming and friendly, and people nodded to Jim as they passed on the street.

Helen watched the way the others interacted with each other. There was a certain distance in the way they dealt with Jim, but there was definitely respect and a bit of admiration—especially from the unaccompanied females. Helen felt like putting her arm around Jim, or making some other overt sign of possession, but she didn't dare. She didn't own him. They'd only kissed.

Sure, if she had her way, they'd be doing a whole lot more than that in the not-too-distant future, but right now, she had no claim on him at all. Even if they had been intimate, she didn't think Jim was the kind of man any woman could hold onto if he didn't want to be held. She'd learned a bit about shifters and their mates. She knew it was all or nothing for them.

Either she was Jim's mate, in which case, they would be together forever. There was no such thing as divorce among shifters. Or she wasn't. In which case, they could have fun while it lasted, but that was it. Helen wasn't sure which way she wanted things to go.

On the one hand, being Jim's mate was a scary concept because, really, they'd only just met. She was learning more about him as they spent time together, but she wasn't sure she was ready to make a lifetime commitment to him. On the other hand, being the mate of a man like Jim was like a fantasy. If she could have more days like this—being with him in a place that didn't draw on her gift every minute—she thought that would be a pretty nice life.

Whether that was the kind of life Jim could offer was another question. He'd been a Navy SEAL. He still worked dangerous missions on his own, as in this case, or, more typically, with his Uncle Arch, who was supposed to be some kind of super-soldier. She'd met Arch and had been impressed by him. He had spooky eyes that had a way of seeing right through someone, as if he saw more than the average person. She suspected he did.

She wondered if she was as transparent to Jim. Did he know how much she wanted to jump his bones right now?

Jim had been feeling some odd vibes from Helen during their meal and now as they strolled back toward the B&B. He wasn't sure if it was wishful thinking on his part, but he thought maybe Helen might be receptive to another kiss...and maybe a whole lot more.

That kiss they'd shared the night before had left him wanting so much more, but their day had been filled to the brim with logistics and planning and flying and settling in. They had barely had a chance to breathe, much less anything else, all day. However, the night lay before them, and he wanted with all his heart to see where the darkness might lead them.

Jim did have one more task he wanted to complete, but not until much later. He planned to go wolf and scout the area around the feed mill, looking for clues. He would do it after midnight, when most folks were asleep, except for the nocturnal hunters, like himself. That left all those hours between now and then for him to savor...perhaps...with Helen. If she was willing.

Something in her manner and the way she smiled at him made him think maybe she just might be. He'd wait until they were back in their suite, and then, he'd approach her calmly. He didn't want to frighten her off. He'd be as gentle as he knew how to be, and he'd coax her, if necessary, though he wouldn't push her past any limit she might want to set. He'd be a gentleman. Even if it killed him.

They climbed the porch stairs to the B&B, and he opened the door for her, remembering his manners. They didn't encounter anyone on their way up the stairs to their room, and he unlocked the door to the suite with his key. She had one too, but she was waiting for him to do the honors, so he took charge. He opened the door and let her go in first, turning to close and lock the door behind them. Then, he turned...and she was in his arms.

Jim wanted to laugh. He hadn't had to coax her at all. Quiet little Helen had seized what she wanted and had taken the initiative. She plastered her luscious body against his and threw her arms around his neck. It took him only a split second to get with the program and kiss her back.

He was pleasantly shocked by her aggressive move and wondered if she'd ever done anything like it in her life before. He'd bet she hadn't. She was enthusiastic but unpracticed, and he found that entirely enchanting.

When she pressed him against the closed door and tried to climb him like a tree, he took hold of her legs and let her wrap them around him. She was fire in his arms, and her kiss was a tempestuous mix of desire and need that echoed through his soul. Her scent filled his nostrils and made his inner wolf stand up and take notice.

He wanted her desperately, and she was giving him every sign that she felt the same. He lifted her in his arms and walked toward the bedrooms at the other end of the suite. Their lips melded and fused, their tongues dueling and playing and driving desire higher with every lingering lick. Her body pressed against him in a need echoed in his own soul. He'd never been so hot for a woman. Not ever.

Had it been almost dying? Had it been the fact that she'd saved his life? Jim wasn't going to put a lot of thought into it at the present moment, but he suspected it was really neither of those things. It was Helen. Pure and simple. Delicious, delicate Helen of the immense power and even bigger heart. Helen the innocent. Helen the man-eater. Helen of the Rockets. Helen of the Land. Healer Helen, the purest soul he'd ever had the good fortune to encounter.

Pure and just a little bit naughty. She bit at his lips while he opened the door to one of the bedrooms. He wasn't sure exactly which. It didn't matter. They both had what he most needed at the moment—a big, soft bed.

As it happened, he'd stumbled into Helen's room. He realized it when he saw the big ubiquitous bag that seemed to hold everything she'd ever need and then some. It was just as well they'd ended up in her room. He still intended to go prowling later, and she'd probably prefer her own bed and being surrounded by her things. If he did it right, she'd never know when he left, and he'd be able to slip back into bed with her when he got back. He hoped.

But for now, they had hours to enjoy before duty, once again, called. He planned to make the most of them.

Helen didn't know what had come over her. One minute, they'd been walking in the door, and the next, she'd jumped the poor man. Thank goodness he'd responded positively to her rather clumsy overture, not that she'd given him much alternative. Still, he could have put her away and then let her live through the mortification of a very embarrassing rejection. Instead, he'd joined her in the most delicious feast for the senses she'd ever had the pleasure to indulge in.

He kissed like a dream. Hard and soft, fast and slow. He seemed to know just what she wanted and gave it to her exactly when she needed it. That boded well for the more intimate activities she hoped they would soon be enjoying. Sweet mercy! She didn't know if she would survive his lovemaking if just kissing the man felt this amazingly good.

She felt motion and then, he dropped her onto a bed. She hadn't even realized he'd been carrying her anywhere. She'd been so focused on the feel of his hard body against her and, in particular, between her legs, she hadn't realized he'd taken the initiative and brought them to a bedroom. Which bedroom, she wondered in one little part of her brain that still had energy to wonder about such things before it was overridden by the more primitive part that was in full control of her body right now.

The beast of desire that wanted Jim's possession. His lovemaking. His mastery.

And if that wasn't a primitive thought, she didn't know what was. Helen surprised herself as those thoughts scrolled through her mind. She'd never been one to revel in the dominance of a male, but apparently she was now. Maybe it was *this* male that lit that primitive fuse in her hindbrain and fired all those seldom-used neurons to life.

Was it because he was a shifter? Maybe his innate magic rubbed hers in just the right way to evoke this amazingly strong response. Maybe it was just that he was the manliest man she'd ever known. A soldier. A warrior. A deadly man who had killed to defend others. It wasn't a pretty thought, but it was a true one. She'd known farmers and other upstanding fellows her entire life, but there was something about the danger of Jim. The sharp edge that was part and parcel of his being.

It could be a shifter thing, but she thought instead, it was a *Jim* thing. Something about him, in particular, flipped all her switches and created a hunger in her that she'd never experienced before. She had the awesome and somewhat scary thought that after this, she might never be the same.

That devil may care attitude that only Jim inspired urged her to throw caution to the wind and just enjoy what would come next. Based on his kisses and the way he touched her as he began to undress her, inch by precious inch, she thought they were both going to enjoy it to the max.

CHAPTER 11

Helen felt needy and hot as Jim undressed her. She wanted to help, but he gently pushed her hands away when she tried to assist. She met his gaze and found the same fire in her veins glowing in his eyes.

"Let me savor this, sweetheart," he said, nipping at her collarbone before he worked his way down her body.

She lay on her back on the bed, Jim hovering over her as he did what he liked. She was powerless to resist or make any effort to do other than what he suggested. Not that she wanted to change anything. Jim was clearly well acquainted with the female form and how to bring a woman pleasure. She felt a little pang at that thought but decided to be thankful for his knowledge rather than jealous. The ugly green-eyed monster had no business in this bed. She couldn't be jealous of a man who wasn't really hers, could she? Not really.

And, if he did turn out to want something more permanent, she knew shifters didn't play around. Not after they found their mate. If lightning should strike and they somehow were fated to be together, then she'd have a whole other set of things to think about. For now, she was done with thinking. It was time to just *feel*.

She loved the way he touched her. He made her feel

special and desirable as he stroked the slinky fabric of her dress up her bare thighs. Packing light meant she didn't have anything like pantyhose or stockings to wear with the dress. Just some panties and a bra under the soft jersey knit fabric. Jim lifted it up slowly, tantalizing her with each inch of skin revealed. He lowered his head to kiss her knee then worked his way up her inner thigh, nibbling and licking his way upward as the stretchy fabric of the dress moved with his hands, out of the path of his lips.

She gasped when the fabric passed over her panties, but he didn't pause there. He went higher, lifting the dress all the way to her midriff. Then, he exposed her lacy bra. She felt the cool air of the room against her skin, along with his heated touch. Everywhere his fingers stroked, they left a trail of fire in their path until she was burning, burning. So bright.

When he lifted the dress off over her head, she helped, lifting up to assist. She wanted the fabric gone. She wanted her underwear gone, too, but Jim, apparently, had other ideas. He touched her breasts through the lace, tantalizing, torturing, oh, so sweetly. Her nipples hardened, yearning to feel his lips, his fingers, his skin, only to be denied. At least, for now.

Jim stroked his way down her torso, hooking his fingers into the elastic waistband of her panties. She was glad she'd packed her sexiest underthings for this trip. When she'd filled her bag with odds and ends, she'd told herself that satin and lace was practical because it was less bulky than cotton, but really, she'd had exactly this situation in mind. Even as she packed for her dash to Virginia Beach, she'd had seduction in the back of her mind, though she hadn't let herself realize it fully until just now.

Still, the satin and lace felt good against her skin, and Jim certainly seemed to appreciate them. He dragged the elastic down the sides of her hips slowly, his fingers hot and slightly rough against her skin. He had big hands, and just the image of them against her creamy skin, holding the satin underwear, made her steam with desire. He was so masculine juxtaposed against the soft skin of her hips and thighs. A man who wasn't entirely human, which gave her just a moment's pause.

Would he be rough, like the wild animal that lived inside his skin? Or would he give her just the right amount of untamed passion that would send her into orbit? Somehow, she thought it would probably be the latter. She wasn't afraid of him. Not in this form or in his wolf form—if she ever got a chance to see it again. He was just...Jim. Steady, solid, sexier-than-anything Jim.

He lowered her panties an excruciating inch at a time. When she lifted her hips to help him over the curve of her rear, she felt a tiny bit wicked, but in a good way. The motion revealed more of her to his gaze, his hands, and—oh, stars!— his mouth. He slid the panties down her legs, tossing them to the floor quickly, then lowered his mouth to the top of her mound, rubbing his lips downward until his tongue licked out and slid between her lower lips to find the little nub that made her want to scream.

She managed to keep it to a strangled moan, but she found it impossible to stifle the sounds of her desire altogether. Jim made a sound, something like a dark, masculine chuckle. Apparently, he liked making her almost lose control. It seemed to make him even bolder, his tongue dipping inward as his hands moved her thighs apart.

The next few minutes passed in a blur of incredible sensations. Helen had never had so much attention paid to her in this way by any man she'd ever bedded. While it was true there hadn't been many lovers in her past, she wasn't a shy virgin, either. Still, Jim managed—in the first few minutes of their intimacy—to put all her past lovers to shame. She couldn't wait to find out what else he had in store.

He made her come with his mouth once, then again, until she was keening with pleasure. She did her best to keep her volume down, conscious of the fact that they were in a building with other people. Make that other werewolves with exceptional hearing. She would be mortified if everyone in the place heard her cries of pleasure, though she suspected

Jim would simply smile smugly.

She'd have to ask him sometime about shifter attitudes toward sex. She'd already heard from other sources—her distant cousins and her sister—that they weren't all that phased by nudity, since they had to strip to assume their other shape. Well, they didn't *have to* strip, technically. Jim's change on the beach in Virginia was evidence of that. But, if they didn't want to mostly destroy their clothing, getting naked before shifting saved their wardrobe. As a result, nudity didn't seem to be such a big deal among them.

It was strange to think of such a society. Helen had been raised in a culture where people covered up even more than most modern folk who lived elsewhere. The so-called *plain people* who lived all around their farm in rural Pennsylvania valued modesty. Women wore long sleeves and below-the-knee skirts and thick stockings, without any skin showing. Men wore long pants and button-down shirts, for the most part, though they did sport short sleeves in the summer.

To be wild and free enough to run around naked. That just boggled Helen's mind. She couldn't imagine how it worked with groups of shifters, but she assumed, if they'd grown up that way, it didn't seem odd to them. Helen thought these stray thoughts as she came down from the second orgasm of the day. Jim moved up her body, leaving her legs spread while he finally attacked the lacy fabric of her bra.

Soon, all rational thought fled as he lowered his lips to her nipple, sucking at her right through the lace on one side, while on the other, his questing fingers peeled back the lace cup to expose her breast first, to the cool air of the room, then, to the heated touch of his talented fingers.

"Sweet mercy!" she swore as his skilled touch drove her toward another climax. She'd never been so responsive to any man. She hadn't known she could respond this way, but Jim was showing her things she never knew about her own body.

"Oh, I like that," he said, looking up to meet her gaze, his mouth still near the tip of her lace-covered breast. "Begging for mercy. I don't think anyone's ever had quite that response to me."

He bared his teeth in a grin then held her gaze as he lowered those pearly whites to the place where lace met skin. He bit at the lace, peeling it back with his teeth in a move that made her squirm with desire.

When the fabric was out of the way, he closed his eyes as he sucked her nipple into his mouth. Helen's eyes rolled back in ecstasy as she gave up to the sensations he was provoking in her body. A moment—or maybe it was a lifetime—later, he left her. She felt momentarily bereft until she opened her eyes to find him standing at the side of the bed, taking off his clothes as he watched her body sprawled naked in front of him in wild abandon.

She tried to close her thighs, feeling a bit too exposed, but he stopped her. "Don't move. Just let me enjoy the way you look while I do this."

This turned out to be getting naked in a slow strip while he watched her body...and she watched his. Her mouth watered when his shirt landed on the floor. She wanted to touch and taste every rippling muscle on his tanned torso.

And when he dropped his pants, she had to lick her lips. Her throat was suddenly dry at the sight of his tall, thick erection. He gripped it, sliding his own hand up and down a few times as he watched her. Then, his gaze shifted to meet hers, and he smiled. A slow, sexy smile that made her fall just a little bit in love with the rogue werewolf who was about to possess every inch of her body. And then some.

"Like what you see?" he asked, stalking closer.

She nodded. "Very much." Why was her voice so breathy? Could it be the insane desire to have him inside her? Yes, that was probably it. Damn.

"That goes both ways, sweetheart. You're a vision," he told her in a soft voice that touched places deep inside. Scarred places that had been hurt by unkind words of other men. She might be the healer, but Jim was healing wounds she hadn't even known she'd had with his approving gaze and compliments. "I hope you're ready because I don't think I can wait another minute," he whispered in a rough voice as he rejoined her on the wide bed.

"I can't wait, either," she told him in that breathy voice that seemed to have taken over her vocal cords. "Come to me, now, Jim. Don't make us wait."

That was all he seemed to need to hear. He knelt between her spread thighs, still holding his hard cock in one hand, using it to guide the head into the channel he'd prepared so lovingly to receive him. He entered her slowly, taking time to be certain she could take him. He wasn't a small man, and Helen wasn't entirely certain all of him would fit. Somehow, he made it work, sliding in by slow degrees, letting her get used to the feel of him before adding more.

Sweet merciful heaven! That felt good.

When he was fully seated, he paused, meeting her gaze and waiting. What in the *world* was he waiting for? She almost wanted to scream, but the moment was too perfect—too beautiful—to mar with angry sounds.

"You okay?" he asked, and her heart melted at the gentle concern mixing with the swirling fire of desire in his gaze.

"Better than okay," she promised him.

He growled low in his throat. A sound of approval from his inner wolf. Then, he started to move.

To say his style was wild and free would be an understatement, but there was also the cunning strategy of the predator in the way he played her body, fast then slow, then fast again. He made her cry out numerous times as completion neared, then he would back off, milking it for all it was worth, drawing out the sensations to drive them both close to insanity.

He nipped at her ear. He even bit her shoulder, but it didn't hurt. It felt sexy...and daring. When he had played with her long enough, he finally allowed her to crash over the edge into a swirling mass of pleasure so deep, it had no beginning and no end. It was *all* pleasure. *All* ecstasy. *All* bliss.

BIANCA D'ARC

He followed where she led and joined her in orgasm a moment later. It was at that point that reality came crashing back. He hadn't worn a condom. Helen had never made love without protection, but she had learned from Kiki that shifters didn't carry human diseases and they weren't exactly fertile unless they were with their destined mate.

She wasn't sure how that made her feel. On the one hand, she wasn't sure she was ready to be a mother, though she'd always assumed children would be in her future at some point. On the other, she really liked Jim. Heck, she was well on the way to falling in love with him. She wanted more than just one night with him. She was thinking relationship, at the very least, if that's what he wanted, too.

But did she want to be his mate? How would she know if they were truly destined to be together for the rest of their lives? Was that something only the shifters knew? Or did their human mates feel it, too? Helen hadn't gotten to ask her sister about that one. At this point, she was almost afraid of the answer.

Helen talked herself down from the ledge. She was getting ahead of herself, as usual. They'd made love only once. Whether or not there would be a repeat was still very much up in the air. As for the lack of a condom, it only really mattered if he was her mate. Since he hadn't said anything to that effect yet, she would assume it was either too early to tell or she wasn't his mate. In which case, it was highly unlikely that what they'd just done would result in pregnancy.

For just a moment, she let herself fantasize about the possibility that they were fated mates and she would get pregnant with his baby. What would it be like? A little girl who could turn into an adorable wolf pup? Or a little boy just like his papa? Either one made her heart fill with joy.

Jim lifted off of her and rolled to his side, but he didn't move away. No, he tucked her up close to him at his side. Like he wanted the closeness after the ecstasy as much as she did. They weren't cuddling, exactly, but it sure felt good to her touch-starved senses.

Helen didn't often touch other people because it always caused her gift to go into action if there was the least little thing wrong. Even a hangnail wasn't too little to set off her gift, but with Jim, it was different. His own metabolism was so high that most of the daily little hurts that affected everyone just disappeared on their own due to his innate magic and the ramped up self-healing abilities of his shifter nature.

Her gift didn't fire, and she wasn't drained. On the contrary, touching Jim, being with Jim, especially making love with Jim seemed to fortify her on a cellular level. She felt invigorated. Replenished. At peace and full of life at the same time. It was a heady feeling that she was very sure she could easily become addicted to, if given half a chance.

"You make me feel good," she told him, wanting to share the revelation of her post-ecstasy thoughts. Her mind drifted in bliss, and everything seemed brighter and more joyful.

He hugged her close. "You make me feel good, too, little one." Jim bestowed a kiss to the top of her head that made her feel warm inside. As if he really cared about her.

"I mean," she tried to explain, "this…refreshes my energy. It makes me whole." She wasn't saying it right. She tried again. "Sex has never felt like this before." No, that wasn't quite what she meant. "It doesn't drain me. It makes me stronger. My gift, I mean." She shook her head. "And it's muddled my brain, too. I can't find the right words."

Jim chuckled and drew her close for a lingering kiss on her lips, this time. "That's okay. It sounds like it's a good thing, which makes me happy. For the record, I've never felt exactly like this before, either. You are one special, special lady, Helen."

He kissed her again, which led to other things… Which led to another, even more intense session of lovemaking that left them both wrung out and in need of sleep.

They slept in each other's arms, dreaming dreams of the future and letting go of things past.

Jim almost couldn't bear to leave Helen's bed, but he still had to do reconnaissance of that old feed mill. Such work was better done in the dark, and there were still a couple of hours left before dawn. With any luck, he could go, check out the place, and be back before she even noticed he was gone.

Jim crept from the bedroom as quietly as he could, watching Helen carefully to make certain she stayed asleep. He could hear her soft breaths and noted no change in the pattern of her sleep as he closed the door and padded, naked, to his side of the suite. Once there, he threw on some of his new clothes and equipment then headed out of the suite.

He encountered no one on his way downstairs, but Miss Felicity was in the parlor, and she saw him as he crossed its open archway heading for the front door. She signaled to him, and he stopped, going into her parlor to see what the old dear had to tell him. She held up a single key with a knowing smile.

"This will get you back in the front door. I may be old, but I'm still a wolf, and I like to prowl at night. I just got back from a little jog down the street. I can't really run like I used to, due to my arthritis, but I still get around a bit. I'll sit here for a little while before I go to my room, but you'll need a way back into the house if you're going to go out prowling." She smiled at him as she handed him the key.

"I'll return this to you," he promised. "Thank you for your trust."

"I talked with young Joseph earlier," she said, making Jim realize just how old this lady was, if that's what she called the Alpha. "He said you were here to help and that he knew your family. I trust his judgment, and therefore, I trust you. Plus, you're a handsome young devil." There was a saucy glint in her eye as she said that last. "I like the way you look out for that girl you brought with you," she added.

"Helen is special," he felt compelled to say, as if he was admitting to his first grade teacher that he'd failed to do his math homework.

"It's good you think so," Miss Felicity said primly. "She'll come to no harm in this house. You have my word on that."

Jim felt her words like the vow they were. "Thank you, Miss Felicity," he said, feeling grateful enough to bend down and kiss her on the cheek. "I admit I've been worried about how the townsfolk would treat her. She doesn't get out much, and she needs a protector. With you on the job while I'm doing mine, I feel much better."

Miss Felicity smiled up at him. "Go on, now. Do your duty and rest easy. Things will be all right here while you go do dangerous things."

He noticed, even as he left, that she didn't bother telling him to be careful. Miss Felicity was used to wolves. She was one herself, and she knew the human warning to be careful just made his inner wolf scoff. Though, he had to admit, if Helen had told him to be careful, he probably would have taken it as a sign that she cared for him. Funny how that worked.

Jim headed out the door, locking it behind him and pocketed the key. Miss Felicity had just given him a measure of trust. He wanted to make sure that any threat posed by those at the old feed mill was eliminated, by way of repayment of that gift of trust. That mission firmly in mind, he headed for the wooded patch on the edge of the downtown area. He'd eyed it before as they walked, as a likely place to stash his clothes while he let his furry side out to prowl.

CHAPTER 12

Jim scented all sorts of interesting things on his way to the old feed mill, including the unmistakable scent of adolescent wolves. It got stronger, the closer he got to the run-down property out beyond the border of the town, and he realized that old feed mill must be one of the places youngsters congregated away from adult supervision. There were a few spots like that in every territory. The shifter version of lovers' lane. Someplace teens could go to bond and explore together.

Oh, the adults knew all about it. They'd probably used the same spots to gather when they were youngsters. Shifter kids didn't go to such places to use illicit substances or get drunk. Most drugs didn't have much of an effect on shifters since they had such high metabolisms, and for the same reason, drinking wasn't that much of a thrill to shifter kids. Smoking wasn't something any shifter with a strong olfactory sense would enjoy, either.

Shifter kids went to places like the abandoned mill to learn the limits of their shapeshifting abilities and run, usually in animal form, with kids their own age. The old mill offered a plethora of scents to learn and discern, and many obstacles to jump or navigate. It was a playground for a shifter teen where they could explore their own abilities and match wits and skills against their friends in a competitive, yet friendly way.

Jim dismissed the teen wolf scents and concentrated on anything else that might be in the area. He began his recon in a wide perimeter around the property he was interested in. He made several passes, closing in a little bit more on each pass. He didn't smell anything, other than those teenage tracks which where a few days old, as he moved closer.

Jim prowled the area, finding the usual scents associated with the perimeter of a Pack territory. The stronger Alpha wolves in the group probably helped check the boundary line between Pack lands and the rest of the world. Joe no doubt had a group of lieutenants whose job descriptions included helping keep this very large territory free from trespass or interlopers. Anybody nosing around the invisible boundary line that marked where the town—and therefore the Pack-owned lands—ended would likely find themselves under surveillance, at the very least.

If they had evil intent, they would discover a very different response. Wolves weren't known for their patience with transgressors. They were more likely to bite first and ask questions later. Periodically, that caused problems with the outside world, and that's where the human positions of mayor and sheriff and the like came into play. Among the Pack, Joe was the Alpha. The leader. To the human world, he was the town's mayor. Same concept, different titles, slightly different levels of discretion and authority.

Likewise, the town's sheriff was also the Pack's enforcer. An enforcer had broad discretion to mete out punishment as directed by the Alpha and Pack law. In a Pack this size, the enforcer was an extension of the Alpha. In fact, in a Pack as large as this one, many functions were delegated to other Pack members. The Alpha of a group this size had a lot on his plate. It only made sense that he would need help keeping everything running and everybody happy.

So it was that Jim scented several very distinct trails running in roughly the same paths, parallel to the town boundary line. He recognized Joe's scent immediately. Likewise, the sheriff's scent trail was very distinctive and strong in the area. There were others, too. Most likely, they belonged to strong members of the Pack who were likely employed as sheriff's deputies or other first-responder types of positions. Police, firemen, ambulance workers, emergency medical technicians, and the like. Those were all good places to put dominant wolves who felt a strong compulsion to protect and serve.

Giving the subordinate dominant wolves respected places within the pack hierarchy also helped to keep the peace and the cohesiveness of the group. Joe was a smart and generous Alpha. He gave the other strong wolves in his group a chance to show their stuff, rather than subduing them into compliance. Experienced Alphas often had such power structures. That was often the mark of a very successful Pack.

Jim was gratified to discover that his initial impressions of Joe and his people were correct. The scent trails told the story. This was a tale of dominant wolves sharing space and authority for the good of their Pack, and an Alpha who knew how to best help his people, by letting them be who they were born to be, without forcing them to suppress their own strengths. Joe was old enough, and wise enough, to let them all be the best they could be and use those talents for the good of the whole.

Jim's brother, Brock, was trying to do the same. With guidance from both Joe and their Uncle Arch, Brock was guiding Jim's home Pack into the successful model Jim saw working here in Big Wolf. Jim was thinking about this as he went along, not really finding anything that concerned him as far as his mission went but learning a bit more about the town and its people from the age and frequency of the different scent trails. Until suddenly... All scent was gone.

In wolf form, Jim stopped short and backed up. Was the problem with him or the area? He retreated a few feet and cautiously put his nose to the ground. Relief hit him when the scents he had been following greeted him once more.

Step by cautious step, he advanced, making special note of any change in scent, but there wasn't any...until... Abruptly, again, the scents just disappeared. What in the world could cause something like that?

Jim sat back on his haunches just shy of the area where everything stopped to think it through. He started thinking about some of the things Jack Bishop had told him about the black magic encounter he'd recently had in that paper mill in West Virginia. Black magic was hidden magic. Unseen. Deceptive.

The man Jim had been tracking from that paper mill to here might well have been a devotee of the black arts, as well, even though it was a rare discipline because of the patience and time it took to master. At least, that's what Jim had always heard. Personally, he didn't know anyone who dabbled in such things himself. Black magic was, in general, practiced by those pursuing evil ends, and Jim was firmly on the other side of that fight.

Very carefully, Jim explored the bounds of the area where the scents all disappeared. It corresponded to the legal property line of the old feed mill, almost exactly. That couldn't be a coincidence. In fact, it could only mean one thing.

Evil had taken up residence in that abandoned property. With a low growl of anger, frustration, and determination, Jim turned tail and headed back to town.

With every step of his four paws, he began to strategize ways to deal with this newest obstacle, but first, he had to report what he'd found. Then, he'd find a way to penetrate the dark shield around that old mill and discover what lay within.

*

Helen was already awake by the time Jim got back to the suite. He'd seen Joe walking into the local diner when he was heading back to the B&B and had stopped to let the Alpha know what he'd found. Joe had invited him inside, but Jim had declined breakfast, opting for a simple cup of coffee while the Alpha got his enforcer, Sheriff Shane, to drop by so they could both hear the sit-rep.

Jim left them after they had heard his report, promising to call his contacts to see what he could learn about combatting black magic of this kind. Neither the Alpha nor the sheriff had ever come across anything like what Jim described, but they had both pledged to be there as backup, should Jim need more firepower behind him when he made his move on the place.

Entering the suite, he could hear Helen humming in the bathroom. He smiled, thinking of her, and sat on the couch to make his calls. First, he fired off a text message to Ezra. It was still the middle of the night there, so he didn't really expect a reply right away. Jim knew his uncle was usually up and at 'em by dawn, so he placed his first call to Arch, filling him in and soliciting his advice on how to handle this development.

He was just ending his call with Arch when Helen came into the room. She smiled at him, and just like that, he was ready for more of the incredible sex they'd shared the night before. Damn. They didn't have time, right now, but later...oh, yes, later...he promised himself he'd do all the delightful things he'd been dreaming about, as soon as they had a little more time alone.

She came over to the couch as he stood, putting his phone in his pocket. "Good morning," he said, his voice filled with the rumble of his wolf. She didn't seem to mind, and the wolf approved wholeheartedly.

"Good morning," she replied, standing before him, her expression so innocently hopeful that he couldn't help but kiss her.

Jim approached slowly, giving her time to turn away, if that's what she wanted, but no. All systems were go as his lips touched hers, and then, all good intentions flew out the window as he lost all sense of time, space, propriety, missions, and everything else. All that existed was him and her. Male and female. Jim and Helen.

He took her down to the couch and kissed her the way he'd been longing to do ever since he'd made himself leave her bed in the dark hours of the morning. He'd regretted that, bitterly, but he'd been trained to his duty since long before he'd discovered girls. Jim had always followed his duty first, all other things came after, and he'd never regretted it.

Helen, though… She could easily make him forget duty, forget everything but her. He wasn't sure what was going on, but Helen was quickly becoming way more important to his happiness than any woman ever had before.

Could she be his mate? The thought gave him pause. Jim drew back to meet her gaze, his thoughts stunning him into a ceasefire, so to speak. She met his gaze, her eyes questioning.

"What's wrong?" she asked gently.

"Do you feel this…?" He tried his best to articulate what he was feeling, but it was difficult. "This thing between us… It's…"

"Magical," she supplied when he couldn't think of a big enough word to encompass what he was feeling.

He nodded. "It feels important, somehow," he went on, still trying to find the right words.

She smiled shyly at him, her eyes holding mysteries he longed to know. "It feels important to me, too," she said finally.

He could only hope she understood the complexity of his simple words. He wasn't entirely sure he understood it all, himself, but he was definitely feeling something very out of the ordinary when it came to being with Helen.

Jim's phone rang in his pocket, and the moment was broken. "I'm sorry. I've got to answer this." He was already off the couch and reaching for his phone as he spoke.

Helen nodded understandingly. Maybe it was wishful thinking, but he thought he saw a bit of regret in her eyes as she got up and straightened her clothes. He felt a little wisp of pride in the fact that he'd been the one to muss her. It was still a marvel that a woman like Helen would even want to be with a guy like him, and Jim thanked his lucky stars every time he thought about what they'd shared the night before.

She was right. It had been magical.

Jim answered the phone, fielding a call from his brother, Brock. As a general rule, Brock didn't keep Jim on a tight leash. Brock was very focused on building the Pack into something to be really proud of while Jim was content to troubleshoot one situation at a time, using his military skills where they were most needed and best applied, but they kept in touch. They were brothers. Even though Jim would go off on missions all over the world, he was still a member of Brock's Pack. White Oaks, in Iowa, was still his home. At least for now.

Jim didn't kid himself. He wasn't entirely sure he would be able to stick it out in White Oaks for the rest of his life. He wanted to support his brother, of course, but he also had his own dreams to fulfill and destiny to follow. Luckily, he knew Brock wouldn't stand in the way of that. Even though Brock wanted to keep Jim home, he knew it was no good. As Uncle Arch had often said, some pups were born with invisible wings, and sooner or later, you just had to let them fly.

Jim took the call from Brock, and they spoke just a short time. It was basically a quick check-in with a promise of a longer call to come. Jim explained that they were on their way to breakfast and that he'd call back later. Brock had made no secret of his curiosity and hinted that he'd spoken to Joe Villalobos at some length the night before about Jim and his very interesting travel companion.

Jim didn't rise to the bait and ended the call as quickly as he could. He really was hungry and Helen was already heading for the door. If he couldn't snack on her, they might as well get some actual food. It was looking like it was going to be a long day, and he'd need the fuel to keep going.

Helen felt a little conspicuous as they headed downstairs for breakfast. She wondered if everyone would realize what they'd been up to the night before. As the only human in a room full of shifters, she suspected they would know, somehow. That was, if Jim's smug expression didn't give them away completely from the get go. She could almost laugh at the way he strutted down the stairs, if he didn't look so darned sexy.

She knew firsthand, now, how incredible it was to be with him. As a matter of fact, she was feeling a little smug herself this morning.

Waking up to find him gone had been disappointing, but she understood. Wolves were nocturnal hunters. They did their best work in the dark. She had to stifle a chuckle as that thought trickled through her mind. Jim certainly did do his very best work at night. At least, he had last night.

Scandalous. That's what she was. Helen had never behaved quite like this in her entire life, but she couldn't find it within herself to regret a single moment. Nothing about what had passed between them would cause her any regrets, ever. The only thing she feared she might regret was when this fantastical adventure came to an end.

She really didn't know how she was going to continue the humdrum existence she had lived up to now. In fact, the more she thought about it, the more she realized that she could not continue as she had been. Things were going to change for her. She was determined the change would be for the better. She actually had to thank Jim for that. He had made her see, viscerally, what her life had become, and that it could be different.

Helen would choose to make things better when she finally had the chance to slow down and reevaluate. After this whirlwind romance and adventure, she would embark upon a new existence. She wasn't sure exactly what that would entail yet, but she was determined to figure it out.

Breakfast was served in the rear dining room of the big Victorian mansion. There were only a few guests in residence, at the moment, so they had plenty of room to enjoy the huge spread on the buffet table. Helen was truly impressed by the vast array of breakfast foods, from cereals to eggs and other hot items kept warm in ornate steaming trays. She took a plate and helped herself, trying not to laugh at how much food Jim kept adding to his own plate. He only stopped spooning things on when he had a truly amazing pile that was in danger of imminent collapse.

At that point, he ushered her to the table—a large rectangular heirloom that could easily seat twelve adults and then some. He pulled out her chair for her, in a gallant act of chivalry, then took the seat beside her. Felicia came out at that point and greeted them, asking if there was anything they needed. She was chipper and friendly, and Helen began to breathe easier when Felicia left without any teasing remarks or significant glances.

"So, where did you go last night?" Helen asked, just making conversation and trying not to sound as if she was prying or chastising him in any way. She had no real claim over Jim, and she didn't want to scare him off too soon by acting like a jealous cow.

"I had to do a perimeter sweep to see if I could find anything out of the ordinary," he said between shoveling food into his mouth. He wasn't a messy eater, but he ate *a lot*.

"And did you? Find anything out of the ordinary, I mean."

Jim nodded as he swallowed his food. He paused to have a sip of water before answering. "Actually, I did." A frown marred his near-perfect brow. "I'm very concerned that we may be dealing was something similar to what your sister found in West Virginia."

Helen felt the bottom drop out of her stomach. "Black magic? Is that what you mean?" She was filled with dread at what he might answer.

When he nodded again, she shut her eyes and searched for her center quickly. Focused once more, she tried to see his discovery in a positive light. At least he knew what to look for now, after that near-fiasco in West Virginia. He had approached the situation cautiously and had probably found something everybody else had missed.

"What does Joe say?" She knew he must have reported his findings to the Alpha of this territory right away. Something that important couldn't wait.

"None of the locals noticed what I did," Jim said quietly.

He wasn't bragging. He was just stating a fact. "Then again, none of them saw what I saw in the aftermath of the action your sister was involved in."

Kiki had been a little more than *involved*. She'd been held prisoner by an evil witch who was using her as bait to catch Kiki's mate, Jack, in werebear form. That sorceress would have killed him for his power, as she'd killed the others they'd since discovered. She'd almost killed Kiki, too, but little sis had outsmarted the witch and brought about her downfall. Helen was so darn proud of that kid.

"But they're going to check it out?" Helen asked, worried for the town and the nice people she'd met here, so far.

"I'm going to check it out, with their help. This may be a little beyond the local talent's experience. Heck, it's beyond some of my experience, as well, but I'm not going into this unprepared. In fact..." He took his buzzing phone out of his pocket and laid it on the table next to his rapidly emptying plate. "Yeah, I figured this would happen," he said as he read the text message that had just come in. "We're doing a conference call in fifteen minutes. Will you be okay for a couple of hours?"

CHAPTER 13

Jim stood from the table and bussed his and Helen's dirty plates to the area set aside for them. She stood as well, any thought of lingering over coffee or a cinnamon bun forgotten.

While Helen was somewhat disappointed not to be included in the strategy session, she understood. She was the new kid on the block as far as Jim's mission went. The boys who had planned it and sent him here were all familiar with their own abilities, but nobody really understood what she could do to aid the mission any more than she already had.

She had probably surprised everybody when she'd saved Jim's life in Virginia Beach. Frankly, she had surprised herself, as well. Of course, she wasn't about to admit that to anyone. Helen was confident that she had more to contribute, but she wasn't altogether certain that she would get the chance. However, she wasn't going to force her way in, if she wasn't wanted. Things would unfold, she was confident, as the Mother of All intended.

With that thought in mind, she decided she was going to spend the morning shopping. Even her enormous bag couldn't hold enough clothing for an indefinite stay. She was down to her last outfit and wouldn't mind picking up a few things that were more suitable to this warmer climate. She would get another bag too, she decided. A real suitcase, since she was going to be flying out of a real airport once this adventure was over and she was on her way home. She'd always wanted a slick wheelie bag that she could maneuver every which way, and she'd seen some colorful examples in one of the shop windows they'd passed on their stroll through town the evening before.

"I'll be okay," Helen told Jim. "I need to do a little shopping, anyway."

"Take my credit card. Get whatever you need," he offered, reaching for his wallet, but she held up her hand.

"Oh, no. I couldn't do that. I'm going to be buying some souvenirs for my family, as well as another outfit and some personal items. You don't have to pay for any of that, and I can afford it." She pushed his arm down when he continued to try to get his wallet out of his pants pocket. "Seriously. Thanks for the offer, but I'm good."

His smile went from concerned to sinful in a second flat. "Actually, you're way better than good," he commented in a voice so low that only she could hear it.

She wanted to purr. Just like that, he'd evoked memories of the amazing night she'd just spent in his arms. A night never to be forgotten.

"So are you," she said, blushing only a little as she dared to say the words.

Felicia bustled in from the kitchen, a platter of hot blueberry muffins in her hands. Even though Helen had just eaten a rather large breakfast, by her standards, she felt her mouth water at the scent of those muffins. Jim's gaze went to Felicia as well.

"I'm glad we agree on that, Helen," he said, sounding deceptively businesslike. Only Helen knew what he was talking about, and it made her grin knowingly. "Maybe we should take a couple of those muffins for the road?"

He was already moving before the question left his mouth, homing in on that warm tray Felicia had just placed on the buffet. Helen followed him at a slower pace. Felicia was way ahead of them, wrapping two muffins in paper napkins and handing them each one.

"Sorry these weren't ready before," Felicia apologized. "You two got up earlier than I expected. The rest of the guests won't be down for a few minutes yet."

"Sorry." Helen felt compelled to apologize. "I live on a farm. We get up with the dawn, most days. The animals don't understand sleeping late, but I promise, I'm going to give it a try tomorrow. This is sort of a vacation for me."

"Oh, it's no problem. I usually have a little more time in the morning, but my great-grandmother was having a rough night last night," Felicia explained.

"I saw her on my way out around four in the morning," Jim said, surprising Helen that he'd been up and about much earlier than she'd suspected.

"That reminds me," Helen said gently to Felicia. "I promised your Alpha that I'd see if I could help Miss Felicity. Is she around? Do you think she'd let me take a look and see if I can do anything?"

"I know she was very pleased with how you helped Angus, so I suspect she'd be happy to learn if you could do anything for her aching bones. Her knees are particularly bad, and at times, she can hardly walk," Felicia confided. "That's a really hard thing to accept for a wolf who's used to running free. She's in her parlor. It's where she spends a lot of her time these days."

Helen sympathized. "I'll see what I can do."

Jim walked her out of the breakfast room then left her at the front door with a kiss. She might've lingered a bit too long in his arms, but he didn't seem to mind. She'd been looking forward to a kiss from him since the last one. She could hardly go a few minutes without wanting to kiss him, now that she knew just how amazing it could be between them.

She was an addict, and Jim was the drug.

He left her to go have his conference call—most likely at the mayor's office—while she headed into the parlor to see

Miss Felicity before she did anything else. The old lady smiled when she saw Helen in the archway.

"Was that your young man who just left?" the old lady asked. Helen realized Miss Felicity had a very good vantage point between the archway to the parlor and the big window that looked out onto the street, with a good view of the front steps, as well.

"Jim has a meeting. Boys only, apparently," Helen joked, rolling her eyes as she smiled. "I was wondering if I could keep you company for a little bit."

"Don't let the males walk all over you," Miss Felicity advised. "They always try, but you can't let them succeed." The old woman had a twinkle in her eye as Helen approached. "If you have to bite him once in a while to get him to take you seriously, my advice is to do so."

Helen laughed. "If I were a wolf, I would definitely do that."

"Come now, you must have your own ways of keeping folks in line," Miss Felicity suggested.

Helen thought about it. "I'll have to think about that. I'm not much of a mage, compared to others in my family."

"Even non-magical folk can do it. I've seen it with some of the human mates in our Pack. They find the right way to remind their spouses that they have a voice, too, and they use it when necessary." Miss Felicity nodded knowingly. "You just need to find your way of doing things. I understand the relationship with Jim is a new one, but you'll figure it out."

Helen wasn't even going to ask how Miss Felicity had come to the conclusion that she was having a relationship with Jim. Maybe it was just an assumption. Maybe there was some way Miss Felicity had of knowing. Or, maybe, she'd heard something last night? Helen felt her cheeks flush with embarrassment at that last thought, but Miss Felicity didn't say anything more on the topic, which was a relief.

Helen sat in the chair that was placed at a ninety-degree angle to the couch on which Miss Felicity sat. The dog was not in his basket, nor was he anywhere in the room.

"No Angus today?" Helen asked, looking around for the little fellow.

"He's out prowling around somewhere," Miss Felicity said, unconcerned. "He always returns for mealtime, when he's had enough exploring.

"I'm not sure if you know, but Joe, your Alpha, asked me to have a look at your knees, if you're willing," Helen said gently. She would never examine or treat someone who was conscious without their permission and cooperation.

"Young Joseph mentioned something to me about your abilities and then, of course, I saw what you did for little Angus. I doubt you can do much, but if it's no drain on your energy, I wouldn't mind an examination. The Pack healer has done as much as he can for my arthritis, so this is about as good as it's going to get for me, at this point," Miss Felicity said, a sad but resigned note in her tone.

"I can't promise anything, of course, but...well...let me just have a look, first, okay?" Helen said, leaning forward in her chair. She reached out, putting her hand above Miss Felicity's knee. "Is it okay to touch you?"

"Certainly, my dear," Miss Felicity replied graciously, holding out her legs and tugging the hem of her long dress up just over her swollen knees.

Helen held back her instinctive wince. Those knee joints looked angry, even without invoking her gift. Swollen and painful, Helen had no doubt. Well, she could probably do something about that, at least temporarily. She'd have to use more of her gift to see if there was a longer-term solution, but first things first. Helen laid her hand on the closer knee and set to work bringing down the swelling and easing the pain.

When she was done with the initial treatment on the first knee, she went onto the other without pause. She suspected Miss Felicity wanted to say something, but Helen didn't allow anything to break her concentration. Her energy levels were high after the night spent with Jim. So high, in fact, that the treatment of the swelling and pain didn't take much of her energy at all. It felt like she had extra reserves now, or something.

Had sex with Jim given her extra magical energy? Helen had no idea that could even be a side effect of great sex. She'd have to do some research in the family archive when she got home. For now, though, she was buzzing with life-giving energy and able to do more than she'd expected. She took away the swelling, sending the fluid out, into the channels it was supposed to travel to leave Miss Felicity's body and reduced what pain was left.

Helen ran her hands downward toward Miss Felicity's ankles and took away the swelling, which wasn't quite as bad, in them as well. She sent her energy out, seeking other places—hips and spine, in particular. She did what she could on this first go-round, noting things for the next treatment, which would come later.

"You're probably going to want to go to the bathroom, shortly," Helen advised as she lifted her hands. "Why don't you try standing and seeing how that feels?"

Miss Felicity did as Helen suggested and stood up. She had a cane not too far from her hand, but she didn't reach for it. She tested her knees and ankles, shifting her weight from side to side.

"Oh, that feels marvelous!" Miss Felicity walked a few steps then turned. "Thank you, dear. You really have a gift. I'll be right back." With a new spring in her step, she practically danced out of the parlor and down the hall.

Helen had to smile. Miss Felicity seemed so happy to be able to move again without pain. Helen loved it when she could give a gift like that to someone. She sat back in her chair and took stock of her own energy levels, marveling at how much she still had to work with. Helping Miss Felicity didn't even dent Helen's energy reserves, which was pretty amazing.

She heard the door down the hall open, and Miss Felicity came out of the powder room, only to be intercepted by Felicia. Helen could hear the conversation.

"Where's your cane, Gran? Do you want me to get it for

you?" Felicia asked, sounding concerned.

"It's in the parlor, and no, I don't need it. That Helen did something amazing. Look at my knees," Miss Felicity said in an excited tone.

"Wow," Felicia said after a moment. "They haven't looked that good in years."

"They feel even better," Miss Felicity enthused. "I feel like going for a run."

Helen got up and went to the archway. "Not yet, Miss Felicity. I still haven't had a look at your arms, and I'd like to discuss further work we can do to make this a more permanent change."

"Permanent?" Miss Felicity walked quickly down the hall to Helen. "You mean there's more?"

"Much more," Helen assured the old lady, ushering her back toward the couch. Felicia followed her great-grandmother into the room, standing in the back, watching with interest. "Now, I presume your shoulders, elbows and wrists are also painful, right?"

"They are," Miss Felicity admitted.

"If you'll allow me," Helen said, taking hold of one of Miss Felicity's hands, she set to work. The inflammation wasn't as bad, but the joints had worn down and showed signs of damage, including thin cartilage and a lack of lubrication, which was probably very painful. Helen did the work of beginning repairs.

Her gift could actually regrow cartilage and repair soft tissues, as well as mending bones, but it sometimes took repeated treatments. She started work on Miss Felicity, with the idea of doing two or three more sessions to achieve the full effect.

Helen finished with Miss Felicity's arms and then discussed the options for further treatment. "I can make these changes permanent in just two or three more treatments. Otherwise, it'll wear off over time," she told the older woman. Felicia was still in the room, listening, as well. "What I'm doing is encouraging the cartilage to re-grow and fill in the bare spots where you have bone grinding on bone. I'm also reshaping any areas that have been damaged by the passage of time and repetitive motion. When I'm done, your joints won't give you trouble for a good long while."

"It's a miracle," Felicia whispered. Helen smiled at her.

"It's just my particular flavor of magic. Healing is what I do." Helen shrugged, glad to be able to give Miss Felicity this gift of her magic.

"And this doesn't drain you?" Miss Felicity looked hard at Helen, as if searching for any telltale fatigue.

Helen put both palms on her thighs and thought about it. "Honestly, this is strange. Normally, this kind of thing would take a lot out of me, but for whatever reason—maybe it's working with shifter metabolism as a boost to my natural abilities—I'm not really feeling drained at all right now." Helen shook her head in wonder. "I'm not going to question it. I suggest we just use this and get you fixed up as well as we can while I've got the zip to do it."

Miss Felicity chuckled. "Whatever the reason—and I think it might have something to do with a certain young male you've been keeping company with—I agree with your plan. I feel so good right now, it's like you took fifty years off. I don't mind being greedy and saying I'd like to feel this good for as long as possible."

"It's not greedy," Helen assured her, studiously ignoring the reference to Jim and their budding relationship. "Everybody wants to feel good. I'm just glad that sometimes, I can help them achieve that goal."

They made plans to meet up again the next day, after breakfast, and then Helen took her leave. She still had some shopping to do, and she wanted to see more of the town in the daylight.

Helen's shopping trip went well, for the most part. She picked up the nifty wheelie bag she'd been eying and a few other things, but the people in the shops and on the street were cool with her. Their reaction to her only changed when she got close to someone, and crazy as it seemed, she thought she caught some of them sniffing her. It dawned on her that maybe these shifters, with their ultra-strong senses, could somehow smell Jim on her, and that's what changed their attitudes.

That made her feel weird. It actually felt both good and bad. Good that somehow what she and Jim had done together had left its mark on her. Bad that these people would have continued to treat her somewhat rudely had she not carried that scent mark. It seemed sort of backwards to her. Like, shouldn't people just assume she was okay if she'd been welcomed to their town by no less than their Alpha and the ladies at the B&B? Why did they seem to look at her as a potential enemy until they got close enough?

She didn't like how suspicious they were. Maybe that was a shifter thing. Maybe they'd been burned in the past and keeping their secrets was the only thing keeping them safe in this increasingly human-dominated world. She supposed she could understand their caution, but it still rubbed her the wrong way to be treated so coldly, at first.

Helen spent the morning shopping and trying to figure out what she could do to *bite* Jim—metaphorically speaking—as Miss Felicity had suggested. He needed a reminder that she could contribute to the mission. She just wasn't sure what it was she could do that would get his attention.

Jim took the conference call in Joe's office. Better to have the Alpha in on the planning from the start, than to run afoul of something local that they didn't know about. Shane was also present, putting in his two cents when necessary. Jim was grateful for all the information Ezra and the others had been able to dig up, but he felt like something was missing.

About halfway through the call, when someone asked how Helen was doing, he realized it was her. She was missing. He'd somehow gotten so used to having her around, voicing her opinions, that he now missed her when she wasn't present. It was a little disconcerting for a guy who'd always been a bit of a lone wolf. How had he become so dependent on her presence in such a short time? It felt like the answer to that question should be right there, in front of him, but then, Ezra asked a question, and Jim was distracted.

"Did you see a dark line on the ground?" Jack Bishop asked. He, of all of them, had the most recent experience with black magic wards.

"Not that I noticed, but it was dark, and I wasn't particularly looking for anything physical. I was more concerned with the magical effects," Jim said, cringing a bit. He should've looked harder. It just hadn't occurred to him that there might be a physical sign of what he'd thought was a purely magical construct.

"That's understandable," Jack allowed. "But, with the potion witch, there was a dark line made by whatever potion she used to erect the black ward. Once we broke those lines, the wards were broken. The first time, I used a deer herd. I had them trample across a freshly laid potion line a few times, and their little hoofs obliterated it, wrecking the ward. The second time was when Kiki used those herbs from her fey garden to break the line."

"Exactly what happened there again?" Jim asked. He hadn't been present when the ward came down. He'd arrived a few minutes later.

"She had the herbs in a cotton pouch. She dropped the pouch on the line of the ward, and it ate through the cotton, releasing the herbs. Once that happened, the ward slammed down," Jack explained.

"So, it was sort of acidic?" Jim asked, something occurring to him. "One of the old ladies in town has a little dog that roams around on his own during the day. Last week, he came back with burnt paws."

"I bet he got into the ward line. At least a little. Like the deer, he could cross over the line with impunity because it's probably set to keep werewolves and Others out, not simpler animals," Jack said.

"Makes sense," Joe said, joining the conversation. "So, we know the ward has been up at least since the dog was injured."

"That's before my target got back to this area—if he is, indeed, actually here—so, that means there's someone else at that feed mill with the skills to cast black wards," Jim told them all. Silence met his words. Nobody was happy to hear there were more evil mages out there practicing black magic.

CHAPTER 14

Jim's conference call went on much longer than he'd expected. When he finally emerged from the mayor's office, the sun was overhead, and he was thinking about lunch. He was also thinking about ways to break a black ward, but that was a problem he'd have to solve later. Lunch was just slightly more important, at the present moment, so he went back to the B&B in search of Helen.

He found her in the kitchen, working alongside Felicia at the counter, with Miss Felicity sitting at the kitchen table, sipping a cup of tea. Jim was enchanted by the domestic scene and wondered what the women had gotten up to while he'd been in conference.

"You all look very industrious," Jim commented from the doorway.

Helen turned, a smile on her face. Felicia turned more slowly, a handful of lavender in her hands. "Helen has been teaching us things we didn't know about our garden," she explained, a bemused look on her face. "Did you know lavender could purify evil magic?"

Jim remembered hearing about how Helen's sister had used herbs to unwind the magic that had been used on the child they'd found imprisoned. He hadn't thought much of it at the time, but Helen must have been taught the same things as her sister. She probably had a vast knowledge of herbal magic. Wolves knew earth magic was potent. They used a lot of it in their daily lives, but he had no doubt that Helen's knowledge was of a different—and, perhaps, even more powerful—kind than theirs.

"I heard something about it on my last mission," he said, walking into the large kitchen.

"We have an herb garden out back," Felicia went on, "as well as a vegetable patch. I had no idea, when we took a little stroll in the garden, that I was going to learn so much."

"It's good of you to share your knowledge," Jim said, walking right up to Helen. He couldn't resist bending down to place a quick kiss on her lips. He'd been wanting to do that for hours.

"It's all simple stuff, really," Helen insisted, "but there's lots of very useful things out there in the garden that could be put to good use in warding this house and others."

"We're making decorative flower sprigs that have the added benefit of preventing evil from passing wherever they're placed. Doors, windows. I'm going to put one on every opening in this house," Felicia said, nodding to herself as she tied a little twine bow on the bundle of flowers and herbs in her hand.

"And they smell good, too," Helen added, finishing up and wiping her hands on a dish towel.

"Can I interest you in lunch?" Jim asked Helen, then looked at the other two women. "You're invited as well, of course," he added politely, but both Felicia and Miss Felicity declined. Felicia wanted to work on her flower bundles, and Miss Felicity said she was going to go for a run.

Jim thought privately that Helen must have been successful in treating Miss Felicity's joint pain if she was thinking about running. Helen picked up her bag from where it lay on the chair next to Miss Felicity and waited for him at the doorway while he made his farewells to the other women. Then, they were out of the house and walking down the street.

"Barbeque again? Or should we try someplace else?" Jim asked as they walked.

"Let's do barbeque again. They had pulled pork sandwiches on the menu that would be perfect for lunch, I thought. We can try someplace else tonight, if you're available for dinner," she replied.

He liked that she was already thinking ahead to when they would be together again. He found it hard to concentrate on his mission, knowing that Helen was nearby. He wanted to be with her, not running around after evildoers. He promised himself that, once he was done with this mission, he'd spend a good long time with Helen, so he could find out where this relationship was going...if anyplace. He had a feeling it was, but he wasn't entirely certain, yet.

Some wolves knew the moment they scented their mates, he knew. Some took a bit longer to figure it out. Jim suspected he was going to be one of the latter, much to his annoyance, but being with Helen felt really, really *right*. If that's how it felt when you found your mate, well, then, he was already there.

"I should be around for dinner," he told her, putting one arm around her shoulders as casually as he could. His inner wolf was adamant in wanting to touch her. He couldn't be close to her without wanting to stroke and pet and kiss. "There's a diner and another fancier American bistro type place. There's also a bakery that serves sandwiches where we could get lunch tomorrow, if we're both free." He was planning even farther ahead than just dinner. He wanted to be with her as much as he could.

"That sounds nice," she answered, seemingly content to walk down the street tucked close to his side.

They lingered over lunch. Helen got her desired pulled pork sandwich while Jim had two and a side of ribs. He liked how daintily she ate, even when the food was inherently messy. She had class, did Helen, and he found himself enchanted by her manner.

He was so enraptured by his lunch companion that he

almost didn't notice when Joe walked into the dining area and did a quick scan. Jim looked up and met Joe's gaze as the Alpha headed straight for their table. Jim went on high alert. The Alpha looked concerned, and Jim figured there was some kind of trouble.

Joe nodded to them both as he joined them at their table. It was a square table set for four, and they were only using two of the chairs. Joe pulled out one of the spare chairs and sat, his expression troubled.

"I hate to bother you at lunch, but we have a little situation that you need to be aware of," he began. Jim put down his fork and gave the Alpha his full attention. "We've got a missing teenager," Joe told them, getting straight to the point. "Calum Ingles is a good kid. Maybe a little wild but basically clean. He's at that age where they like to go exploring and sometimes get into trouble." Joe sighed, shaking his head. "Thing is, they usually go off in groups. The teens stick together, generally speaking, but Calum went off on his own two days ago, and nobody's seen him since."

"Two days ago?" Helen asked, concern clear in her tone. "How did nobody notice until now?"

"Miscommunication," Joe told her. "His grandmother thought he was staying over at a friend's. Apparently, that fell through when the friend's mother put the kibosh on the sleepover, but Calum didn't go back home. Nobody knows where he went, but I'm half afraid he might've gone to the old feed mill. The friend lives out near there, and the teens sometimes prowl the outskirts of town in that area because they know nobody has been at the mill for years."

"I scented a lot of teenage wolf scents on my prowl out that way," Jim admitted. "I discarded those as of no interest, so I can't be sure if one was stronger than the others. They were all pretty recent, though. Within the past week, or so."

"That makes sense. Like I said, that area is popular with the teens who are learning their skills. They know nobody really goes out that way, except those of us running perimeter checks. They're out from under watchful eyes and able to test their boundaries a bit. We all did it, as young pups," Joe said, trying unsuccessfully to hide his worry. "What concerns me," he finally admitted, "is that bear child that was kidnapped in Pennsylvania. You found her in West Virginia, right? Which is where you were following this target of yours from?"

"Yes, Alpha. And I can understand why you'd be concerned about that. The sorceress that was killed in the West Virginia op had stockpiled a bunch of bodies in her warehouse. The man we followed from there was overseeing the body storage area, in fact. They were keeping them in chest freezers."

"So, if he's familiar with the technique of draining magic from one being and taking it for himself..." Joe let the sentence drift.

"Or if whoever laid the black ward can do the same," Helen put in, making the men frown.

"Then, we've got a problem," Jim finished the thought. "I'll go check out that feed mill right now. I was going to wait until dark, but if Calum's there, he doesn't have time for us to sit around waiting for dark." Jim stood and reached for his wallet. He dug out a few bills, which would more than cover their lunch tab, and put them on the table.

Helen stood also. "I'm going with you."

"No—"

"He might be hurt," she insisted, not letting him finish what he was going to say. "I'm going with you, and that's that."

Damn. Her little chin was lifted in a stubborn, adorable line. She was going to insist, and he'd be a cad to leave her behind. Still, he had to try.

"Sweetheart, this could be very dangerous. And besides, we don't have a car. I can run, but you need some kind of transport." He hoped she would leave it at that and accept his decision, but the set of her jaw told him his hope was in vain.

"Then, we'll get a car, and I'll drive." She looked at the Alpha. "Surely, there's a car rental place here somewhere, isn't there?"

Joe pulled out his phone and started tapping. "I'll have a car out front for you in ten minutes. Thanks, Helen. If he is hurt, I'd be grateful for your help, but I also don't want to put you in unnecessary danger. You stay in the car unless and until Jim finds Calum. Understood?"

Helen nodded. "I promise," she told the Alpha. "I just... I feel like I need to be there."

Helen didn't know why she'd said that, but once the words were out of her mouth, she realized the truth of them. She had a feeling she just had to stay with Jim and be there, with him, when he explored the site of the old feed mill.

"I've got the sheriff, the deputies and anyone else who's good at tracking out looking for this kid. I'll keep you posted on our progress, if we have any. Likewise, if you need backup, we'll all be out in the field, all around town and the perimeter. All you have to do is call, and whoever is closest will come," Joe said, looking from her to Jim.

Jim nodded. "Thank you, Alpha. We'll call if we need assistance. With any luck, Calum will turn up on his own, no harm done."

Joe left the table, grabbing a few people on his way out the door, who left with him. Probably trackers who would help with the search.

"You don't really believe he's going to show up on his own," Helen said quietly, gathering her things.

Jim shook his head. "Probably not," he admitted.

"Do you think he's at the mill?" Helen asked as they walked out of the restaurant. They waited on the sidewalk for the promised car.

"Only one way to find out," he told her. He looked preoccupied, as if he was already thinking through the actions he would take when they got where they were going.

A minute later, a young man drove up in a rental car. He hopped out and held the keys up, looking at them. "You called for a car?"

Helen stepped forward and took the keys from the

youngster. "Do you know a young man named Calum Ingles?" she asked, on a hunch.

"Cal? Sure. He's a lot of fun. Why?"

Jim stepped closer. "Does he ever go out toward the old feed mill on the edge of town?" Jim took a rather obvious sniff of the kid. "I know I caught your scent out that way. Yours and a lot of other young pups."

The kid looked as if he'd been caught with his hand in the cookie jar. "It's just a place we go, you know? There are cool obstacles we can try without everyone watching and criticizing when we screw up. We have our own competitions."

"You have an obstacle course out there? Outdoors or inside one of the old buildings?" Jim asked, his tone patient. "I won't get you in any trouble. I just really need to know."

The boy seemed hesitant but relented. "You know how there are a bunch of silos, and they have these conveyor things? We start the course through the rusty hole in the half-collapsed silo then run up the conveyors to the top and then down into the mill building, itself. There's a lot of machinery in there that we go up over, jump and slide under, that kind of thing, then we take another conveyor back out to the silos and do a final long jump from the roof of the shortest silo. The finish line is when you make it to the ground, and how far out you jumped is taken into account in the awarding of points."

He sounded eager as he described the acrobatic course the children had devised. Helen thought it sounded altogether too dangerous, but she wasn't a werewolf, so she didn't know what was easy for them. For certain, human children could get really hurt if they tried something like that.

"You won't tell my dad I've been out there, will you?" the boy asked, looking a bit sheepish, for a wolf.

"I think that's something you need to tell him yourself," Jim said, his tone unyielding. "But don't be surprised if he already knows. Nothing much gets past the Alpha in a Pack like this."

The youngster brushed his toe in the imaginary dirt on the sidewalk. "You're probably right, but I'll tell him. I promise."

"Good lad," Jim praised the kid and patted him on the shoulder. "Tell him I'm going to check out your obstacle course. Calum's missing, so if you hear from him, call your father right away. He's mobilizing half the town to look for him."

The boy's eyes widened as Jim opened the passenger-side door and got in. Helen took that as her cue to walk around to the driver's side. She got behind the wheel and adjusted the seat and mirrors before putting the car in gear and heading down the street. Jim gave her directions, since she didn't really know her way around town, yet.

"Was that boy Joe's son?" Helen asked once she was heading in the right direction.

"His youngest," Jim confirmed. "I've met him once or twice before, when he was younger. Good kid, as far as I know. He has the makings of an Alpha when he gets older, too. He might even be strong enough to lead this Pack after his dad, if he continues as he's going."

"You can tell that so young?" Helen was surprised.

Jim shrugged. "Sort of. There's a lot that goes into a good Alpha wolf. The training he's getting just by watching his farther counts for a lot, but there's the dominance issue, as well. He's very young, but his wolf is definitely of a dominant type. How strong he proves to be will depend on the rest of his experiences as he grows and all sorts of other factors that can't really be quantified."

Helen found that fascinating, and said so, but Jim still seemed preoccupied by what would come next. He gave her the instructions for turning off the main road then had her drive out over open land and into some light tree cover that still had enough room for her to fit the car through. She could see the tops of silos just over the hill they were cresting, and then, there they were. An old building with a number of big metal silos attached by spindly conveyors.

"Stop here," Jim said. "I'm going in on foot, and you can

watch from the car up here. Do you have your phone?"

She stopped the car and turned off the engine. "In my bag," she said, reaching for the big bag she'd slung into the back of the car. She dug through it until she found her phone then held it up triumphantly.

"Put Joe's number in your contacts list." He waited while she did so, reading off the number when she was ready. "If you see anything happening that looks bad, call him. He's got people all around the area, and he can get someone here to help more quickly than you'd think."

Helen nodded, worried now that the moment was upon them. "Be careful," she told him, unable to stop herself from worrying about his safety.

"I will. You stay in the car and keep the doors locked. Be ready to leave in a hurry, if you need to, and don't hesitate to call for help, if something happens," he reminded her. He moved closer for a deep kiss that was over all too soon, then he was out of the car and heading toward the old buildings in the distance.

Helen didn't feel right watching him jog into danger. She wasn't sure why, but she had a really bad feeling about the old feed mill. The place looked creepy and sinister to her, and it was broad daylight. She couldn't imagine how bad it must be at night.

She stayed in the car but sent her magical senses out, probing delicately at the land around her, moving outward, toward the feed mill. What she found was not reassuring. There was the black ward, all right. She could feel its malevolence all around the area, but it was concentrated on the main building, which was off to one side of the property. The feed mill itself didn't seem to be within the ward. Curious, she probed farther.

There were others in her family better suited to this kind of work, but even with her minimal traditional magic skills, she was able to discern that there was a presence in the main building, and she'd bet the feed mill had been very deliberately left out of the ward. Why? If the young wolves used the place for their obstacle course, it would be a honey of a trap to catch them.

Helen knew, all of a sudden, why Calum had disappeared. Even before her magical senses brushed past his terrified presence within the walls of the old feed mill, she knew what she was going to find. He was there! Definitely there. Imprisoned.

She had to tell Jim, and she had to get to the boy. She could feel how low his magical reserves were. He was near death and so very scared. Poor kid. She had to help him. First, though, she had to get the word out.

She called Joe and told him what she had discovered in as few words as possible as she got out of the car. She didn't wait for his questions. She just told him to hurry getting over here, and ended the call. Tucking her cellphone into her pocket and arming herself with a bundle of lavender she'd put in her purse after her afternoon in the B&B's garden, she headed out after Jim.

CHAPTER 15

Jim was able to follow a scent trail he could only assume belonged to Calum all the way through the maze of the abandoned part of the feed mill. Where things got tricky was the area where the black ward began. In this case, it looked like whoever had laid this ward had deliberately excluded the part of the mill used by the teens for the obstacle course. It was only at the point where they left the dilapidated silos and entered the sturdier structure of the building that the ward ran through the path.

Jim hesitated. The ward was likely set in such a way that he could enter here, but he wasn't altogether certain he would be able to get out again. This enemy had baited their trap for the pups, but would it also catch him, if he crossed over that boundary? He wasn't sure, but the possibility was real.

Of course, folks knew where Jim was, and if he didn't surface to report his findings in a reasonable time, they'd come looking. Plus, Helen was out there. She'd call the cavalry if he didn't come back soon. The kid, though... The kid couldn't wait. Jim had to take the chance and go in to help that teen who'd been caught all too long in this tangled web of deceit.

Black magic. It made Jim's skin crawl. Hidden magic. Unseen and deceptive. He held his breath and crossed over the barrier. As he'd thought, it sprang up behind him, the trap sprung. No matter. He'd deal with that later, on the way out. Right now, he had to find the boy.

Jim picked up the scent trail once the barrier was behind him. The boy had come this way on his own, but then, another scent intruded. Someone had intercepted Calum, and there were signs of a scuffle. Jim proceeded cautiously, lest there be some kind of physical traps set to catch whoever came this way. He picked up another scent. This one he knew from the warehouse in West Virginia.

Bingo. He'd found his man. Buford—or whatever his real name was—had been here no less than a few hours ago. Jim followed the mingled scents until he came to a door. Pausing to listen, he didn't hear anything that would tell him what was behind the door. There was just one way to find out without specialized equipment he didn't have on him.

Jim readied himself for what he might find and opened the door. A quick visual scan of the room showed it was empty, except for a large crate of the kind people kept dogs or other large animals in. Inside, wrapped in a tight circle—almost a fetal position—was a young wolf, looking at Jim with tired, scared eyes.

"Calum?" Jim whispered low so that only the wolf in the crate could hear him.

The wolf's head lifted, but every motion seemed a struggle. The wolf had been drained of most of its magical energy. That much was clear to Jim.

"I'm an ally of your Pack. Your Alpha sent me to find you," he told the boy.

There was more to Jim's presence, of course, but Calum didn't need to know about any of that right now. No, at this moment, Calum needed reassurance. Jim wasn't part of Calum's Pack, and he might very well suspect a trick. It was up to Jim to convince the teen that he had legitimately come to rescue him.

"Everybody's on the hunt for your trail, and I was asked to check out this location because I came here on the trail of a very evil individual who was thought to be in the area." Jim walked closer as he talked, noting the way the wolf's ears moved to catch his words. "I'm guessing you fell into their trap, and they've been stealing your energy for the past day or two." Jim crouched down in front of the crate and casually broke the small lock that had kept the latch closed. "I'm going to let you out, and if you can walk, we're going to get out of here. If you can't walk, I'm going to carry you, okay?"

The wolf tried to stand, but it was too weak as Jim opened the wire door.

"That's okay, Calum," Jim told the wolf. "I'll help you, all right?" Jim was about to reach in when he froze in place at an unexpected sound.

"I don't think so."

A man's voice came from the other side of the long room. There was an archway there, and fans blowing the air out of it, which was why Jim hadn't scented the newcomer. Jim stood and turned to face the man in the archway.

"Well, if it isn't Buford Somersby. I've been looking all over for you," Jim said, trying to evaluate the threat level posed by the man and any help he might have hidden around here somewhere. Jim had to remember, this guy practiced black magic—the art of the unseen. Jim could take nothing at face value.

The man made a dismissive gesture. "That's just one of my names. You may call me master."

Jim scoffed. "Fat chance."

Buford smiled, and it was an evil looking thing. "You don't think so?" He moved a step farther into the room. "I will have you begging for mercy before you die. Mark my words."

"Funny," Jim said, taking up a casual pose, leaning against the crate and thereby shielding the teen within as best he could, "I was just about to say something similar to you. Only, I don't go in for long goodbyes. When you die at my hands, I promise to make it quick. You'll have time enough in the next realm to be tormented by what you've done here."

Buford's eyes narrowed, and his expression grew cold. "Perhaps you are unaware, but you cannot leave the circle. Once you stepped inside my ward, you were trapped here, never to leave."

"Maybe. Maybe not," Jim said, as if it didn't matter to him. "Just tell me one thing, if you wouldn't mind satisfying my curiosity... Were you Carol's apprentice or merely her errand boy?"

Carol, the potion witch in West Virginia, had used a very similar kind of ward, and Jim wondered if Buford had learned it from her. If so, maybe he wasn't as advanced a mage as the woman had been.

"My husband went north to liaise with the potion witch, nothing more." A female voice sounded from a side door that had opened noiselessly. Jim regarded the woman who stood in the opening with wary eyes.

"That's not how I heard it," Jim said, as if this new development didn't worry him at all. In fact, he was starting to wish he'd called in the cavalry before setting foot over that ward. "From what I understand, old Buford here was in charge of the warehouse freezer section where Carol stored her victims. Pretty gross, if you ask me, putting them on ice like that."

"It was I who showed Carol the benefits of the blood path," Buford stated proudly. Jim's stomach turned. Not only black magic, but blood magic. This couldn't really get any worse. "My lovely Otalla and I have been practicing the bloody arts for as long as we've been together," Buford went on while his wife frowned. "She set things up here while I checked out Carol's operation, but in the end, it wasn't really worth my time, and it got *you* on my trail." Buford's expression spoke of his disgust for that little gem.

"We did learn one thing from Carol, though," Otalla put in as she stepped into the room and raised her hands. "She really was very good at draining the magic out of her victims."

Otalla tried something on Jim at that point. He felt it, but it didn't quite connect. Was she trying to drain his magic from a distance? If so, it wasn't very effective. Jim reached for one of his new throwing knives and sent it her way. It didn't hit her—she had some kind of shield around herself—but it thunked into the wall next to her head and made her stop whatever it was she'd been attempting.

"That tickles," Jim told her, deadpan. Her expression showed deep rage. She was good and pissed and liable to make a mistake. He hoped. "So, what made you pick this place to set up shop?" Jim turned to ask Buford, as if Otalla were no threat. He knew that would only feed her ire.

"A town full of werewolves?" Buford asked rhetorically. "You've got to be kidding. This place is ripe and ready for the picking."

"Maybe. Maybe not," Jim repeated himself. "How did you find out about this place?" Jim's question was open enough not to be construed as agreement with Buford's claim that the town was full of shifters. Jim could mean the old feed mill, or he could mean the town.

"Found it in my travels," Buford said offhandedly. "I flew through the airport and realized the place was overflowing with shifter magic. Then, I started looking for a way to get closer. This old wreck fit the bill, and it was easy enough to convince the owner to sell."

Jim wondered what kind of pressure Buford had applied to make the former owner sell. Jim knew for a fact that Joe had made offers on the land over the years, but they'd all been rejected. Why should the owners suddenly turn around and sell to Buford, unless he'd done something to make it happen. Something that had probably been entirely unpleasant for the people who had owned the land before.

Jim made a mental note to have someone check on those poor souls, whoever they were. Joe probably knew. He had that nifty color-coded map and probably a hefty file of information to go along with it. Jim would tell the Alpha, and Joe could check what had happened there—as soon as Jim got himself out of this neat little trap.

*

Helen approached the mill cautiously. She didn't go through the maze of rusty metal that the kids were using as an obstacle course. If she dallied there, she'd likely get tetanus or something. Instead, she honed in on the area she'd sensed. The building where the boy was being tortured. At least, she assumed it was torture that had caused him to become so very weak.

She'd called Joe, and she knew the cavalry was on the way. He'd said he had some people close—within about ten minutes of her location—but she couldn't wait. Calum might not have ten minutes to spare.

The first thing she noticed as she got closer to the building was a queasy feeling in the pit of her stomach. There was something evil here, and she could only assume this was where the black ward passed. Closing her eyes for a moment, she concentrated. This wasn't her best skill, but she could sense magic, like most of her siblings. She just had to look a little harder than the others, but she could find it.

Then, she did. A near-invisible line of considerable strength lay across the threshold. A black ward. Hidden. Powerful. Disgusting enough to make her want to puke.

She held her breath and divided the bunch of lavender she had brought with her in half. The purity of the cleansing herb might just be enough to disrupt the line of the ward, bringing down the entire circle. She bent to place half the lavender on the hidden line on the ground, keeping the other half in reserve, in case she ran into something else that needed its cleansing power.

She watched, her magical senses open, as were her eyes. She saw only a faint shimmer when the ward fell, but on the magical plane, she saw a catastrophic failure as evil succumbed to good, the sacred lavender breaking the line and collapsing the field. A moment later, she heard a scream of outrage from inside the building.

She ducked in quickly and found a place of concealment. She wasn't quite ready to confront anyone just yet. First, she wanted to find Jim and Calum and see what was happening.

Only then, could she decide what she could do to help.

*

Otalla screamed as the ward came crashing down. Jim felt it and wondered who had caused it. He had a sneaking suspicion Helen might be involved, which meant she was either in the building already, or about to enter. He'd run out of time to play with these morons. It was time for action.

While Otalla screamed, Jim acted. He sprang at Buford, who was closer, going straight for the man's throat. The momentary distraction of having the ward fail was just enough opening for Jim to catch the bastard by surprise.

There was no mercy. No offer of repentance. Jim knew it would do no good to hesitate. This pair had shown their true colors in every act he was aware of, including most recently, what they'd done to poor Calum. For that alone, they deserved to die.

Jim killed Buford clean. One slice with his new Bowie knife, and the man was down on the floor, bleeding out. Otalla surprised him, though. Instead of a magical attack, she launched herself at him physically, scratching at his face and clamping onto his back, screaming like a banshee right into his ear.

Then Otalla bit him, breaking this skin, and licked at his blood. At that point, Jim lost track of what was going on. Otalla was doing something… Something magical…

Helen heard the uproar from the next room and knew the time for caution was at an end. Something was going on in there, and she had better go in and see what she could do to help. She entered, taking a quick look around. She saw the wolf in the cage. The door was open, but the wolf was so weak, he was unable to move.

Then, she saw Jim a few yards farther away. A man was lying on the floor, unmoving, blood pooling all around, practically at Jim's feet. A woman was clinging to Jim's back, screaming obscene dark magical words, her mouth wet with blood.

Jim's blood.

Helen's stomach turned, but she knew she had to act. She stepped fully into the room and used her loudest, most authoritative tone.

"Stop!" she ordered, holding up the remaining lavender as a shield before her.

Helen walked closer, advancing steadily, showing no fear. Her goal was to get between the woman and the wolf in the crate, so she couldn't hurt the boy anymore.

"I said stop," Helen repeated, letting the ancient words flow from her lips. Words she had learned alongside her magical siblings, taught by their mother. Words passed down for generations from the old country, meant to quell and banish the forces of evil.

High German poured from her lips. Words she had never spoken in a real-life situation like this. Words she had practiced and memorized, then tucked neatly away, never to be used. Only, she was using them now, and they seemed to be having quite an effect on the woman whose lips still glistened red with Jim's blood.

Helen would have to purify Jim's blood after this, she knew. That woman was evil, and she'd no doubt injected some of her poison into him with her bite. Sickened by the thought, Helen nonetheless pressed on, reciting the ancient formula and repeating the words that weakened the evil woman.

The woman dropped off Jim's back, unable to cling to him any longer as her power fled from her being and melted into the earth, never to return to her. It seemed to be affecting her hair as she writhed in what looked like pain. The long hair on her head had gone from a lustrous black to dull gray and then to a sickly white. Helen couldn't see her face, but the skin of her hands also appeared to be wrinkling in a somewhat nauseating way.

Helen repeated the ritual words for a third time, moving closer with each step, though careful to stay out of the weakened woman's reach, lest she try some sort of physical attack, like she had with Jim. The woman was on the ground now, her head down as she struggled to stay stable on all fours.

There was a moment when she looked up at Helen, her hair draping around a face that was almost unrecognizable from what it had been only moments before. She had...aged. There was no other way to describe it. She'd gone from temptress to crone in almost the blink of an eye. Helen had never seen anything like it.

Jim stood between the evil woman and Helen, just a little off to her right, watching. Ready. He would act if the woman tried anything. Meanwhile, Helen said the final words and watched the remaining energy of the evil sorceress fade into the earth, grounded and banished from her for all eternity. Any power that remained to the woman had to come from some new source. As it was, the woman began to fade, and Helen felt the moment she ceased to exist on this plane.

Helen had killed her? She hadn't meant to. It went against her healer's sensibilities to end another life. She stood there, shocked, as the woman faded away.

"What happened?" Helen breathed. "I only meant to drain her magic, not her life force. She should still be alive."

"She isn't," Jim confirmed, going over to examine the woman. "Her name was Otalla, and she was Buford's wife. I suspect she died because all her energy came from others. Energy she stole from other living beings to support her own life. Look how she's aged."

"I've heard of this," Helen breathed. "Mages who extend their own lives with the life force of other people. Blood path..." Helen gasped, appalled. "Sweet Mother of All." She turned to Jim. "She bit you! Quick, bend down here and let me get a look. She probably infected you with something."

Helen still held the lavender in one hand as she examined the twin half-circles of the bite mark on Jim's back, up high, just below his neck. The lavender reacted, meaning Helen was right to worry about contagion.

"Hold still. This might be a bit uncomfortable, but it's

necessary," she told him. Using her power to cleanse his system, she sent the Lady's Light through his bloodstream, burning out the evil the woman had planted.

"Feels warm," Jim commented as she finished the treatment. "Was it bad?"

"Not as bad as it could have gotten. She poisoned you with her evil." Helen zapped the bite marks with her power, healing them. "It's gone now. You'll be okay."

"Thanks, love," he told her, tugging her into his arms for a quick squeeze. "Now, did you call for help before storming in to the rescue?"

"I did," she admitted, giving in for just a moment, to the need to be close to him. "Joe said ten minutes, but I didn't want to wait once I sensed Calum inside this building. I knew you were probably walking into a trap."

"You broke the ward, didn't you?" Jim asked as they walked, arm in arm, over to the crate where Calum lay, watching all.

"I did. The lavender from the B&B's garden is particularly potent." She smiled at the young wolf as she crouched down in front of the open door of the crate. "Hi, I'm Helen, and this is Jim. You're Calum, aren't you? Your Alpha is on the way, and he's bringing help, but maybe I can give you a little help before they get here, huh? This way, you can stand on your own feet when they show up. I'm a healer. What do you think?"

The wolf submitted, reaching out of the open crate with his nose and licking her hand. Helen took that as permission and sent a tendril of healing power into the teen. Almost instantly, his eyes looked more alert.

"That felt okay?" she asked, waiting for a little nod from the wolf's head. She let her power diagnose what might be wrong with the youngster and was relieved to find it wasn't as bad as it could have been. "I think mostly you're just underpowered right now. They were draining your magical power and your life force, weren't they?" she asked. "Well, I can give you enough of a boost to let you walk out of here with your dignity, at least, but time will repair the rest. Time, food, and rest, and you'll be good as new in a few days."

"Thanks be to the Mother of All," Joe said, entering the room on that last declaration. He went immediately to the open crate and reached in to touch Calum, offering the comfort of the Alpha to his Packmate. He kept his hand on Calum's ruff while he spoke with Helen and Jim. "Thank you for finding him."

Joe didn't get choked up, exactly, but Helen could definitely feel the emotion in his words. He spent a moment more just looking into the eyes of the young wolf, offering reassurance that everything would be all right now, then he stood and went over to Jim, getting a full report on the action. Helen ignored them while she did what she could for Calum, knowing that others would be joining them shortly.

CHAPTER 16

Jim stood with the Alpha while Helen got to work on the boy. He was in awe of her power, and her bravery. His inner wolf had just about howled when she'd walked in, concerned for her safety, but he needn't have worried. Helen was *formidable!* He'd had no idea she had that kind of power. She seemed so innocent, so demure, but when push came to shove, she had guts. Real guts. He'd have her at his back in a fight any day, and he was going to be sure to tell her as much, once they were alone.

"You got them both?" Joe asked, bringing Jim back to the matter at hand.

"I got the male. Helen got the woman," Jim clarified. It was important to him that Helen get credit for her deeds.

Joe glanced over at the white-haired body. "An old woman?"

"She was younger looking than Helen when she attacked me," Jim said. "Buford said her name was Otalla, but whether that was her real name is anybody's guess. We figure she was using the life force of others to prolong her life. When Helen let loose with the chanting, Otalla's power drained away, and she started to age right in front of my eyes. One of the freakiest things I've ever witnessed."

"I thought Helen was a healer?" Joe said, looking over at

her, kneeling in front of the crate and running her hands gently over Calum's furry back.

"She is, but her heritage is very magical, going back many generations. I think maybe her magical education is more extensive than any of us realized. I suspect her strongest skill is healing, and that's always taken precedence, but she knows other things too. Such as how to banish evil. She was chanting in ancient German, which makes sense when you realize her ancestry is from that part of the world, and her folks still live alongside the Amish and Mennonite communities of Eastern Pennsylvania." Jim thought about what he had learned of the Richards family. "Her sister, Kiki, is non-magical, but she knew enough herbal lore to break a dark ward. I bet Helen did the same. She told me she used that lavender she picked this morning from the B&B's garden to break the dark ward around this place. Their mother is a strong clairvoyant, so maybe she has a bit of that, as well."

"I don't claim to know much about mages," Joe said, holding up both hands, palms outward. "All I can say is that I'm glad she's here. I'm not sure Calum would have survived another day with these people."

"Joe," Jim pitched his voice low, "Buford knew about the town. He deliberately bought this land and set this trap to capture and drain shifters. He and his wife said they were both blood path mages who dabbled in black magic. This was going to be their honey hole, where they could capture nice, juicy, powerful shifters and drain them of their life force, for their own evil ends." Jim shook his head in disgust. "It really sounded as if Buford had gone to West Virginia to trade knowledge with the potion witch up there. He was showing her blood path nastiness, and she was teaching him black wards, and the like."

"Now, that's a partnership made in hell," Joe observed, his expression hard. "Did he give you any indication if he'd passed on information about the town to anybody?"

"It didn't sound like it, but I can't be one hundred percent certain. For what it's worth, I believe they wanted to keep Big

Wolf all to themselves, but you should be wary of travelers. He said he discovered the town when he flew through the airport. It might be wise to hire a few non-magical folk to deal with unknown flights that find their way here. Too many shifters in one place is too attractive a target these days. Just ask the bears in Grizzly Cove how much trouble they've attracted by grouping together in that little town of theirs."

"Bears are a lot more magical than us, and we've always lived in Packs," Joe said, pushing back a bit.

Jim relented. "I hear you, but even though we won here today, evil is growing stronger and bolder all over the world. Things seem to be coming to a head, and we all have to be extra careful right now."

"Agreed," Joe said, moving to intercept as Shane walked in the door.

"Perimeter secure," the sheriff reported, moving into the room. He glanced at the two bodies and then at the wolf slowly getting to its feet and walking out of the crate as Helen helped him.

"If you could clean up here," Joe suggested to the sheriff, "we'll take Calum home to his family."

"The woman's body is safe. No magic left," Jim reported to Shane as he passed. "But be careful with the male. He might be booby-trapped or something."

"Understood," Shane replied quietly, already on the radio to his deputies, speaking in codes so that anyone listening in on a police scanner wouldn't notice anything different about this sheriff's department from any other in the country.

Helen and the boy in wolf form walked slowly to where Joe and Jim waited. Joe crouched down to look at the young wolf, talking quietly with the boy, even though the youngster couldn't answer back in his present form. Helen went to stand next to Jim, and he put his arm around her shoulders. She slumped against him, and he realized she'd given the boy a lot of her energy.

"You okay, sweetheart?" he asked gently, leaning down to nuzzle a kiss to her temple.

"I'll be fine. Just give me a minute, and we can head out. I suspect Calum's going to need a little help, though. He was as close as I've ever seen someone to being drained dry."

Jim frowned and snuggled Helen closer into his side. Joe reached out for the wolf pup and gathered him into his arms. He caught Jim's eyes and jerked his head toward the exit then walked out with Jim and Helen following behind.

Joe carried the teen all the way to where Helen had left the rental car. He got in the backseat with Calum still in wolf form, sitting on the bench seat with his head resting on Joe's knee. Helen took the passenger seat and immediately rested her head back with her eyes closed. Jim drove and headed back toward town. Joe gave him directions to Calum's home.

When they arrived, Calum's mother and father were outside, waiting to meet them. Tears ran down the woman's face as she saw her boy carried in Joe's strong arms. They followed their Alpha into their home, pointing the way to Calum's room, where Joe placed him on the bed.

Jim had followed behind, tugging Helen along with him when she would have held back from entering a stranger's home. Jim knew they would be welcome for Calum's sake, and with Joe there, as Alpha, Calum's family wouldn't turn them away.

They stood in the doorway of the teen's room while Calum's mother fussed over her child and his father talked in low tones with Joe. The man kept glancing at Jim and Helen, and Jim realized he must be asking the details of his son's rescue. After a few minutes of this, the conversation ended, and the man came over to Jim, his hand outstretched.

"Thank you for finding my son," he said as Jim shook the man's hand.

"Jim Hanson, Helen Richards, this is Ephraim and his mate, Audrey," Joe made the introductions. "Audrey is our Pack healer," he added, looking at Helen. "She went to medical school, and in the human world, she's a doctor. She's actually the town's only licensed General Practitioner, and her clinic is just next door," Joe explained. "Audrey doesn't do magical healing, but she understands the concept and will accept any further help you can give, once she settles down and reassures herself that her pup is whole and mostly undamaged."

"I can't imagine what you both have been going through," Helen said, offering sympathy to Calum's father. He shook her hand, in turn.

"Thank you for all you've done to help our son," he said, and Helen could feel the true emotion behind the man's words. This was a father who deeply loved his child.

"It was our pleasure to be able to help," Helen assured the man. "And I'll happily do what I can to restore his energy, but he'll definitely be able to heal on his own, with time, food and rest."

"That's really good to hear," Ephraim said, his hand over his heart, as if feeling her reassuring words very deeply. "Let's talk in the hall for a moment while Audrey gets Calum comfortable."

Joe stayed behind while Helen, Jim and Ephraim moved out into the hall. Their home was built on a large scale but wasn't ostentatious. It was just big and comfortable in a way that told Helen a lot about the couple. They were clearly doing well for themselves, but they didn't live in a grandiose manner.

"Audrey's been just about going out of her mind," Ephraim said as he closed the door to his son's room gently. "It's been all I could do to keep her calm and wait for news. We both searched all over town before calling for help."

"It was good you called when you did," Jim said, his expression grave. "I don't know how much Joe's told you yet, but your son got caught in a trap set by a couple of evil mages."

"Joe gave me the bare bones of it, and I'm sure I'll get all the details once things settle down, but please know that we owe you a debt of gratitude that we can never repay. You saved our son, and that means…" His voice wobbled, and he stopped talking. Helen reached out to touch Ephraim's arm in sympathy.

"I believe the good we do for others comes back in a multitude of ways. The good you've done allowed this blessing into your life," Helen told him. "The Mother of All put us in the right place to help, and as far as I'm concerned, there is no debt. I did what I did because I serve the Light. I could do no less."

"You're not what I expected of a human mage," Ephraim told her candidly. Helen laughed.

"We're not all alike. Even in my family, we all have different talents and specialties. I'm one of the more docile ones since my strongest gift is healing, but some of my siblings are a bit more like the stereotype than I am." Helen looked down, still smiling. At that moment, the door to Calum's room opened, and Joe beckoned to Helen.

Jim stayed with Ephraim while Helen went into the room to find the young wolf had transformed into a teenaged boy. His mother was helping him put on a T-shirt over the pajama bottoms he already wore, and then she tucked him into bed. Helen hung back with Joe while the mother fussed over her son. When it looked like she was done tucking him in, Helen walked over.

"Is it all right with you both if we do another treatment now? It'll help him sleep, and that will bring back even more of his energy," Helen told Audrey.

They agreed, and Audrey watched carefully as Helen sat on the edge of Calum's bed and took his hand in hers. She closed her eyes and concentrated on transferring energy to the youngster, seeking out the damaged pathways in his system and curing them with an influx of healing Light energy. She let her mind wander in a sort of wordless prayer as she worked, as she often did in these kinds of situations. Helen wasn't sure, but she thought maybe, when she healed, she was somehow channeling just a little bit of the Divine.

She did what she could for Calum before her own strength gave out, then opened her eyes and smiled at him. He looked better to her. There was more color in his cheeks, and he had a healthier—if fatigued—look about him. She let go of his hand and tried to stand, but her knees were a bit wobbly.

Jim was at her side in a flash, supporting her with an arm around her waist. Audrey looked worried as Jim guided her from the room, but Helen waved at her and smiled. "I'm fine. So is Calum. We just both need a little rest to restore our energy. That's all." Helen's voice faded as they walked out of the room, and then, Jim surprised her by lifting her into his arms as if she weighed nothing at all.

Helen clung to Jim, looping her hands around his neck, but she was in no danger of falling. Jim was so strong, and his steps were sure as he walked back through the house and out to the car. Joe followed behind, shaking his head. Helen could just see the Alpha over Jim's muscular shoulder.

Jim paused by the passenger door of their rental vehicle for Joe to come and open the door, then he placed her into the car as gently as he could. She knew he was concerned by the hard cast to his features.

"I'm all right," she told him, touching his cheek as he buckled her into the passenger seat. "Just tired. I'll be good as new in a little bit. I promise."

His mouth formed a tight line. "I'll see that you keep that promise, sweetheart. We're going back to the B&B."

"I'll arrange for dinner to be delivered," Joe added. "You just rest up now, Helen, and thanks again, for what you did for my Pack. I won't forget your generous heart."

Helen felt the impact of the Alpha's soft words. He was a good man, and she really liked the way he looked out for his Pack. They were all his extended family, in a way, and it was clear he cared for each and every one. No wonder this group was so successful. With a leader like Joe in command, caring for every soul under his protection, they couldn't help but succeed in all they did.

Jim drove them back through town, to the B&B. He parked out front and wouldn't let Helen walk. Instead, he carried her again, and Felicia flung open the front door even before they got to the steps. Helen felt a bit conspicuous, but it also felt wonderful to be in Jim's arms, no matter the circumstances. He was really pulling out all the stops in his care for her welfare and the way he looked after her touched her deeply. It felt like... Like he really cared.

He walked right in, muttering a quick greeting and thanks to Felicia as he made for the stairs. Helen expected he'd put her down, but instead, he mounted the stairs, holding her as if she weighed nothing. He wasn't even the tiniest bit out of breath when they got to the top. She'd known he was strong, but this was ridiculous...in the best possible way.

Shifter strength must be even greater than Helen had thought. He turned to their door and backed up to the electronic lock. Normally, all they had to do was wave their cards the sensor and the door would unlock. Helen heard the latch pop open as Jim's back pocket came into contact with the sensor, and he grinned at her.

"I put the card in my back pocket." He looked so proud of himself she had to laugh. "Always think ahead, that's what Uncle Arch says." He moved a little, sort of rubbing against the door, and Helen realized he was pushing the handle on the door downward with his butt. The door opened a moment later, and his grin widened. "I love it when a plan comes together."

"You're quoting *The A Team*?" she asked, surprised.

"I loved that show when I was a kid," he told her.

"When you were a..." A few explanations raced through her mind, but he was a shifter, after all. They aged differently than normal folk. "Wait a minute. Just how old are you?"

He gave her a wolfish grin. "Older than you, baby doll, by at least a couple of decades." He walked through the open door to her bedroom and lay her on the bed then sat on the side, looking down at her. "Does it really matter? Do you think I'm a dirty old man now? Or a cradle robber? I'll live a few hundred years if I don't screw up and get killed," he said, his tone almost speculative. "I won't look much older than I do now, for a good two centuries or so."

She was stunned by the concept, though she'd been learning a bit about shifters for the past few months. Ever since her distant cousin had mated a werewolf, in fact. Still, the idea of just how long they could live caught her by surprise. It had been a nebulous concept before, but now, it was real. Jim was real.

Jim was, slowly but surely, taking little bits of her heart. She was very much afraid she was falling in love with him, but knowing how long he would live, how could such a thing work?

"Even with all the magic in my family, the most I'll likely get is about a hundred and fifty years, and that's only if I'm one of the lucky ones," she told him, her tone and expression turning serious.

"That's still a lot more than most non-magical folk, even in this day of modern medicine," he offered.

She noticed he'd avoided any talk of a possible future shared between them. She'd heard from her sister that mating with a shifter often had the effect of extending the human mate's lifespan to match the shifter's. Either Jim was being obtuse or evasive. She'd bet on the latter because, if there was one thing Jim was not, it was stupid.

Their conversation was interrupted by a knock on the outer door of the suite. Jim got up and went out into the main room, talking quietly with a woman. Probably Felicia, Helen thought, but she was too tired to get up and be polite at the moment. She'd given a lot of her own energy to Calum, but she wasn't too concerned about it. She knew Jim would keep her safe.

Even if he wouldn't keep her forever.

CHAPTER 17

Jim chatted with Felicia when she delivered the bags of food Joe had ordered to be sent over from the diner. Two big shopping bags full of various things in containers that smelled really good. Jim thanked Felicia and assured her that Helen was fine, just a bit tired. Felicia left, asking him to pass on her good wishes to Helen, and he closed the door behind her.

He knew he'd been evasive with Helen just a few minutes ago, but he honestly didn't think she was ready to hear what he wanted to say. Increasingly, he was starting to feel incredibly possessive of her. So much so that he was seriously considering whether or not they could make a go of a more permanent relationship. Permanent, as in…forever.

There were no half-measures with shifters when it came to mating. Either she was his forever mate or she wasn't, but he had been having a hard time reconciling his inner wolf's thoughts about Helen, and how awesome she was, with his human half's confused expectations. He'd always imagined that, when he met his mate, he'd be hit by a lightning bolt of recognition and just know, right away, that she was the one.

That hadn't happened with Helen, though he did recall feeling an immediate attraction toward her. They'd had chemistry from the first moment they'd met, though he hadn't really recognized it at the time. He'd been so focused on his mission and so...in denial, really...that a human could be his fated mate. How pompous he'd been in his own thoughts. What a fool he'd been. What an unmitigated ass he'd been.

Jim could kick himself now, for wasting all that time. He should have been wooing her, and instead, he'd packed her off home with a half-assed goodbye. It had been Helen who'd listened to her instincts and come to his rescue. Helen—who didn't have the benefit of an animal side—who had been more in touch with her intuition than he had. What a joke he was for a shifter. He hadn't listened to the wolf who had wanted to keep her near at all times. He hadn't understood the wolf's desire to be with her and keep her safe. He'd been an idiot.

And now, it was probably too late. She was clearly confused by his behavior. Hell, he was confused by his own actions toward her.

He still didn't understand how it could work between them. Their most recent conversation about the vast differences in their ages and life expectancies was something he didn't know the answer to, and something that needed to be figured out if he really was going to entertain the idea of anything permanent between them.

All he knew for now, was that he wanted to be with her. He wanted to take care of her and make sure she was safe and healthy. He wanted to protect her while she was so drained from putting herself out for others.

She had such a generous heart. A brave heart, as well. That stunt on the beach where she'd scared off the hyena pack with a few fireworks impressed the hell out of him. He couldn't imagine the courage it took for her to do all that. For him.

She'd been so good to him from the moment they'd met. He'd known she was attracted to him. He was older than her. He'd been around the block more than a few times, and he wasn't unaware when a woman found him attractive. He'd chosen to ignore it, for the most part. A foolish move, in retrospect. Why? Because she was human, and he'd had a mental block against getting involved romantically with humans—even magical ones.

Stupid.

He cursed himself as he set out the boxes and cartons of food on the table. He'd make up a plate with a little of everything and bring it in to her. Then, he'd find out what she liked best and get more of whatever it was, so she could eat and regain her strength. He was going to treat her like the queen she was and make sure she didn't suffer for her kind act this day.

Jim put little bits of meatloaf, mac and cheese, baked chicken over seasoned rice, turkey with stuffing, and salmon on a plate and brought it in to her. Helen was laying on the bed, in the position he'd left her in, her eyes closed. He thought she might actually be asleep, but when he drew closer, her eyes opened, and she sniffed appreciatively at the scent of the food wafting toward her.

"That smells good," she said, "but also confusing. I smell fish and turkey and beef?" She sat up, leaning against the headboard of her bed.

"I brought a sampler. A little bit of everything on offer. Taste it and tell me what you want, and I'll go get it for you from the other room. There's also a tossed salad with tomatoes and a vinaigrette dressing, some vegetable side dishes, and a selection of desserts." He handed her the plate and watched as her eyes lit with pleasure. "Were there any green beans?" she asked as she nibbled a bit of the turkey.

He nodded. "Green bean casserole. With the mushrooms and fried onions. There was also cranberry sauce in that bag and mashed potatoes."

"Like Thanksgiving dinner," she said, grinning. "I'll have a little of each of those, please. Turkey, stuffing, cranberry sauce, mashed potatoes, green bean casserole, and applesauce, if there's any. Just a spoonful of each, okay?"

Jim moved to take her plate, but she jerked it out of his reach. "Nope. You can't have this back. I'm going to nibble," she told him with a crafty grin. "Just bring me Thanksgiving on a plate, and I'll be happy. You can have the rest."

Jim laughed as he headed back into the other room. He was still chuckling over her reaction as he made up the plate as she'd asked. He felt very domestic. Rarely had he taken care of another person this closely. He was more the man of action, parachuting in to save the day. The aftermath was for other people to deal with. He found he liked this. Taking care of another person—particularly Helen—was something he didn't mind in the least.

He fixed up her plate, adding a few bites of salad in an empty spot and a slice of apple pie on a dessert plate, then brought it in to her. Going back out, he heaped some of the other selections onto two plates for himself then went back into her bedroom and set himself up on the nightstand. Helen had already cleared it off, so she could use it as a make-shift dining table.

There was just enough room for one of his plates, as well. He put the other within easy reach at the foot of the bed and dragged a chair over so he could sit opposite her. That's when he realized he hadn't brought in anything to drink, though he had remembered silverware and napkins. He dashed back out and got a few bottles of spring water, then returned and sat back down. They ate in relative silence, each savoring the meal and, at least in Jim's case, running through the events of the day in his head.

Helen seemed so tired, but the food was perking her up a bit, for which he was grateful. "You were really magnificent today, Helen," he said a moment after the thought crossed his mind. He needed to let her know how much he valued her input and abilities. She'd surprised him, and he was never more grateful to have been taken unawares.

"Oh, you did most of the heavy lifting," she told him. "I'm just glad it was something I could help with. That poor boy. He really suffered at the hands of those people."

"Are you okay with what happened? I mean, I know sometimes a first kill can be tough." He wanted her to talk to him and open up about her feelings if she was having trouble with what she'd done. He wanted her to know he was willing to listen.

"What makes you think that was my first kill?" she asked, challenging him. He loved how she was constantly making him rethink his assumptions.

"It wasn't?"

"That's not what I said," she replied, giving nothing away. "I grew up on a farm. I've seen death. I've caused it a time or two, though you're right. I'll admit I've never killed another person before. Of course, that woman was just about as far from being a decent human being as it's possible to get." Helen sipped her water and regarded him steadily. "I admit, I felt very odd about it at first, but I've been pondering whether my actions were right or wrong, and I realized that the gift the Mother of All has given me would not work had my actions not been righteous. All of my power—magical and otherwise—comes from the Goddess. It stands to reason that, if I tried to use it in a way She didn't approve of, it wouldn't work. That's how it's always been for me, at least." Helen shrugged as she ate a dainty spoonful of her mashed potatoes.

She went on after a short pause to swallow, before he could say anything. "Then, of course, I saw the full extent of what she and her husband had done to Calum, and I almost wished I could kill her, all over again. That poor boy." She blinked a few times, and he realized there were tears glistening in her eyes. "He was so close to death, Jim. So close." She held it together and sipped her water again. "That's why I gave so much of my own power to him. He really, really needed it. Plus, I knew you wouldn't let anything bad happen to me while I was so run down."

"You've got that right," he said, meaning every syllable. "Are you feeling better now? You already look a lot steadier."

"The food is really helping," she told him, forking another bite of turkey and stuffing into her mouth. She chewed and swallowed before going on. "This is really amazingly delicious. As good as my mother's, though if you tell her I said that, I'll deny it." Helen smiled at him then concentrated on her plate for a bit.

He'd never seen her eat so much, and it gave his inner wolf a warm feeling to feed her. Providing for one's mate was a basic need of the wolf, though Jim couldn't be sure that a mating between them would work out. There were a few obstacles that had to be overcome if this was going to work.

Helen was starting to feel much, much better. The meal was helping, though the turkey had its usual effect, making her a bit sleepy. Still, she wasn't close to crashing from fatigue anymore. She was just happily sleepy, but she didn't really want to sleep. No, what she wanted was sitting across the little table from her.

Jim. She wanted him like she wanted her next breath.

She did her best to hold in her impulses until they were finished eating, but when he rose to take the plates out into the main room, she grabbed his forearm. Jim paused, meeting her gaze.

"Don't go far," she said, trying to find a way to say what she really wanted that didn't sound too brassy.

"I'm just going into the next room to clear up," he told her. Damn. He wasn't getting it.

"I mean, go ahead and do that but then come back."

His brow furrowed slightly. "Why don't you just get in bed and get some rest?"

She shook her head. "Not without you."

His expression cleared, but she wasn't sure he totally understood what she wanted. Still, he looked more agreeable. She could work with that.

"Okay. You get in bed, and I'll be back in just a few minutes," he told her, bending to place a chaste kiss on her forehead.

From that, she surmised he was under the impression that she wanted him to hold her while she slept or something. While that would be nice, what she wanted went a lot farther than just being held. She wanted him. His possession. His lovemaking. His full attention.

Jim cleared the nightstand and went into the main room with the plates. Helen took a few moments to put the nightstand back in its original position. Then, she went into the shared bathroom between the bedrooms, trailing her clothing like breadcrumbs along the path to the bathroom door, which she left ajar.

Once inside, she turned on the shower, nice and warm, and stepped under the spray. She'd been through a lot that day, and the warm water was just what she needed to get the knots out of her shoulder muscles. She washed her hair, and the slide of the lather down her body felt unaccountably sensual. She might have even moaned a little, but the answering growl made her nipples peak and her tummy clench.

Her eyes shot open, and she turned her head. Jim had followed her trail of discarded clothing and was standing just outside the large walk-in shower stall, looking at her. The growl had come from his throat, and it was deliciously clear that he was more than interested in what he saw.

"Join me?" she asked, looking at him over her soapy shoulder. He answered with a new growl that flowed over her nether regions like a caress.

As she watched, he peeled off his shirt, kicked off his boots, and shucked his pants, all without breaking eye contact. She held his gaze as he opened the fogged glass door and entered the shower stall. He was a big man, but the bathroom had been built with shifters in mind, and the shower was luxuriously large with a wide bench built right in and multiple showerheads.

Jim touched one of the controls, and a wide rain head came on over the entire enclosure. It felt like being caught in a warm summer rain. The mood Helen was in, it felt sensual and seductive. Just like the man who caught her in his arms and slid against her, both of their bodies slick with warm water.

He helped her wash the few remaining suds out of her hair with gentle hands then took her chin in one hand, tilting her face up to the rain. She closed her eyes, and then, the rain was replaced by him. His presence. His lips on hers. His kiss.

It was one of the most erotic experiences she'd ever had, and they hadn't even done much of anything, yet. She couldn't wait to find out what else he had in store.

She'd been extremely tired and low on energy, just a moment ago, but as they kissed, she could feel the fire in her soul rekindling. Her energy started to flow more easily, and she was able to meet him, kiss for kiss, touch for touch. She ran her hands all over his hard body, reaching between them to stroke his hardness with a gentle but firm touch. She loved the growl that came from deep within his chest, especially when he rubbed against her, and she felt the growl in her skin, as well as heard it.

He moved back so that she had to let go of him, but he didn't go far. He came up behind her and pressed against her back, cupping her breasts from behind, playing with her nipples under the warm rain of the shower. Bending, he kissed her neck and nibbled gently on her earlobe as his fingers trailed over her body, no part of it left untouched or unexplored.

Jim's talented hands delved between her legs, one from the front and one from the back, cupping her rear then sliding between her cheeks to tease and tantalize. No man had ever touched her so intimately as a precursor to lovemaking. No man, she realized only now, had ever really cared that much about her enjoyment of the act, as to prepare her so thoroughly.

The irony was that all Jim had to do was crook his little finger—and not even necessarily in the position it now enjoyed—and she was ready for him. Although, when he did crook his finger...and a whole lot more...she found it hard to stand because her knees almost gave out at the deliciously decadent sensations he was causing to course through her body.

But he was there to catch her. Jim held her securely, and she knew he would never let her fall. She'd never felt so sure about any man. He was unique in her experience. Unique and wonderful.

She felt herself being lifted off the ground and turned. His strength continued to take her breath away. He was muscular and sleek, but those lean muscles of his provided a strength all out of proportion of any regular man. Maybe it was shifter magic. Maybe it was the power of his animal spirit. She didn't know what made him so incredibly strong, but she liked it, whatever it was.

His power made her feel delicate and feminine. Her. A farm girl. Born and bred to work a full day and never complain. She had seldom felt delicate in her entire life, but being around Jim made that fantasy a reality. He made her feel soft and feminine and so very desired.

It was a heady experience for a farm girl who had never really felt the zap of instant attraction as she had for Jim. She didn't know, for sure, if he felt the same, but she was suspending reality for this time out of time with him. She was going to enjoy it for all she could, just in case she never got the chance to be with him, again.

Their earlier discussion about their relative ages brought harsh reality all too close to her mind. He was older than her. Substantially so if he'd watched 1980's television shows when he was a kid. She knew shifters aged differently than other beings. She just hadn't expected to have that reality displayed so openly when an off-hand remark made her realize their differences, all over again.

She resolved to forget it. At least, for now. She wanted to enjoy this time with him, and besides, the way he touched her pretty much drew all coherent thought from her mind so that only pleasure remained. She'd focus on that. The incredible pleasure only Jim had ever brought to her.

He lifted her and turned her so that she was facing him and her thighs straddled his hips. Then, he made use of the wide bench at the back of the shower. He sat, draping her over him, her thighs splayed open directly across from his erection. Oh, yeah. That's just what she wanted. He rubbed their bodies together, his warm hands playing over her hips and spine.

"Are you ready?" he asked, his words clipped and his excitement evident in the labored nature of his breathing.

"Definitely," she told him, unable to speak more than that single word.

"Thank heaven," he gasped, bringing them together and sliding deep inside.

CHAPTER 18

Jim's eyes closed, and Helen watched the tight lines of his face with fascination. She'd never really watched a man in passion before. She'd always been a bit embarrassed by the whole thing and kept her eyes closed or on something else, for the most part. But, with Jim, she wanted to see it all. His restraint, his surrender to passion, and most of all, his pleasure.

She felt the deep penetration of his length within her. It felt good. It felt like coming home. Right. Tremendously satisfying...and they hadn't even really gotten started, yet.

The warm rain of the shower poured down around them as Jim began to move, guiding her hips so that Helen understood the rhythm he wanted her to take. Her knees on the tile of the bench seat for leverage, she did the best she could on the slippery surface to hold it together long enough to bring them both pleasure. She began moving slowly, at first, figuring out how best to position herself on this unique surface. Jim was there, guiding her hips, holding her steady. He was her anchor. Her rock.

Heaven knew, he was definitely hard as one as she rode him in the steamy rain of the shower stall. She doubted she would ever take a shower, again, without thinking of this moment. It was perfect. Their bodies straining together, Jim having given control of their motion to her—at least for now. She liked it. She liked the feeling of power he gave her. He was such a good man, and he made her feel so good. She might die of the pleasure, but she'd die happy.

Helen increased her pace, riding him with confidence, now that she'd figured out just how to move on the slick surface and how deep to take him. All the way felt right. Like he would become part of her forever, which she didn't mind in the least at that moment.

She panted as she rode him, encouraged by his hand on her ass. He surprised her with a wet slap that smarted a bit but also, oddly, turned her on even more.

"You like that?" Jim asked, his smile full of deviltry. "I'll have to remember that."

Helen was beyond replying in words at that point, and when he smacked her ass, again, this time on the other cheek, she went off like a rocket, coming hard around him. She squeezed him with her internal muscles, milking his cock until he, too, joined her in climax.

Jim's inner wolf growled as he came, setting off more aftershocks inside her body. It was like fireworks and lighting all at once. Rain poured down around them, but it didn't douse the flame. It only fed the sensations as the orgasm they shared went on and on.

Eventually, she was able to catch her breath, and Jim just held her, his arms looped around her back, holding her steady. Her legs were beginning to cramp, so she moved off him, and he helped her stand. She wavered a bit, unsteady on her feet at first after the blue haze of pleasure that had caused her to nearly black out for a moment.

As she came back to herself, she realized something amazing. Her internal energy levels were not only restored, but overflowing with life energy. Being with Jim had done that. She had no doubt in her mind.

She leaned down to kiss him and smiled as she drew back. "You restore me," she said simply. "My energy is back, even better than before."

"You're kidding." Jim looked unconvinced.

"Nope," she told him, smiling as she stood and rinsed off in the continuing warm rain of the shower. "Both times we've done this, I've come out of it reenergized. I think it's you, lover." She sent him a smile over her shoulder and was gratified by the dazed look in his eyes as he watched her body.

He cleared his throat before he replied. "Wherever you're getting the energy, it's not from me. I feel fine. Better than fine, in fact." He frowned a bit. "Do you think we could be creating the energy between us, somehow?"

She touched her nose and winked playfully. "I think that's exactly what's going on," she told him. "We're not draining each other. We're creating life energy between us and sending it out into the universe, keeping some for ourselves, of course. It's a beautiful thing."

"Speaking of beautiful things…" Jim stood and took her into his arms from behind. "You are amazing, Helen. Have I told you that lately?"

"I think you just did," she replied, feeling young and carefree in a way she seldom had in her life.

"Good. Let's dry off, and we can make some more universal energy. In a bed, this time." His growl was the sexy key that started her engine, all over again.

"You're on," she told him, reaching for the door and preceding him out of the shower.

They dried off and spent the rest of the night making love then eating some of the extra desserts Joe had sent over. Then, they made love, again, finally falling asleep in each other's arms.

The next morning, Jim's wolf woke him with a snarl. It wanted him to claim Helen as his mate. The night they'd just spent together had clinched it as far as his wolf was concerned, but the human half of him still had doubts. Mating was about more than the physical. It had a spiritual component, as well, but there was also the nitty-gritty details of everyday life to be considered.

Helen was so young and innocent compared to him. She was human. Okay, she was a magical human, but still human. How would that work? He knew, theoretically, that humans and shifters had been mating for centuries, but what about magical humans, like Helen? And what would her family say? Would they flip out about getting yet another shifter in the family?

He didn't know exactly how Kiki's mate, Jack, had been received, but Jack was a bear and had a lot more magical power just by his very nature. Bears were like that. Jim was a wolf. A shifter, but nowhere near the magic rating of a bear. Would Helen's folks turn up their nose at a mere wolf? He had no idea, though her distant cousin had reportedly mated with a wolf, but still, these thoughts plagued his mind.

He got out of bed before she woke, unable to face her while his mind was in turmoil. Besides, she deserved to sleep in after the excitement of the day before. Jim tiptoed out and closed the bedroom door behind him. He had to check in with Joe and his current employers.

Which was another problem he'd have to overcome if he wanted to convince Helen to be his mate. He'd been living a rather vagabond existence up 'til now, taking jobs as they came along, never really staying in one place for long. If he had a mate, that would have to change. He didn't want to scar a gentle soul like Helen's with his tramp lifestyle.

Ostensibly, he still lived in Iowa, but really, he hadn't been home for long in years. He'd only paused there between assignments, and even Uncle Arch knew that eventually Jim would have to find a place where he fit. Not that Jim didn't love his brother. He did. He supported Brock, as Alpha, as much as possible. Jim just hadn't fully made the transition from the military life he'd lived for so long back to civilian life, yet. Maybe he never would.

He'd talked it over a time or two with Uncle Arch, and the last time the subject had come up, Arch had surprised Jim by suggesting he check out what the ex-military bears had built in Grizzly Cove. Arch had thought Jim might find that town easier on his senses, since just about every damn bear in it was ex-Special Forces. Either that or Arch had suggested hooking up with Jesse Moore's mercenary team and living in Wyoming with them.

Jim hadn't wanted that. He'd given up the military and didn't want to be a full-on mercenary. He preferred doing what he'd been doing. Running specialist jobs for friends of friends or those who came with good credentials and high recommendations from people he trusted. He liked being a troubleshooter.

Come to think of it, Ezra Tate had hinted more than once that he was looking for more people with Jim's unique skills to help clean up the mess left behind by SeaLife Enterprises' former CEO. Jim might just have to sit down with Ezra when this mission was over and discuss that possibility in more depth. If he did go to work for SeaLife, he'd have a legitimate reason to rent an apartment in Grizzly Cove and check the place out to see if that was where he was meant to be.

If he had a real house, he could offer some stability to a mate, but would Helen want to live clear on the other side of the country from her close-knit family? Jim didn't think so. Yet another obstacle in their path. At this rate, he'd never find a way for them to make a go of it. Maybe it just wasn't meant to be.

Discouraged, with his wolf howling denial inside his brain, Jim got back to work. His first call was to Joe. He knew Joe had sent his investigators over to the old feed mill to go over everything there with a fine-toothed comb. Shane had probably spent all night working through whatever evidence he could find in the building and on the grounds. Jim was interested to learn if they'd found anything actionable.

"Glad you're up," Joe said, his voice filled with energy. "There have been some developments. Can you come over to my office?"

"I'll be there in about ten minutes," Jim answered right away and ended the call after a quick farewell. He dashed off a note for Helen, so she'd know where he was when she woke, then headed out to see what had been found.

*

Helen woke by slow degrees. She felt deliciously lethargic after the rather acrobatic night she'd spent in Jim's arms. He'd surprised her with some of the positions he'd coaxed her into, but it had been worth it. She felt decadent when she thought about the incredible pleasure they'd shared. Never in her life had she reached such highs as she did with Jim. She'd come to the conclusion that he'd thoroughly ruined her for any other man, but she couldn't really bring herself to care. Not right now, at any rate. Not when she felt so sated.

She put on a satin robe she'd picked up during her shopping yesterday and padded barefoot out into the rest of the suite, looking for him. She didn't find him, but she found a note, along with a single rose she recognized as having come from the B&B's garden. Her heart just about melted. Whether he'd picked the rose himself or saw it somewhere in the house and purloined it for her didn't matter. What mattered was the thoughtful gesture.

His note indicated that he was already working, over at the mayor's office, examining the evidence haul. She felt decadent for having slept in but was thoroughly enjoying herself. She took a shower, remembering all the naughtiness they'd gotten up to in that shower stall the night before with fond delight, then dressed and headed downstairs to see if there was any breakfast still available.

There was, and she spent a few minutes chatting with Felicia and Miss Felicity while she ate then worked with Miss Felicity for a few minutes, doing another healing session that went even better than Helen had expected. The extra energy boost she got from making love with Jim seemed to give her even more power to work with when she healed.

"You know, I may have overestimated how long I'd need to treat you," she told Miss Felicity when she was done with the morning's healing session. "You're taking to this better than I'd expected, and I've had a bit more energy to work with since being…uh…in this town."

"Being with young Jim, you mean." Miss Felicity grinned as she gave Helen a knowing look.

Helen felt her cheeks heat with a telltale flush but realized Miss Felicity must have learned a thing or two in her time. Maybe she could explain what was going on.

"I don't understand it," Helen said, gauging Miss Felicity's reaction to her words. "I've never gotten such an energy boost from anyone. Being around Jim does something unexpected." Helen shook her head. "Have you ever heard of anything like that before?"

Miss Felicity nodded. "It's the combination of shifter magic with yours. I've seen such things go either way. Sometimes, they work together and feed each other, making both people stronger than they were before. Sometimes, they clash. The times I've seen it cooperate were among mated pairs who had very strong emotional bonds and very happy lives together." Miss Felicity smiled broadly. "I'm glad to see you two doing so well. I expect great things to come of your relationship."

"If we even have a relationship," Helen muttered, forgetting, for the moment, about sharp shifter hearing.

"Do you mean to tell me that boy hasn't declared himself yet?" Miss Felicity seemed a bit outraged.

Helen felt the odd need to defend Jim from the old lady's ire. "He's hardly had time. We only just met a few days ago, and we've only been…um…together…well…not long at all." Helen felt herself blushing again. People didn't talk much about sex in the culture she'd been raised in—and especially not with their elders.

Miss Felicity scoffed. "Things were done differently in my day. Not to say we didn't have our fun, but mating was serious business, and we didn't screw around when it came to that." Miss Felicity seemed to think about it then shrugged. "I suppose he must be confused," she finally said. "I've seen that happen more than it should. Some men just don't know what's good for them when it's standing right in front of them. He'll figure it out eventually. They always do. It just takes some longer than others." She shook a finger at Helen. "Don't make it too easy on him when he does. A woman deserves to know where she stands, and if he makes you wait, you give him what-for when the time comes, understand? It's the principle of the thing."

Helen could do nothing other than nod and agree with Miss Felicity, even if her words were a bit bewildering. Helen still had no idea if she and Jim were meant to be together long-term. After last night, she'd love it if that was the case. They already knew they worked well together under pressure, and they had complementary skill sets. She also enjoyed his company and thought he felt the same, and when it came time to make love…well…that was pretty darn fantastic, so it was clear they were compatible that way.

If that was enough to make a mating among shifters, they were already there. The thing was, Helen wasn't a shifter, and she wanted that one elusive thing that they'd never even hinted at. She wanted love.

For her part, she was already most of the way in love with Jim, but she wasn't sure what he was feeling, at all. The topic had just never come up. Sure, he'd showed her he cared with his gestures and gentleness, but was that enough to build a life on? Was it love?

She didn't know. She was downright afraid to even hint at the subject, lest it ruin what they already had together.

Helen left Miss Felicity, who was feeling as well as Helen could probably make her. If they were still here tomorrow, Helen would try another treatment, but she really thought her work was done. On her way out the door, she spotted Felicia and told her as much. Felicia surprised her by giving her a big hug and a tearful thanks for helping her great-grandmother, which made Helen's heart fill with joy. She loved helping people, and by helping Miss Felicity, she'd helped Felicia, as well.

What was it Jim had said? He loved it when a plan came together. Yeah, Helen thought, she agreed wholeheartedly.

Helen smiled as she walked toward the mayor's office. It was time she reasserted herself as part of the team.

Jim ran into Helen on the steps of city hall. He was just leaving the meeting with Joe and Shane.

"I was just heading back to the B&B to talk to you," he told her.

She smiled up at him, and he felt his heart skip a beat with happiness. "What's up?"

"They found some evidence that needs to get to Grizzly Cove as soon as possible." Jim took her arm and escorted her down the block, heading back toward the B&B. "I volunteered to fly it there, but we have to leave, right away."

"I can come, too?" she asked, as if surprised.

Jim stopped walking and turned to look at her. "If you want. I didn't mean to imply you had to, but I thought maybe you'd want to see this through." Did she want to go home? Was their partnership at an end, now that she'd saved him, more than once?

Why did that thought hurt so much? Damn.

"You bet I want to see it through," Helen replied, and he found he could breathe, again. "I just wasn't sure you'd want me around, now that your mission is fulfilled."

"Not want you around? Is that what you think? Even after last night?" Jim cursed under his breath. "Honey, if you couldn't tell how much I want you around, then I wasn't doing my job right last night." He bent down and kissed her gently. "For the record, I definitely want you around, for as long as you want to stick around."

"That sounds good to me," she said in a low, sexy voice.

If they weren't standing in the middle of the sidewalk on a busy street, he probably would have kissed her a whole lot more. As it was, he turned, tucking her under his arm as they resumed walking back to the B&B.

"Are you okay with leaving today? Were you going to do more for Miss Felicity?" he asked as they walked. "Maybe we can stop through here on the way back, so you can do more for her."

"No need. I think I've done about all I can for her. I just did a treatment with her, and it went better than I expected," she said. "I think I might've mentioned the power boost I get from being with you? That seems to give me even more ability to heal than I usually have, so the treatment was extra strength. She's about as good as I can get her, right now."

Jim was glad to hear it. He hadn't wanted to leave that old lady in the lurch, but the entire population of Grizzly Cove needed the evidence they'd found in the old feed mill. The words on the documents could be relayed by phone, but the actual physical documents had more to them. Potentially, they had a magical aspect that the leaders of Grizzly Cove wanted their specialists to examine firsthand.

"That's great," Jim replied to Helen as they neared the B&B. "Joe already has people working on refueling and resupplying the plane. He also talked to Sal and rented the plane officially for us. Joe will meet us at the plane with the bags of evidence. He's stocking us up with food and drink, too, so we should be able to just drop off the rental car at the airport, load and go."

"Sounds like you boys thought of everything," Helen commented as they mounted the steps to the porch. Little Angus was just inside the door when they entered and leaped excitedly at Helen's heels.

"I think you've got a fan," Jim observed, grinning at the little dog's antics.

"He just likes me because I took the pain out of his paws." Helen bent down to pet the dog and took a quick look at his paws. "All better," she said with satisfaction as she stood, again.

They packed quickly then headed downstairs. Felicia was already waiting for them, Miss Felicity beside her.

"The Alpha called and explained you were leaving," Felicia said. "We just wanted to see you off and thank you for all you've done for our town and for us." Felicia hugged Helen. "I can never thank you enough for what you did for my gran," she said quietly.

"I was happy to help," Helen said with a smile and a shrug. "It's what I do."

Felicia laughed with her, and Jim was glad to see that Helen had made friends among these people. Miss Felicity gave her a hug next, and then, she beckoned to Jim, having him bend down so she could kiss his cheek.

"You take care of that girl," Miss Felicity whispered for his ears only. "She's going to make you a fine mate, if you ever get your head out of your ass and figure things out. Don't let her get away."

Shocked a bit by her crude language, Jim was nevertheless floored by her presumption. He wished he had more time to talk to the old lady, but duty called, and he would just have to muddle through and figure this emotional stuff out for himself. Goddess help him.

CHAPTER 19

True to his word, Joe had set everything up, and all they had to do was take possession of the evidence bags—two big suitcases Jim stowed in the back—and get going. There was plenty of food in the galley, and Helen served lunch after they'd been in the air for an hour or so. Joe had filed a flight plan for them that included a quick fuel stop in Colorado at a small airport owned by a family of cougar shifters. It was nowhere near as big or fancy as Big Wolf Airport, but it was perfectly positioned and run efficiently.

They were able to fuel and go, taking only a few minutes to climb out of the plane and stretch their legs. The cougars weren't overly friendly, but cats were like that, sometimes. They went their own way, but they did a good job. Jim watched, to make sure.

He fielded a call while they were on the ground from Ezra, in Grizzly Cove. They talked about how the flight was going and when they'd arrive. Ezra said he'd try to have someone drive up to the closest airport, in this case, Seattle-Tacoma, or SeaTac as it was called. There were smaller airstrips, but the big airport had better services, and the plane needed a going over by a mechanic before they flew it back.

Jim had discovered a slight problem with one of the switches that he'd like to have fixed before he returned the plane to Sal. He was certain there would be crackerjack mechanics at SeaTac who could handle just about anything they might find. Jim wanted to make sure everything was perfect when he brought the plane home to Sal. He'd been more than kind in loaning it to Jim, and even though Joe was paying for this additional voyage, Jim knew it wasn't normal for Sal to rent his baby to other pilots. If they used this plane for charters, it was likely only family allowed at the controls. Sal or his daughter, and that was it.

They left the cougar air trip and arrived at SeaTac a couple of hours later. The food was gone, and all they had to remove from the plane was their bags and the two bags of evidence, which was packed in suitcases to blend in with their personal luggage. A rental car had been arranged, and they were on the road in short order, heading south along the coast.

The drive down to Grizzly Cove wasn't long as the crow flies, but once out of the metro area, the roads became rather twisty, and the speed limits lowered to match. Helen drove. She'd argued that he'd done all the flying, so the least she could do was the driving. Jim hadn't minded. He didn't expect trouble, but if it found them, he'd be ready. Plus, he was able to devote his attention to the phone, which hadn't stopped since they'd landed.

Joe had requested a call at each point along their journey, and Jim felt it only polite to ease the Alpha's concerns by calling. Jim had also called Ezra, to fill him in on where they were. Ezra had apologized for not meeting them at the airport, but he'd been delayed leaving the cove. Jim told him not to bother. They were making good time and would be there within the hour.

Jim next called Big John Marshall, as a courtesy. It was only polite to talk to the Alpha of a territory before entering. Jim told Big John about Helen and that she was magical but not a shifter. Big John seemed to take that news in stride and didn't ask for details. At that point, Jim had to wonder if all he'd heard about Grizzly Cove becoming a haven for all sorts of magical folk was true. That would certainly explain the

Alpha bear's easygoing attitude.

Jim was about to check in with his Uncle Arch when the hairs on the back of his neck stood on end. If he'd been in wolf form, he'd have said his hackles rose. Whatever it was, he knew that feeling. Trouble was coming and coming fast.

"Something's about to happen," he said, warning Helen as best he could. "Be alert. Something bad is coming."

In the last moments before the shit hit the fan, Jim placed a call to Ezra. "Better send the cavalry. Something's going down," Jim said shortly, giving Ezra their location just as lightning struck a tree ahead and sent it crashing across the road. Helen stood on the brake, and the rental car stopped just shy of the massive pine. Jim was alert, giving a terse recap of events to Ezra, even as he armed himself and got ready for action.

Then, there was no time left.

"Get out of the car!" Jim yelled at Helen, diving for the driver's side door as she rolled out of it. A woman approached the passenger side, lightning playing about her hands.

He realized in an instant, that she'd felled the tree, not lightning from the sky. For one thing, the few clouds above weren't storm clouds. It was a beautiful day with no rain. The lightning was a mage bolt, and it had come from the woman.

Jim got a good look at her face, and a sinking feeling filled his stomach. She looked familiar. She looked a lot like the late, unlamented Otalla, in fact.

Helen scrambled for cover at the side of the road as Jim pushed her to hurry. A shimmer of electricity went down his spine as he received a glancing blow from the mage bolt the woman threw at them. As a shifter, he had some natural defenses to magical attack, but Helen had none that he knew of. If the bolts were going to fly, he'd have to cover her, but he could only take so much without faltering. He prayed as he'd never prayed before, for the Goddess to keep Helen safe.

"You killed my sister!" the woman shrieked, and Jim had

his suspicions confirmed. "I don't know who you are, but I followed your magical trail all over the damned country with my scrying bowl, and you came almost to my front door. You bastards!"

She let go with another bolt, but they were off the road, in the trees, which offered a little cover, though not enough. Jim tried to stall.

"I don't know who you are or who your sister was, lady," he called out, signaling to Helen to go farther away, under better cover. He was going to draw the woman's fire and hopefully give Helen a chance to hide.

"How soon they forget," the woman scoffed. "I am Maura Dunlevy, and you killed my sister, Otalla. She was partnered to that great lump, Somersby, or whatever he was calling himself this week. I told her she could do better." Little lightning zaps leapt from her fingers to the road as she stalked closer, hunting them. "I kept magical surveillance on them, always. I saw what happened. I saw what you did to her!" A large bolt took out the tree next to Jim, and he dove the other way as it toppled onto the road. "I want you both dead, but I want that witch to suffer, like my dear Otalla suffered. You hear me, witch?" Lightning danced through the trees, taking out a few, here and there.

This woman had power, Jim would give her that, but was she stable mentally? And what could he do with that? Jim thought hard about how to destabilize her enough to get her to make a mistake and leave herself open for attack. It would be tricky, but he might just be able to pull it off.

"So, you're an old lady, like your bitch of a sister?" he asked, almost conversationally.

He saw no reason to continue denying he understood what she was going on about. She was pissed, and she was going to attack them, no matter what he said. He might as well use what he knew to throw her off balance, if he could.

She screamed and threw a mage bolt at where he'd been standing when he spoke. Luckily, he was long gone from that spot. A column of smoke went up from the small fire her magic had started, but luckily, the area was too damp from the near-constant rain that was typical of this part of the world for the fire to really get going.

"We were born of the old world and the old ways," Maura proclaimed. "When power meant something, and only the strong survived. I don't know how you managed to end my sister, but you will not do the same to me. I don't have a parasite of a husband leeching off my power the way she did. I stand alone, and I kill those who dare try to block my path or do me wrong." She made a sweeping gesture with her hands. Jim wondered if it was some kind of magical spellcasting, but nothing happened, right away. "You have done me wrong. Both of you."

Maura repeated the motion, and Jim started to look around more closely. She was definitely doing something. He felt her power against his natural shielding like someone rubbing his fur the wrong way. Uncomfortable. Annoying. Unwanted.

"We killed her because good always triumphs over evil," Jim said, moving quickly to a new bit of cover. None too soon, because the boulder he'd been crouching behind split in two when Marua hit it with one of her mage bolts.

Did the woman not tire? Did she really have that much energy at her disposal? If so, they were in trouble. Jim kept track of where Helen was hiding, all the while trying to figure out how to save this situation.

His phone vibrated, and he glanced at it. The cavalry was on its way, but would it get here soon enough?

Helen hid behind a tree and tried to think. No way was she going to go out like this—cowering behind a tree. It went against every principle she'd been raised with, and it didn't suit her personality at all. No, if she was going to die today, she was going to meet her fate with courage, and fight back, darnit!

Helen might not have learned much of the combative magic her brothers excelled in, but she'd seen them work. She knew how mage bolts were launched and where the power came from. At least, in theory. She'd never been able to conjure offensive magic at all, but her defensive skills were pretty good, even when compared to her more apt siblings. Just because she was more healer than mage didn't mean she couldn't use what power she had to protect the man she loved.

And there it was. She was in love with Jim. Against all odds and counter to common sense, she'd fallen in love with the big galoot. Goddess help her.

No way would she stand by and watch him take chance after chance at getting his handsome ass fried to kingdom come and do nothing about it. Helen thought hard about her next move, and then, when she was sure she'd conjured the best protection she could muster, she stepped out from behind the tree.

She called on Mother Nature, the forest, and all living things to help defend her. She called on the Light of the Goddess and the goodness of the Mother of All to aid her in her time of need. She beseeched the Lady in all Her forms to help protect those who served the Light in this situation, and she put all that energy into a shield that stood as a wall between the roadway and the forest, through which she would allow no evil power to pass.

The sorceress saw her and immediately threw a powerful mage bolt her way, but the invisible shield blocked it, shimmering in the air for a moment as it absorbed the power and drove it into the earth, to harm none. Maura screamed in frustration and launched, again, with the same results. Helen watched the health of her shield wall carefully. So far, it was holding up nicely against whatever Maura threw against it, but Helen didn't know for how long she could keep it up. Something would have to give at some point, but for now, they could at least breathe and strategize.

Jim looked concerned but hadn't said anything. She was glad he hadn't told her to run. She would never leave him behind, and if she was going to try to convince him that they should be together long-term, she had to show him that she could be the partner he needed, not some wimp that had to be protected all the time.

More than that, though, she needed to stand on her own two feet and help. It was her deepest nature to offer aid—of whatever type she could—when there was trouble. While she hadn't been in too many combative situations in her life, she was learning through her adventures with Jim that she could contribute. Perhaps in unexpected ways, but she definitely could make a difference.

Helen walked closer to her side of the shield wall to confront the woman. She had a few things to say, and if this situation was going to end badly, she at least wanted to have her thoughts heard before it happened.

"You sister was a cruel and evil woman, Maura Dunlevy," Helen said in a clear voice. "I've never ended a life before. I'm a healer. I save life and value it, but I don't regret what the Lady's power, working through me, did to Otalla. She kept her youth by killing others, and that is one of the definitions of evil in my book. She needed to go on to the next realm, and I was the instrument of sending her there." Helen paused while Maura steamed and launched useless attacks against her shield wall. "I'll do the same for you, if you continue to attack."

"Oh, I'm so scared," Maura said in exaggerated tones. "You hide behind a shield like a coward, instead of fighting me mage to mage."

Helen wasn't going to fall for Maura's taunts. She would not play this game by Maura's rules. She'd watched her brothers learn battle magic and knew that way lay certain defeat. Helen would not be distracted into doing something stupid or dared into idiocy.

"I do not attack. I defend. You can lob mage bolts at us until the cows come home, if you want, but I'm not going to dance with you. I'm a healer, not a fool." Helen kept her expression serene, knowing it would really bother someone like Maura to see her unruffled at the threat she posed.

"What you fail to realize is that I've only been playing with you up to now," Maura said after a long pause, during which she seemed to regain a bit of her emotional control.

Helen feared what that might mean. She was in the open, right near the line where the roadway began and the grassy area ended. The trees were behind her—too far to get to quickly without protection. If Maura made a move that dissolved the shield, Helen would be all too vulnerable.

Jim was off to her right. Somewhere. She'd sort of lost track of him while focusing on Maura, but Helen knew he could take care of himself. Heck, he was probably better equipped—even without battle magic—than she was for this kind of confrontation. He probably had some plan in mind, so the longer she kept Maura talking, the better chance he had of pulling off whatever it was he was trying to do. Helen certainly hoped he had a decisive move up his sleeve, or this was probably going to end badly.

Maura was conjuring something, keeping her focus on Helen and the shield. She was gathering her energies, and Helen actually felt them as a slimy sensation over her skin. She shivered, unable to help herself. Whatever Maura was planning, it was going to be bad. Helen only hoped she could withstand it.

When Maura let loose with her spellcasting, several things happened simultaneously. Helen felt like everything went into slow motion as Maura launched shield-cracking energy bolts at her shield wall, one after the other in rapid succession until the wall could stand no more. It went down, and then, all hell broke loose.

Helen got hit with more than one of those slicing, painfully sharp mage bolts, the energy cutting her skin to ribbons, even as she fell to the ground. Helen put her hands out, calling up what energy she could from Mother Earth, trying to form a little bubble of protection around her huddled form, but it wasn't quite enough to keep out the continued attack. It did help, a little, but she was still catching the occasional glancing blow, and she couldn't move from the spot. She was terribly exposed, and Maura moved right up on her, standing over her like some sort of avenging demon.

Helen looked up, meeting the death she saw in Maura's eyes with calm. She didn't want to die, but if that's the way this was going to go, she would meet her fate with dignity. She had few regrets, but not getting to spend any more time with Jim was right at the top of her list.

She couldn't even look at him. The sorceress took up all her vision, and she didn't even know where he was. A single tear leaked from the side of her eye that she couldn't control, and she saw Maura's expression fill with hateful glee.

And then...

Her head exploded.

Helen registered a very loud bang and realized the sorceress had forgotten one very important element to this scenario. Jim wasn't just a werewolf. He was also a Navy SEAL, familiar with weapons of every sort. Somehow, at some point, he'd armed himself with something that could literally blow someone away.

Helen sagged in relief as Maura's body slid to the side and collapsed, lifeless. Thanks be to the Mother of All, and the U.S. Navy's finest.

Jim was there the next moment, holding her with gentle hands. "Are you all right, baby?" He looked worried, but she found it hard to articulate everything that was running through her mind. She also felt unaccountably weak. Whether from blood loss or the magical drain, or both, she didn't know, but she was viewing the world through a gray haze.

"I love you," she told him, wanting him to know, just in case this was the end for her. "I've loved spending time with you," she went on when his face paled. "Thank you for some of the best adventures of my life," she finished her thought, unable to say more. She just didn't have the strength.

"Helen! Don't you leave me, now," he told her in a commanding, pained voice. "I need you to stay awake, sweetheart. Help is on the way, but you need to stay awake."

Helen thought she heard motorcycle engines—a lot of

them—as she faded into unconsciousness, but maybe that was just wishful thinking.

CHAPTER 20

Helen woke someplace else. She was in a hospital bed, in a strange room with monitors and other medical equipment. A hospital? No, it felt more intimate than that, and she had the room all to herself. A strange man walked in. He was tall and blond, and he bristled with magical power. Shifter power.

"Where am I?" she asked, feeling blurry, blinking her gummy eyes.

"Grizzly Cove Clinic," the man replied with a smile. "I'm Doctor Olafsson, and you've been unconscious for about twenty-four hours." He came over to her, checking the monitors. "Welcome back to the waking world. You had my buddy, Jim, very worried. He's barely left your side, but Big John made him take a break so he could brief the Town Council on what went down in Texas and explain a bit more about the documents and the run-in you had on the road."

Helen remembered, now. "An evil sorceress calling herself Maura Dunlevy. Claimed she was the sister of Otalla, who I ended in Texas."

"Wait. You ended her?" The doctor seemed surprised.

Had Jim not filled them all in on events to this point yet? Or was he withholding the fact that she'd killed someone for a particular reason? She wasn't ashamed of her actions. She knew, in her heart, they were sanctioned by the Mother of

All.

"It had to be done, and the Goddess gave me the strength to do it, so I did." Helen shrugged. "I've never done that sort of thing before, but it was okay."

"Some people don't understand how I can be a bear, who kills, and also a doctor," he said, his expression going solemn. "I probably understand, better than most." His expression lightened as he went on. "As my mate would probably say, we tend to be a bunch of chauvinists in this town, even though we have plenty of evidence that our females can be just as fierce as us, whether they have claws, magic, or no special abilities, at all." He grinned at her, and she smiled back.

"Thank you for looking after me," she told him, not sure what would come next. She really wanted to see Jim, but it sounded like he was closeted with the men in power in this town, and she probably couldn't bust in on that sort of meeting.

"I texted Jim, as he made me promise to do, and he should be here—" The sound of a door slamming in the other room made the doctor look up and grin. "I suspect he's already here. I'll leave you two to talk. Just don't get out of bed yet. I want to make sure you're completely stable before I let you go, okay?"

"Sure thing, doctor," she told him, already looking past his large form, looking for Jim.

And then, he was there. Filling the doorway, his face looking a bit haggard but every bit as handsome as always. He came into the room, and the doctor went out, pulling the door shut behind him.

"How are you feeling?" Jim asked, looking unsure of himself for the first time in their acquaintance.

"Awake. Alive. Better than when I passed out," she reported with a smile. "I really thought I was done for. What happened?"

"The Grizzly Cove contingent showed up a few minutes after you passed out. Luckily, Sven was with them, and he was able to treat your wounds and stop the bleeding. We all helped. Most of us have had advanced training in first aid, so there was no shortage of skilled assistants, but Sven is an actual doctor, so he took charge of your treatment," Jim said, walking closer to her bed. She noticed a chair had been placed right beside the bed, and she wondered if he'd been sitting in it while she'd been unconscious.

"Sven is the guy who just left? Doctor Olafsson?" she asked, just to make sure she had the right bear shifter in mind.

"Yeah, Sven Olafsson. He's a polar bear, believe it or not," Jim told her, shaking his head.

"I believe it," Helen admitted with a chuckle. "He said you were in a meeting with the Town Council."

"I didn't want to leave your side, but when an Alpha bear tells you to do something in his territory, it's wise not to argue too much," Jim said with a rueful grin. "I think he just wanted me to take a break from my vigil. I've been sitting in this chair since they brought you in." Jim patted the back of the chair. "I wanted to be here when you woke up because of what you said…" His words trailed off, and she searched her memory to come up with a meaning for them.

Then, she remembered. She'd told him she loved him. Oh, boy.

She was searching for the right thing to say when he went on. "You see, I realized something when you blacked out on me." He sat in the chair and took her hand in his. "I realized that, if you died, right then and there, so would I. I realized that you were my mate, and there was no use fighting it—not that I had done so intentionally, in the first place. I was just sort of slow on the uptake and not sure how I could rightfully subject a beautiful soul like yours to my style of life. I was fighting against the change that I now know was inevitable, and for the better."

He lifted her hand to his lips and kissed her knuckles, one by one, as her heart melted. He lifted his head, and his gaze met hers.

"I love you, Helen. I want you to be with me forever, and

I want to share my life with you. There will never be another woman who completes me the way you do. Please say you'll be my mate." His eyes were beseeching, his expression endearing, and there really was only one answer she could give him.

"Yes," she said through happy tears. "Yes, yes, yes!" she repeated, just to be sure he understood. "I love you, Jim. I think I have for a long time, now."

He jumped up from the chair and leaned over to place a deep, delicious kiss on her lips.

Sometime later, the door to her room opened, but she barely noticed. Jim didn't seem to think it was a threat because he took his time breaking off that amazing kiss. He rose and turned to face whoever had come to disturb their intimate moment.

It was a big man, who bristled with power. Helen could feel his presence from across the room. Maybe this was the Alpha bear?

"Your timing could be better, John," Jim told the other man, who just laughed as he walked farther into the room.

"If I hadn't interrupted, Sven's monitors would've exploded. She's still hooked up, you know." The man nodded toward the wires that protruded from Helen's hospital gown.

She blushed, realizing that her response to Jim's proposal had been visible in the elevated respiration, the speeding heartbeat and the rising pulse rate reported to the monitors in the room, and likely outside, as well. Helen swatted at Jim's arm to get him to move over so she could meet the Alpha bear with as much dignity as she could muster, under the circumstances.

"Helen Richards, this is John Marshall, Alpha bear of this town, as well as mayor. Most folks call him Big John." Jim made the introductions.

"Thank you for your assistance, Mayor Marshall," Helen said politely. "I've heard quite a bit about your town."

John smiled broadly as he stood at the foot of her bed. "You're welcome to stay until you're better. Sven's taken a liking to you, and for some reason, more than a few of my men seem to like this crazy wolf." John put his hand on Jim's shoulder. Jim just smiled. "In fact, you're welcome to stay as long as you like, and we don't usually extend that invitation to just anyone." John tried to look grave but failed. Helen liked this bear who didn't take himself too seriously. "My mate, in particular," he went on, "wants a chance to talk to you about magical stuff. Her heritage is Italian witchcraft, and she's really curious about *Germanic-origin craft*, as she calls it."

"I'd be happy to meet her," Helen said, meaning it. She didn't often get to talk to practitioners of other styles of magic. This would be interesting.

Another man entered the room and moved to stand next to the Alpha. "Sorry to barge in, but I wanted to see how you were doing, ma'am. I'm Ezra Tate. That mission Jim—and you—were on was for my employer, SeaLife Enterprises. The owners wanted me to come down and see how you were. They would've come themselves, but Sven doesn't like a crowd to gather in his clinic, so I was deputized. I'm glad to see you're finally awake."

"Pleased to meet you, Mr. Tate," she said. "Thank you, and your employers, for checking on me. I'm feeling better all the time." She smiled, feeling the truth in her words. "I hope the records Jim liberated will be of some use to you all."

"Oh, they'll keep us busy for months," Ezra assured her, his expression growing serious. "Maybe even years. There are lots of leads to track down." He cleared his throat and looked at Jim. "In fact, I wanted to make it clear, before too much more time had passed, that there's a job here for you, Jim, if you want it. You've already proven you've got the right stuff for doing this kind of work, and Trevor and Beth wanted me to extend the invitation to join SeaLife full-time, if that's what you want."

Jim seemed surprised and pleased, if Helen was any judge of his expressions. He ducked his head, looked at her for a moment and then shifted his attention back to Ezra. "I'm flattered by the offer, and I'll have an answer for you as soon as I figure out a few other things."

"No rush," Ezra assured him. "We all just wanted to make sure you knew you had a job here, if you wanted it."

"Thanks," Jim said. "Really. I'll definitely have an answer for you within the next couple of days, if that's all right."

"Any time, is fine. Just think it over and let me know." With that, Ezra took his leave and exited the room. These bears really did have big presences on the magical plane. If Helen was going to be around them more, she'd have to get used to that.

"There's a hotel in town, and we've got a room reserved for you," the Alpha said, taking charge of the conversation once more, speaking directly to Helen. "Once Sven gives the medical clearance, you can go rest up in private. We have a few more days of debriefing with Jim planned, but I think we'd like to hear your perspective on what you've just been through, as well, once you're up to sharing it."

"I'm at your disposal, Alpha," she told him. "And I definitely want to get out of this hospital bed, nice as it is, and get back to normal as soon as possible. I want to be with my new mate." She tugged on Jim's hand and smiled up at him.

"What's this? You've accepted him?" John asked, a wide smile on his face. "Here, we were taking bets on how long you two would take to finally get together. We all knew, from the moment we saw Jim, that he was a goner. I'm glad you didn't keep him in suspense too long." John patted Jim on the back, shaking his balance, but Jim recovered nicely. "Congratulations to you both. When you're feeling up to it, we'll have a party."

Jim felt like a million bucks, knowing Helen had agreed to be his mate. He couldn't wait to take her out of the clinic and go someplace private, but he also wanted to be certain she was well before they left the care of the town's only doctor. She'd scared him so badly when she'd collapsed. He'd thought she would die, but timely intervention had saved her life—and his, too.

After Ezra's surprising offer, Jim felt like, finally, everything was falling into place. He had the promise of a real job. Stability. Something to offer Helen as a mate. He'd gladly give up his nomadic existence, if that's what she wanted. He wasn't sure where she'd want to live, and that was one of the things they had to discuss before he could give Ezra an answer, but wherever she wanted to go, he'd find a way to make things work.

She was now his number one priority in life. His mate. His happiness. His joy.

"Can we get out of here, yet?" Helen asked Jim after Big John had taken his leave.

"I don't know. It's up to Sven, really," Jim told her, brushing her hair back from her eyes. "Do you want me to go check?"

Helen nodded. "I know I'll heal a million times faster if we can just be together. Remember the way our power feeds off each other?"

Jim hadn't thought of that, but she did have a valid point. He left her side with a quick kiss and went out to track down the polar bear doctor.

An hour later, Jim carried Helen into the hotel room that had been reserved for them. It was a nice room, with a view of the cove and new sturdy furniture in calming shades of ocean-y blue. The whole hotel looked to be very recent construction, as did most of the town. Grizzly Cove was up-and-coming, that was for certain. A guy could make a place for himself and his mate in a town like this.

The hotel was at one end of what could be considered *the strip* in Grizzly Cove, where the vast majority of the businesses were located. It was the Main Street that followed the contour of the cove at its apex, for a ways, then meandered its way back out of town, eventually meeting up with the main coastal highway. The town was definitely a detour from the main drag but well worth the visit.

From what little Jim had seen of it, so far, there were many small art galleries featuring all sorts of art. A few restaurants were also located on that main road. Everything from a relatively fancy Cajun place to a bakery that also served sandwiches and light meals, including delicious-smelling breads and pastries.

Jim had made a note to call in an order once they got to the room, so they wouldn't have to go out again, but when he looked around after setting Helen down on a chair, he found a note beside a large bakery box. It let them know that the small fridge in the room had been stocked just an hour before with fresh sandwiches from the bakery as a gift from the Alpha to welcome them to the town. Jim whistled through his teeth as he read the note then handed it to Helen when she held out her hand.

"Wow," she said after reading the note, "they must really like you."

"Maybe," Jim allowed, bending down to nuzzle her cheek. "Or, maybe, it's you they like." He moved to kiss her gently. Thoroughly. He loved the heavy-lidded look of desire on her face when he broke the kiss. "I know I do," he said, brushing another kiss across her lips in a feather-light caress.

"I'd like to test my theory now," she told him with a teasing light in her eyes.

"Yeah?" He continued to place lingering kisses along her jaw. "What theory is that?"

"The one where I'll heal ultra-fast if we make love," she told him breathlessly.

He growled, liking the sound of that.

While it was true that Helen felt a little grungy with all the bandages, she wanted to heal first, then take a long, hot shower. Preferably with Jim there to wash her back...and other things. The doctor had tended the wounds, cleansing them and applying antibiotics and sterile dressings, but the deep lacerations were still there, hurting when she didn't remember to dampen the pain.

"I can't do much of the energetic stuff right now," she told Jim. "But I do love you, and I want you to make love to me. I think, given a bit of the mutual energy flow that always seems to evolve between us, the injuries will heal, and I'll be able to…um…participate a bit more." She raised the arm that hurt the least and cupped his jaw. "Think of it as an experiment."

"An experiment where I get to do things to you while you lay back and enjoy it?" he mused. "I think I like the sound of that."

He surprised her by lifting her into his arms again, and carrying her over to the large bed. He lay her down as gently as a feather then proceeded to kiss her clothing off her body. She wasn't wearing all that much. Just a cotton sundress she'd bought in Texas with nothing underneath. Putting on a bra and panties had been beyond her with the painful wounds she still had, and she knew she wasn't going far.

The wide-cut, soft cotton of the dress would work just as well as a nightgown, and she figured if she had to, she could sleep in it. Though, to be honest, with Jim in the same room, she preferred to sleep in nothing at all. Sleep itself was optional, at best, when Jim was near. She'd rather be skin-to-skin with him anytime, than wearing any sort of fabric that could get between them.

As Jim made love to her, she felt the pain slough off as if it had never been. When he gave her the first orgasm of many, her hips lifted off the bed, his mouth and hands following as he gave her the most intimate of kisses. She began to move with no pain and suspected the bandages weren't necessary anymore.

When he lifted the dress higher to expose her breasts, she lifted her shoulders off the bed and demanded he remove it completely. He complied, something dangerous in his eyes lighting as her movements became more fluid.

"Are you feeling better?" he asked, pausing to remove his shirt by ripping it off over his head and throwing it after her dress, across the room to land on the chair.

She sat up and checked the bandage on her arm, peeking beneath. She saw pink skin, not the raw red that had been there before. Biting her lip, she removed the bandage completely and was amazed—though she'd expected this would happen—at the complete lack of a wound. There was just a pink slash of newly healed skin where before there had been an angry red slash of an open wound.

"See what you do to me?" she said, holding up her arm as he shucked his pants and got completely naked.

"That is pretty awesome," he allowed, turning back to her and lifting her arm to his lips. He kissed the healing pink line gently.

"I take this as more proof that we were meant to be together. Something this miraculous has to be a gift from the Divine, don't you think?"

He nodded, kissing his way up her arm until he reached her lips. Then, he took her back down to the bed, covering her body with his.

He slid into her, and all was right with her world. Their energy was unbelievable, and she was sure that any remaining injuries on her body would not survive this delectable experience. He was as gentle with her as he had ever been, probably in deference to her healing body, but she wasn't going to sit idly by. No, she wrapped her legs around his hips and urged him on with her heels against the backs of his thighs.

"Are you sure?" he asked, his voice nearly a growl as he held himself above her. The rigidity of his muscles made her mouth water.

"Absolutely. Do it, Jim. Do it, now." She panted as he increased the pace, powering into her and building the inferno between them to majestic heights.

She clung to his shoulders and did her best to move with him as they strained together. Something so perfect had to be truly blessed. She knew for certain that she had found her destiny with this man, and no matter where they ended up living, all would be well, as long as they were together.

When the crisis came, they faced it together, going over the edge of oblivion, secure in each other's arms. Jim growled as Helen moaned, joined in bliss, together in ecstasy.

CHAPTER 21

A long time later, Jim carried Helen into the attached bathroom. She didn't need to be carried due to injuries. No, her injuries were long gone, she was sure. He carried her because she was boneless from his lovemaking, and she liked this evidence of his incredible strength.

He sat her on the counter, a towel beneath her bottom to prevent her from feeling the chill of the stone countertop. Then, he filled a truly massive bathtub with steamy water and a small dollop of herbal-scented bubbles. It wasn't a strong scent. Helen surmised that shifters didn't like overpowering scents in their toiletries, but it was lovely. Fresh and green and wild.

He spent a few moments taking off the remaining bandages that had made it through their lovemaking, discovering healed skin with not even a scar beneath each one. The pink line on her arm was gone, too.

"That really is some amazing stuff," he observed as he looked closely at her arm. "If I hadn't seen you fall beneath those mage bolts, and the aftermath, I would never know you'd been hurt at all."

"Only rarely can I achieve this kind of complete healing with my power," she told him. "Usually, there's some kind of mark left behind."

"More proof that we are magical dynamite when we're together," he said with a grin as he lifted her and placed her into the half-filled, sudsy tub.

A moment later, he joined her, and they took turns washing each other and just enjoying being together. When they inevitably made love, again, it was a bit of a miracle that they didn't flood the bathroom, but they managed to keep all the water in the tub, where it belonged.

They ate the sandwiches and the delicious pastries in the box then made love again, all through the night. When the next day dawned, Helen playfully demanded to see a bit of the town, and they took a walk down the beach in the early morning. Helen thought she saw a mermaid's tail glistening in the early morning sun, but when she blinked, it was gone.

They breakfasted at the bakery, meeting Nell, one of the sisters who owned the place, and her mate, the sheriff of the town, a fellow named Brody. He and Jim were already acquainted, of course, but everything was new to Helen, and she enjoyed meeting new people. She particularly liked the way they seemed to respect Jim, and their genuine friendliness would be hard to fake.

"Thank you for sending all that food to the hotel for us," Helen told Nell as the men discussed meeting times for Jim to attend the Town Council.

"Glad to help. I'm actually surprised to see you up and around. The news from the clinic was pretty bad that first day." Nell's expression invited an explanation, and Helen figured, *why not?*

"It was pretty bad, but there's some kind of amplification effect when Jim and I are together." She looked at him fondly as she tried to find the words to explain. "I'm a healer. I'm used to healing other people with my energy, but there's usually only so much power to go around without draining me too low that I start to falter. But, with Jim… It's all so different. It's like we feed each other's magic, and we both grow stronger as a result. Just spending time with him healed me completely. It's miraculous, even to me, and I've been healing others pretty much my whole life."

"I'm not magical at all," Nell said, her expression completely open, "but I've seen a lot of strange stuff since coming to this town, and my mate has explained a bit more. What you've got is something special with Jim. I'm glad you found each other."

Helen smiled. "Me too."

*

They walked along the Main Street, arm-in-arm, window shopping and getting to know the town a bit better. Often, people would stop to say hello to Jim and be introduced formally to Helen. Many of them had taken part in her rescue from the road outside of town, and she found herself thanking them for their help. One and all, they were gracious and kind, if a bit overwhelming. Bears, she was learning, were quite different than wolves.

They were friendly and outgoing, for the most part. The town wasn't exactly a bustling metropolis, but there were enough people moving around to indicate a thriving community. Helen liked the feel of the place, and the vibe of the art all around made her feel good right down to her soul. There were so many beautiful things to be seen. From the impressive art in all those gallery windows to the majestic beauty of the cove itself. This was an enchanted place, and she felt blessed to be able to see it.

Something about this town just felt so *right* to her. Big Wolf had been nice, but Grizzly Cove felt…like home. The revelation hit her, and she stopped walking. They were in front of another gallery, so Jim paused beside her and looked in the window. Helen looked too, finding a blonde woman on the other side of the glass, behind the window display, looking back at her with wide eyes.

As Helen watched, the blonde woman called to a man in the backroom of the small gallery, and he walked out, his pose attentive. He was a big man and shaggy like some of the other bear shifters she'd seen so far in this town. The woman, though, she was more petite. Lean and tall, kind of like Jim.

Was this a male bear and female wolf couple? Helen didn't know why she thought that, but it felt right.

The woman smiled and picked something up then headed out the door with it. Helen looked up at the sign at the top of the two-story structure. It read *Spirit Bear House*, but the sign above the display window said *White Wolf Gallery*. She looked at the front of the building again, and realized that there was more than one gallery inside, and each had its own name.

In the time it took Helen to figure that out, the woman had come outside. She walked right up to them, a reserved smile on her face.

"I'm sorry, but I just had to show you this." She lifted the item she'd taken from her gallery and showed it to them.

It was a small canvas with a painting done in soft shades of cream and gold. It was of a woman…and a wolf. The wolf looked a lot like Jim's wolf, and the woman…

"That's me," Helen said, surprised and mystified by the painting. "How did you…?"

"I'm Laura, and this is my mate, Gus." She stepped back a little to reveal the man who had come outside to back her up.

Gus reached forward to offer his hand to Jim. "I've heard about you from Big John and Ezra," he said. "Was hoping you'd come by."

"You're the shaman," Jim said, surprising Helen as he shook the other man's hand.

"And you're the SEAL," Gus replied with a grin.

"He's not a seal," Laura insisted. "He smells like a wolf."

Jim chuckled. "You're right, of course, ma'am. I'm from the White Oaks Pack out of Iowa, but what Gus meant is that I'm a former Navy SEAL."

"Of course you are," Laura said, understanding dawning on her face. "Honey, just about every guy in this town is some kind of super soldier," she said to Helen with a conspiratorial grin. "You'll fit in really well here," she told Jim.

She handed the canvas to Helen. "I painted this for you," Laura told her. Helen was bemused.

"How could you have known? Did you do this, like, last night or something?" Helen marveled at the likeness. There was no doubt the painting was of her and Jim.

Laura laughed. "I painted that more than a month ago," she claimed, making a tingle race down Helen's spine. Did this wolf woman have a clairvoyant gift? "I knew it was one of the special ones when I did it. I just didn't know who it would be for. Now, seeing you two, I know. Consider it a mating gift and a welcome to town, from me to you."

"You paint the future?" Helen asked. She hadn't heard of shifters endowed with other magical gifts before. This woman felt special. Like she was more than just your average shifter. Helen wanted to know why. Then, she realized she was being rude and apologized. "I'm sorry to be nosy. My mother is a seer, and I'm just curious. You don't have to answer."

Laura laughed good-naturedly. "It's all right. I'm a wolf, but I'm also a little bit fey," she revealed, and suddenly, it all clicked into place for Helen. "I see things in my painting, sometimes, and I think you and I are going to be good friends."

"If you can pardon my unforgivable rudeness, then I'd say we're off to a good start," Helen agreed, grinning at Laura's enthusiasm. "Just so we're even, let me tell you that I was born a Richards, but my mother is a Llewellyn, which means a long legacy of magic and a big family. Some of the extended clan has fey blood, and some have recently married shifters." Helen looked at Jim and grinned. "I guess I'm one of the latter. Jim and I are newly mated."

"Congratulations," Gus said, and Helen could feel that he truly meant it. He was happy for them as he patted Jim on the back and offered Helen a wide smile. "If you want a ceremony, we have a sacred circle at the southern point of the cove, and I'd be happy to officiate. Or, if you'd rather have a priestess, we have one in town now."

"It's all so new we haven't talked about any of that yet," Helen admitted, "but we'll definitely keep it in mind. It's very kind of you to offer."

They talked about the town and the things they should see and try for a few minutes before leaving. Helen and Jim both thanked Laura for the painting. Jim even offered to pay for it, but Laura refused, and he subsided.

"Let that be the first bit of décor for your new den," Laura said, as if she knew things they didn't about their future. Perhaps she did.

Helen and Jim continued on their walk as the other couple went back into their gallery. Helen couldn't stop thinking about their encounter. "I suppose she's the white wolf. Does that make him the Spirit Bear?"

Jim looked at her. "I've heard about the Grizzly Cove shaman, and he really is a spirit bear. It's a rare kind of bear from this part of the world that has creamy white fur. Very special. When a shifter spirit bear is born, they almost always follow the path of the shaman or priestess."

"Wow," Helen said, surprised even more by their encounter. "He seemed so down to earth."

"The very best shaman do. It's the ones who think themselves better than everyone else who do the worst job at their calling. Or so I've observed," Jim mused, then shrugged. "Are you feeling hungry?"

"I could eat," she replied.

"Good. Let's try out *Flambeau*'s. I hope you're okay with spicy food. It's a mostly Cajun menu, I hear." He looked so eager to try it she couldn't let him down.

They went to the restaurant and enjoyed a delicious meal. Helen ate one serving while Jim wolfed down three, but nobody raised an eyebrow in a town full of bear shifters. They were greeted by just about everyone at some point during their meal, and Helen really felt the welcome of these people, more than she had in Big Wolf. That was for certain. Bears really were different. They were definitely more open with those they had decided to let in.

They spent the rest of the day together and walked all over, perusing the shops and dipping their toes in the cool waters of the cove. Helen was enchanted by the place, and when dusk started to fall, they went back to the hotel and sat on the beach down by the water. Jim shifted to his wolf form and sat at her side while she stroked his fur.

At one point, a bear ambled past, looking up at them and growling what sounded like a greeting. Jim growled back and went back to resting his head on her thigh. They watched the sun set together then went back to their hotel room and made love all night long.

The next morning, Jim got a surprise. A text on his phone at oh-dark-thirty from his Uncle Arch, who had just rolled into town. What in the world was Arch doing in Grizzly Cove, Jim wondered as he got dressed. He did his best not to wake Helen. He'd kept her up half the night, making love in all sorts of new and interesting positions. She'd earned her rest, but Jim wanted to see Arch and find out what was going on.

When he slipped out of the hotel room, he found not just Arch, but Ezra and Big John out there in the hallway, waiting for him. The four of them headed to the empty lobby to sit and talk. There was also coffee in the lobby and a tray of pastries from the bakery, to which they all helped themselves before sitting down.

"Bet you're wondering why I'm here," Arch started the moment they sat down with their coffee and sweets. "John gave me a call, and we had a long talk about things. One thing led to another, and he issued the invite for me to come here and take a look around. I told him how things stood at home and all the reasons it would make sense to go lone wolf more officially than you and I have been doing. John offered an alternative that I think you're going to like as much as I do."

"Wait a minute, Arch. I support Brock as Alpha. He knows that." Jim wanted that point to be clear.

"He does," Arch agreed. "But he also knows that you and I don't fit into the mold of the Pack he's creating. There's no room for the kind of work we do in White Oaks. It was fine when the Pack was smaller, and there were less vulnerable

Pack members, but the work we do can have repercussions, and it's safer for the Pack if we're not seen to be part of it. I have never wanted to lead trouble back home to Brock and all those families under his rule."

Jim sat back in his chair, just looking at his uncle. They'd never come out and said these things aloud, but they'd both known the day to break from White Oaks was coming sooner rather than later. Brock was building a Pack on the Big Wolf model. There were no mercenaries working out of Big Wolf. Jim suspected the Alpha there wouldn't stand for that kind of thing, and he'd probably already talked to Brock about Arch and Jim's presence and how it could negatively impact the rest of the Pack.

"For the good of the Pack, it's time for us to make a decision," Arch said in a solemn tone.

"There's something else you may not know that has to be considered," Jim said, needing everything out on the table so they could make fully informed decisions. "Helen is my mate. I'll be going wherever she wants to go. If she wants to go back to Pennsylvania to be near her family, then that's where I'll be."

"Understood." Arch nodded. "And congratulations. I was hoping you two would make a go of it."

"You were?" Jim was surprised, but then, he realized he probably shouldn't be. Arch was one of the best at observation. He'd probably pegged Jim and Helen at a hundred paces. Jim shook his head. "Of course you saw what I didn't. Question withdrawn." He chuckled at the way Arch just shook his head and grinned.

"Look," Big John spoke for the first time since sitting down, "I know you have things to work out, but I wanted to be here to let you know that the invitation is open for you both to stick around here for a while. A long while."

Jim was surprised, all over again, at the Alpha bear's willingness to let a wolf—now two wolves—make a home here in the haven he'd set up specifically for bear shifters. He was going to ask why, and maybe, finally, he might get an answer.

"With all due respect, Alpha, but just why is that? Neither of us were part of your unit. We're wolves, not bears. Why the red carpet treatment?" Jim tried to keep his tone respectful, but he really wanted to know.

Big John sat back and sighed. "There are a few reasons, son, and I see I'm going to have to give you some of them to satisfy your curiosity. Hell, you sure you're a wolf and not some kind of cat?"

Arch laughed, and Ezra chuckled, but Jim just waited patiently to hear what John would say.

"I'll vouch that he's one hundred percent wolf," Arch said playfully, "though he does swim like a fish."

"Which could come in handy in a town that was created for bears but has become a haven for a mer pod and all sorts of magical Others that I never could have expected," John said, his tone only slightly exasperated. "You may not realize this, but your uncle and I go way back," John revealed, surprising Jim.

"You never said anything," Jim said, looking straight at his uncle.

Arch shrugged. "What was there to say? I've worked with a lot of people in my time, but yeah, I've always had a high regard for Big John. A better tactician I have never met, and I've met more than a few men who were very gifted in that area. Johnny's the best of the best."

John nodded respectfully at Arch, acknowledging the compliment. "And you wrote the book the rest of us studied from, Arch," John said, returning the kudos. "I think every last one of my men would revolt if I didn't invite you to stick around, now that you're finally here. I've been inviting him every time we spoke, but he never quite got around to making the trip," John directed those last comments to Jim.

"Well, that explains why Uncle Arch is welcome, but why me? Why Helen, for that matter?" Jim insisted

"While you would be welcome for Arch's sake, you should know, Jim, that you've been earning quite the reputation of your own, working at his side. We respect that, but there are other reasons, not the least of which is your recent work for SeaLife. Which is why Ezra came this morning rather than lazing in bed with his pretty mate."

"The task of cleaning up all the various businesses associated with SeaLife is bigger than any of us expected when we took it on," Ezra admitted. "We've already hired a few troubleshooters. Some have worked out, and some haven't. All three Bishop brothers are the ones who have worked out. Plus you. We need to speed up the rate at which we clean up the company. Trevor and Beth don't want to let the evil linger any longer than they have to. In fact, they're out there, right now, working on one of the problem companies while I hold the fort. We've been taking it in turns, staying here to keep things rolling. What we need are more reliable operatives that we can send out to do the work, and you're right at the top of our list. We'd really like you to take the job." Ezra looked at Arch. "You too, Arch, if you're willing."

Arch tipped a casual salute Ezra's way. "We'll talk more later."

Ezra nodded agreement to this proposal and subsided.

CHAPTER 22

"There's also the matter of those documents you brought here from Texas," John reminded them all. "While some of them pertain to SeaLife, there's also a treasure trove of information about the *Venifucus* structure and their *Altor Custodis* infiltration. We could use your help with that, perhaps, as well."

Jim nodded. "I looked at some of it, and I can help with parts, but you're going to need specialists for the bulk of those documents."

"I've already put out some feelers," John assured him. "Your Helen has proven herself a kind and resourceful woman," John went on, going back to Jim's previous question. "I have reports of her daring from Joe Villalobos in Texas and have heard rumors about her adventures with fireworks in Virginia. That healing talent of hers is something special, from all accounts, as well." John sighed. "I never envisioned this town would have such a thing as a magic circle, but it does, and they've lobbied me to extend the welcome to Helen because they all know of and respect her family's magical heritage. It doesn't hurt that more than one has had some kind of vision that showcases her as a future member of their magic circle. The painting Laura gave you was just the beginning," John promised.

"I'm not sure if I should be impressed or afraid," Jim admitted with a rueful grin. "I'm not sure what Helen will think of all this."

"That's why I wanted to talk to you first," John admitted. "We're all shifters. We all have a common background, if different peculiarities. Although I mated a powerful witch, I have to admit, I still can't begin to guess, sometimes, how she'll react to things. You know Helen best. That's why I think this will work better if you're the one explaining our position to her. You two also need to arrive at your decision together, so you'll have to spend some time talking it all over."

"Actually, that won't be necessary."

Jim jumped to his feet, hearing Helen's voice behind him. She'd dressed in one of the outfits she'd bought in Texas and looked a vision to his eyes. He went to her side.

"I woke, and you were gone. I decided to go hunting, and here I find you, having a club meeting where, apparently, no girls are allowed." She chuckled to soften her words, and he knew she wasn't mad at him. Thank goodness.

"How much did you hear?" he asked.

"Most of it, I think. They want us to stay?" she asked, talking to him, but Jim knew the others could hear her soft-spoken words.

He nodded. "Ezra needs more troubleshooters, and they want me. The magic circle wants you, and all the ex-military guys want Arch to stick around," he added with a grin.

"So, you'd be able to keep working with your uncle if he stays?" she asked.

"Looks that way. But what about your family? I thought you guys were tight-knit."

"We are, and sometimes, it drives me crazy," she admitted. "Kiki went out on her own, and ever since, I've wondered what there was out there for me. I think my mother knew." Helen rolled her eyes and then smiled. "Of course, my mother knew. She was the one who sent me to Virginia Beach and told me to stop and buy fireworks on the way. She saw all of this." Helen shook her head. "I bet she even knows that I really want to stay."

"You do?" Jim asked, surprised.

"If you do," she backtracked a bit. "Not because I don't love my family. I do love them, fiercely. But I also need to find my own way, with you. We need to stand on our own for a while, until we know who we are as a couple. I think we can do that here. If you want to stay, of course."

"Arch was right. There's really no room for what we do in the Pack my brother is trying to build. We can't stop being who and what we are, so it's about time we found a place that welcomes our kind and our skills. This is that kind of place, so yes, if you want to stay, so do I," he told her, feeling a weight of worry lifting off his shoulders as she smiled.

Helen felt her phone vibrate in her pocket and reached for it. She just shook her head when she read the text message that had just come in.

"It's from my mother," she told Jim, then turned to address the rest of those gathered. "My mother wants you to know, Alpha, that she's already spoken to the rest of the family, and they've decided that I'm to be your liaison to the Llewellyn archive. They've already decided to call me the Llewellyn Liaison." Helen shook her head, grinning at the alliteration.

"I know my mate will be thrilled to hear this," John said, grinning as he stood. "It's settled, then. Welcome to Grizzly Cove."

*

Jim and Helen spent the morning looking at places to live. There were a few apartments in town still available, though they were building as fast as they could to create more accommodations for the mer who wanted places on land. Still, there were a few places Jim and Helen could rent, and they decided on one of the units on the top floor of Gus's building that had a nice view of the cove.

There were actually two units available in the building, and

Arch decided to rent the one that faced Main Street. Jim wasn't sure, but it seemed like Arch was more than a little interested in the new gallery going in directly across the street from his windows. Jim caught a few glances of a very pretty older woman directing the work of setting up the place and looked speculatively at his uncle. Arch may have been a bachelor all his life, but there was always hope.

They moved in after lunch, and the first thing Helen did, even before unpacking her suitcases, was to hang the little painting Laura had given them. It held a place of honor in their new apartment, in the living room where they could see it all the time.

Jim came up behind her as she stood, admiring the canvas. He wrapped his arms around her from behind, snugging her back against his chest. She put her arms over his and settled into his embrace as if she'd been born to fit there.

"Are you happy?" he asked, hoping she felt as good about the decision to live here as he did.

Jim had called his brother just before lunch and explained that he wasn't coming back to Iowa right away. Probably not for a good long time. It had been emotional for them both, but Brock had understood. They'd both seen this day coming for a while now, and although it was heart-wrenching, it was also good.

This change meant that Jim had found his mate, which was something to rejoice over. It also meant that Brock would be able to guide his Pack in the direction he wanted it to go without any more complications. Both were good outcomes. They just had to focus on that.

Arch had taken the phone from Jim and said his piece to his nephew, the Alpha, as well, and when he was done, the Pack ties had been broken, though not totally abandoned. They were all still family and would continue to be close. They just weren't going to live in each other's pockets anymore. Not that they really had been doing that for the last couple of years. Now, it was official. Jim and Arch had both broken away from the Pack and were considered lone wolves.

Only, they both knew they had just exchanged a wolf Pack for a bear Clan. It might be a bit unorthodox, but it worked because, while they may carry different animal spirits, the men were the same at heart. They were all warriors. Special Forces veterans with deep senses of duty and honor. They had been tested in some of the worst hellholes on the planet, and they had each proven their metal.

That was a bond that could, and did, form strong alliances, regardless of their differences. Jim and Arch would do well with the bears in Grizzly Cove, and Helen had already made a few new friends among the magical folk. Gus and his mate, Laura, had invited Jim and Helen to join them for lunch, where they got to meet John's mate, Ursula, and her sister, Mellie, who was mated to another of the bear shifters. Both women were highly magical, and they welcomed Helen with open arms.

"I'm very happy," Helen replied to Jim's question, squeezing his hands with hers. "Ecstatic, in fact. I never thought I'd find a life like this, or a man like you."

"Then, we're even," he told her, rocking her a bit, from side to side. "I never dreamed of a love so deep and true, or a place where we could be ourselves and learn and grow."

She sighed happily and he felt the same deep sense of satisfaction that he sensed in her. Helen leaned back against him as they both gazed at the prophetic portrait of them both. Her words summed up how they both felt.

"I think we're going to like it here."

# # #

ABOUT THE AUTHOR

Bianca D'Arc has run a laboratory, climbed the corporate ladder in the shark-infested streets of lower Manhattan, studied and taught martial arts, and earned the right to put a whole bunch of letters after her name, but she's always enjoyed writing more than any of her other pursuits. She grew up and still lives on Long Island, where she keeps busy with an extensive garden, several aquariums full of very demanding fish, and writing her favorite genres of paranormal, fantasy and sci-fi romance.

Bianca loves to hear from readers and can be reached through Twitter (@BiancaDArc), Facebook (BiancaDArcAuthor) or through the various links on her website.

WELCOME TO THE D'ARC SIDE…
WWW.BIANCADARC.COM

OTHER BOOKS BY BIANCA D'ARC

* RT Book Reviews Awards Nominee
** EPPIE Award Winner
*** CAPA Award Winner

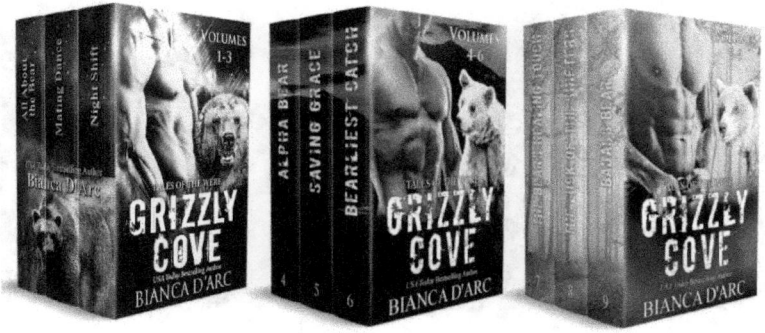

Welcome to Grizzly Cove, where bear shifters can be who they are - if the creatures of the deep will just leave them be. Wild magic, unexpected allies, a conflagration of sorcery and shifter magic the likes of which has not been seen in centuries... That's what awaits the peaceful town of Grizzly Cove. That, and love. Lots and lots of love.

This series begins with...

All About the Bear
Welcome to Grizzly Cove, where the sheriff has more than the peace to protect. The proprietor of the new bakery in town is clueless about the dual nature of her nearest neighbors, but not for long. It'll be up to Sheriff Brody to clue her in and convince her to stay calm—and in his bed—for the next fifty years or so.

Mating Dance
Tom, Grizzly Cove's only lawyer, is also a badass grizzly bear, but he's met his match in Ashley, the woman he just can't get out of his mind. She's got a dark secret, that only he knows. When ugliness from her past tracks her to her new home, can Tom protect the woman he is fast coming to believe is his mate?

Night Shift
Sheriff's Deputy Zak is one of the few black bear shifters in a colony of grizzlies. When his job takes him into closer proximity to the lovely Tina, though, he finds he can't resist her. Could it be he's finally found his mate? And when adversity strikes, will she turn to him, or run into the night? Zak will do all he can to make sure she chooses him.

Phoenix Rising

Lance is inexplicably drawn to the sun and doesn't understand why. Tina is a witch who remembers him from their high school days. She'd had a crush on the quiet boy who had an air of magic about him. Reunited by Fate, she wonders if she could be the one to ground him and make him want to stay even after the fire within him claims his soul...if only their love can be strong enough.

Phoenix and the Wolf

Diana is drawn to the sun and dreams of flying, but her elderly grandmother needs her feet firmly on the ground. When Diana's old clunker breaks down in front of a high-end car lot, she seeks help and finds herself ensnared by the sexy werewolf mechanic who runs the repair shop. Stone makes her want to forget all her responsibilities and take a walk on the wild side...with him.

Phoenix and the Dragon

He's a dragon shapeshifter in search of others like himself. She's a newly transformed phoenix shifter with a lot to learn and bad guys on her trail. Together, they will go on a dazzling adventure into the unknown, and fight against evil folk intent on subduing her immense power and using it for their own ends. They will face untold danger and find love that will last a lifetime.

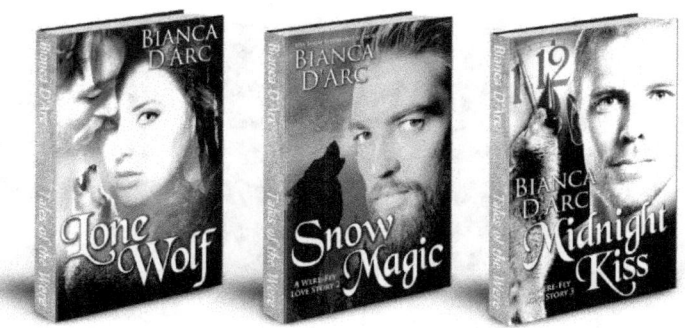

Lone Wolf

Josh is a werewolf who suddenly has extra, unexpected and totally untrained powers. He's not happy about it - or about the evil jackasses who keep attacking him, trying to steal his magic. Forced to seek help, Josh is sent to an unexpected ally for training.

Deena is a priestess with more than her share of magical power and a unique ability that has made her a target. She welcomes Josh, seeing a kindred soul in the lone werewolf. She knows she can help him... if they can survive their enemies long enough.

Snow Magic

Evie has been a lone wolf since the disappearance of her mate, Sir Rayburne, a fey knight from another realm. Left all alone with a young son to raise, Evie has become stronger than she ever was. But now her son is grown and suddenly Ray is back.

Ray never meant to leave Evie all those years ago but he's been caught in a magical trap, slowly being drained of magic all this time. Freed at last, he whisks Evie to the only place he knows in the mortal realm where they were happy and safe—the rustic cabin in the midst of a North Dakota winter where they had been newlyweds. He's used the last of his magic to get there and until he recovers a bit, they're stuck in the middle of nowhere with a blizzard coming and bad guys on their trail.

Can they pick up where they left off and rekindle the magic between them, or has it been extinguished forever?

Midnight Kiss

Margo is a werewolf on a mission...with a disruptively handsome mage named Gabe. She can't figure out where Gabe fits in the pecking order, but it doesn't seem to matter to the attraction driving her wild. Gabe knows he's going to have to prove himself in order to win Margo's heart. He wants her for his mate, but can she give her heart to a mage? And will their dangerous quest get in the way?

The Jaguar Tycoon

Mark may be the larger-than-life billionaire Alpha of the secretive Jaguar Clan, but he's a pussycat when it comes to the one women destined to be his mate. Shelly is an up-and-coming architect trying to drum up business at an elite dinner party at which Mark is the guest of honor. When shots ring out, the hunt for the gunman brings Mark into Shelly's path and their lives will never be the same.

The Jaguar Bodyguard

Sworn to protect his Clan, Nick heads to Hollywood to keep an eye on a rising star who has seen a little too much for her own good. Unexpectedly fame has made a circus of Sal's life, but when decapitated squirrels show up on her doorstep, she knows she needs professional help. Nick embeds himself in her security squad to keep an eye on her as sparks fly and passions rise between them. Can he keep her safe and prevent her from revealing what she knows?

The Jaguar's Secret Baby

Hank has never forgotten the wild woman with whom he spent one memorable night. He's dreamed of her for years now, but has never been back to the small airport in Texas owned and run by her werewolf Pack. Tracy was left with a delicious memory of her night in Hank's arms, and a beautiful baby girl who is the light of her life. She chose not to tell Hank about his daughter, but when he finally returns and he discovers the daughter he's never known, he'll do all he can to set things right.

Dragon Knights

Two dragons, two knights, and one woman to complete their circle. That's the recipe for happiness in the land of fighting dragons. But there are a few special dragons that are more. They are the ruling family and they are half-dragon and half-human, able to change at will from one form to another.

Books in this series have won the EPPIE Award for Best Erotic Romance in the Fantasy/Paranormal category, and have been nominated for *RT Book Reviews Magazine* Reviewers Choice Awards among other honors.

WWW.BIANCADARC.COM